PENGUIN

FASCINA

William Boyd was born in 1952 in Accra, Ghana, and was brought up there and in Nigeria. He was educated at Gordonstoun School and at the universities of Nice, Glasgow and Oxford.

His first novel, *A Good Man in Africa* (1981), was published while he was a lecturer in English at St Hilda's College, Oxford, and won the Whitbread First Novel Award and a Somerset Maugham Award. He is also the author of the novels *An Ice-Cream War*, which won the John Llewellyn Rhys Memorial Prize for 1982 and was shortlisted for the Booker Prize; *Stars and Bars* (1984); *The New Confessions* (1987); *Brazzaville Beach*, which won the James Tait Black Memorial Prize for 1990 and for which William Boyd was awarded the McVitie's Prize for Scottish Writer of the Year; *The Blue Afternoon*, which won the 1993 Sunday Express Book of the Year Award and the 1995 Los Angeles Times Book Prize for Fiction; *Armadillo* (1998); and *Any Human Heart* (2002). He has published three collections of short stories: *On the Yankee Station* (1982), *The Destiny of Nathalie X* (1995), and *Fascination* (2004), and a book of autobiographical pieces, *Protobiography* (2005). All of his books are published in Penguin.

William Boyd is married and lives in London.

Fascination

WILLIAM BOYD

PENGUIN BOOKS

PENGUIN BOOKS

Published by the Penguin Group
Penguin Books Ltd, 80 Strand, London WC2R ORL, England
Penguin Group (USA) Inc., 375 Hudson Street, New York, New York 10014, USA
Penguin Group (Canada), 10 Alcorn Avenue, Toronto, Ontario, Canada M4V 3B2
(a division of Pearson Penguin Canada Inc.)
Penguin Ireland, 25 St Stephen's Green, Dublin 2, Ireland
(a division of Penguin Books Ltd)
Penguin Group (Australia), 250 Camberwell Road, Camberwell, Victoria 3124, Australia
(a division of Pearson Australia Group Pty Ltd)
Penguin Books India Pvt Ltd, 11 Community Centre, Panchsheel Park, New Delhi – 110 017, India
Penguin Group (NZ), cnr Airborne and Rosedale Roads, Albany, Auckland 1310, New Zealand
(a division of Pearson New Zealand Ltd)
Penguin Books (South Africa) (Pty) Ltd, 24 Sturdee Avenue, Rosebank 2196, South Africa

Penguin Books Ltd, Registered Offices: 80 Strand, London WC2R ORL, England

www.penguin.com

First published by Hamish Hamilton 2004
Published in Penguin Books 2005

4

Copyright © William Boyd, 2004
All rights reserved

The moral right of the author has been asserted

Set by Rowland Phototypesetting Ltd, Bury St Edmunds, Suffolk
Printed in England by Clays Ltd, St Ives plc

ISBN-13: 978–0–141–01924–6

for Susan

Contents

Acknowledgements

The following stories first appeared in the *New Yorker*: 'Adult Video', 'Varengeville', 'Fascination', 'Beulah Berlin, an A–Z', 'Loose Continuity' and 'Visions Fugitives'. 'A Haunting' was published in *Le Monde*; 'The Woman on the Beach with a Dog' in *Modern Painters*; 'The Mind/Body Problem' in *Areté*; and 'Fantasia on a Favourite Waltz' in *Three*.

Adult Video

PLAY ▶

Springtime in Oxford is vulgar, anyway, but something about this particular spring in Oxford is having me on. Really, these cherry trees are absurd. One wonders if just quite so many flowers are necessary. It is almost as if the cherry trees on the Woodstock Road are trying to prove something – some sort of floral brag, swanking to the other less advanced vegetation. Very Oxford in a way. Could I work this observation into the novel? 'Only in Oxford do the cherry trees try too hard.' Good opening for the Oxford sequence?

REWIND ◀◀

My meeting with my new supervisor was not a success. Dr Alexander Cardman. 'Call me Alex,' he invited almost immediately. He referred to me as Edward without permission.

'How old are you?' he asked.

'Thirty-one. How old are you?'

'Thirty-three. And you've been writing this thesis for . . . ?'

' – For, oh, six years. Seven. Seven and a bit. I left Oxford for three to teach. Then came back.'

'Teach? Where was that?'

'Abbey Meade. It's a prep school in Wiltshire.'

'Ah.' I could hear the sneer forming in his brain. 'And you came back –'

' – To finish my thesis.'

'I see . . .' I was disliking him quite intensely by now. He looked like he had gel on his hair. The small trimmed goatee was rebarbative and the faint West Country burr in his voice struck me as an affectation.

PLAY ▶

Summertown. The Banbury Road. I push through the front gate of 'See Breezes' (sic) to meet my new student, Gianluca di something-or-other. He is blind, so the language school has told me, and he needs to be walked to my flat. Not every day, I hope.

A cheery plump woman opens the door and leads me through to a living room where Gianluca sits. He is a tall boy – eighteen or nineteen, I would say – with thick, blond hair and a weak-chinned, sad face. His eyes are open and as I introduce myself and shake his hand they seem to stare directly at me, disconcertingly, with only a faint glaucous, bloodshot hue to them.

We walk back to my flat on the Woodstock Road. His right hand rests gently in the crook of my left elbow, his left carries a briefcase and a folded, white cane. We don't speak as he had said, in good English, that he needed to concentrate and count.

We stroll through Summertown's shops and halt the traffic at the beeping pedestrian crossing. Along Moreton Road to Woodstock Road and then a hundred yards or so to the house.

'Ring this doorbell,' I say, guiding his hand to the gleaming brass knob, 'and I'll come down to get you.'

In the hall Gianluca stops and sniffs the air.

'What is this place?' he says.

'A dentist's,' I say, as breezily as I can muster. 'I live on the top floor.'

PAUSE ∎∎

Felicia has gone to Malaysia for a week to try to sell Internet stocks in the Pacific Rim market, or something. Perhaps it's bonds, or fluctuations in other stock markets, that she's selling; or she might even be selling other people's hunches about fluctuations in stock markets in the next decade. I don't even try to understand. She has given me the key to her house so I can feed her tropical fish while she's away. When she left at dawn she kissed me goodbye, told me she loved me and said, ominously, apropos of nothing, that she thought I would make a wonderful father. I suppose it's as close as she'll ever get to issuing an ultimatum.

PLAY ▶
'There is,' I read, 'as every schoolboy knows in this scientific age, a very close chemical relation between coal and diamonds –'
' – Please,' says Gianluca, 'there is a preface by Conrad, no?'
'Yes.'
'Could you please begin with that.' He taps something into his little portable Braille typewriter and I go back to the beginning. You would think that to be paid fifteen pounds an hour to read Joseph Conrad's *Victory* to a blind Italian boy is, well, money for old rope, but I find my heart is curiously heavy with prospective fatigue.

In our first two-hour session we manage five pages. Gianluca listens with almost painful concentration and asks many, many questions, the answers to which he painstakingly types into his braille notebook. I walk him down to the front door where he unfolds his white cane and sets off back to 'See Breezes' with an amazingly unfaltering step. As I turn back into the hall, Krissi, the actually-not-unattractive New Zealand dental nurse, leans out of the door of the surgery and says, 'Mr Prentice would like a word at end of business today.'

As I plod back upstairs to my little flat beneath the eaves I think that 'end-of-business' is a classic Prentissian trope and that I must add it to my collection.

MEMORY
I think, perhaps, that I was at my happiest in Nice. Nineteen years old. At the *Centre Universitaire Méditerranéan*. No family. No friends. No money. Just freedom. My frowsty room in Madame D'Amico's apartment. The young whores in the rue de France. The French girls. The Tunisian boys. Ulrike and Anneliese. All those years ago. Jesus Christ.

REWIND ◄◄

Dr 'Alex' Cardman handed me back my chapter: 'Social consequences of the 1842 Mines Act in South Yorkshire, 1843–50'

'What do you think?' I asked. This guy did not frighten me, I had decided.

'There were fifteen errors of transcription in your first quoted passage,' he said. 'I didn't read on.'

'It's only a draft, for Christ's sake.'

'Even a second-rate examiner will refer you for that kind of carelessness,' he said, reasonably. 'You don't want get into bad habits. Bring it back when you've checked everything.' He smiled. 'What made you so interested in mid-nineteenth-century mining legislation? Pretty arcane subject – even for an Oxford doctorate.'

Its very arcanity, you fool, I wanted to reply, but instead I chose a lie, hoping it might cancel the Abbey Meade blunder. 'My father was a miner,' I said.

'Good God, so was mine,' he said. 'Tin. Cornwall.'

'Coal. Lanarkshire.'

FAST FORWARD ►►

INTERVIEWER: You don't seem embittered, even bothered, by the attack in *The Times* by Sir Alexander Cardman.

ME: It's a matter of complete indifference. Wasn't it Nabokov who said the best response to hostile criticism is to yawn and forget? I yawned. I forgot.

INTERVIEWER: It seems unduly personal, especially when your book has been so widely acclaimed –

ME: I think people on the outside never fully realize the role envy plays in literary and cultural debate in this country.

PLAY ►

Prentice is wearing his track suit and trainers: he likes to go jogging at the end of a day's dentistry. I offer him a glass of wine which he, surprisingly, accepts.

'South African Chardonnay,' I tell him. 'Your neck of the woods.'

Prentice actually comes from Zimbabwe. He has had his gingery-blond hair closely cut, I notice, which makes him look burlier, even fitter, if that were possible. He is always very specific about not being identified as South African, is Mr Prentist, the dentist.

'I prefer Californian,' he says.

'What can I do for you, Mr Prentist?'

'Prentice.'

'Sorry.'

He smiles, showing his small immaculate teeth. 'Bad news,' he says. 'I have to put the rent up. From next month.' He mentions a preposterous figure.

'That's a –' I calculate, trying to keep the rage out of my voice, '– a 120 per cent rise.'

'The going rate for two-bedroom flats on the Woodstock Road, so an estate agent informs me.'

'You cannot call that broom cupboard where I work a second bedroom.'

'Market forces,' he says, sipping, then nodding. 'This is actually an excellent wine.'

FUNCTION

Felicia is unnaturally blonde, has a tendency to plumpness and is devoted to me. I taught her for a term when she was at Somerville. We had an affair, for some reason. She went to work for a bank in the City. She came back to Oxford three years ago. I think, now, that she came deliberately to seek me out. She makes twenty times more money a year than I do.

DISPLAY

My as yet unfinished novel. Five years in the writing. Which today I have decided to re-title: *Morbid Anatomy*.

FAST FORWARD ▶▶

INTERVIEWER: Why did you resign the Trevelyan Chair of Modern History?

ME: I did not approve of the new syllabus.

INTERVIEWER: It had nothing to do with internecine strife within the History Faculty, professional jealousies?

ME: As far as I was concerned it was purely a matter of principle. It was my duty.

PLAY ▶

Gianluca looks at me – his sightless eyes are directed at me. I read on, hastily: '"Meanwhile Shomberg watched Heyst out of the corner of his eye" – ah, notice that glorious Conradian cliché –'

'Why is Heyst so passive?' Gianluca asks. 'He's like he's *stagnante* . . .'

'Same word,' I say, wondering why, indeed. 'Well, he's a bit of a drifter, isn't he, Heyst?'

Gianluca types – I suppose – 'Heyst = drifter' into his Braille notebook.

'Going with the flow,' I improvise. We have reached page 67. I don't think I have ever paid so much attention to a text, and yet I can remember almost nothing. Each day it's as if I'm starting on page 1 again.

REPEAT

'He meant to drift altogether and literally, body and soul, like a detached leaf drifting in the wind currents.'

PLAY ▶

Mrs Warmleigh has left her Hoover on the stairs. I go to look for her and ask her to move it, as Gianluca is due.

'The blind boy? He's amazing that one, the way he comes and goes. Fantastic, it is, bless him.'

I concur, wearily. Mrs Warmleigh has a warty, smiley face and, oddly for the cleaning lady in a dentist's, many pronounced gaps in her famous smile. 'Warmleigh by name, warmly by nature,' she says, at least two or three times a week.

'You'd look at him,' she goes on, 'and you could swear he could see. Amazing.'

A nasty little sliver of suspicion enters my mind.

REWIND ◀◀

Felicia started talking about children on the day of her twenty-eighth birthday. We had been 'going out' for two years by then. I asked her why she chose to live in Oxford with its tiresome, lengthy commute to London when, on her salary, she could have lived in town, conveniently and comfortably. 'I was always happy in Oxford,' she said. 'And besides, you're here.' The logic doesn't hold up. She came back to Oxford, bought her little house in Osney Meade and then we met up again and, as these things will, resumed our affair. There is a character in *Morbid Anatomy* loosely, very loosely, based on Felicia. I think she dies in a plane crash.

PLAY ▶

This is vaguely shaming but I know I have to do it. Gianluca leaves and thirty seconds later I am out the door following him. I watch him for a while and, as he waits at the pedestrian crossing, I use a gap in the traffic to overtake him. I jog ahead up through the Summertown shops until I have a hundred yard start on him and, hidden in a doorway, I watch his progress, steady and sure, towards me. It is true, as Mrs Warmleigh had observed, without the white stick there would be nothing in Gianluca's stride or progress to tell you he was blind. Is it a sad subterfuge, some mental problem, I find myself wondering – wondering with slowly stirring anger, rather than commiseration, as I'm a significant victim of this subterfuge? Or is he merely partially sighted and playing it up for more sympathy?

I let him go by. 'Oi, mate,' I disguise my voice with a bit of Oxford demotic. 'You drop vis money.'

He turns. 'Excuse me?'

My empty palm proffers an invisible ten-pound note.

He steps towards me his eyes moving. 'Some money?' he digs in his pocket, producing a wallet. He *is* blind, all right, blind as a stone, stone-blind, bat-blind, and a small pelt of self-loathing covers me for an instant. 'I dropped money?' he says, fumbling with his wallet's zip.

'Gianluca?' a girl's voice calls. We both turn.

'Gianluca,' I say. 'Is everything all right?'

'Edward,' he says with relief, 'I thought someone talking to me.'

The girl is up to us now and she takes his arm. She's small with wiry brown hair and a mischievous look to her face, half laughing, half smirking. She wears black and she's smoking.

'Is my sister, Claudia,' Gianluca introduces us. 'This is Edward. Claudia is coming to stay for a few days. She take me back home.'

I reach out to take her proffered hand, once she transfers her cigarette.

'Gianluca has told me everything about you.'

'Not everything, I hope,' I say, looking into those thin, brown, sightful eyes. And I know.

PAUSE II

It is a kind of watershed, I realize. When you know instantly. And when the other person knows you know. It is, in its own way, an infallible sign of adulthood – a threshold crossed. All your imagined, wistful, striven-for worldliness suddenly coalescing into a simple, blunt adult recognition. The last shreds of adolescent insecurity finally gone. From now on there will never be any doubt or ambiguity. You can look into a person's eyes, and, wordlessly, the question can be asked – if you want to ask it – and you will know the answer: yes or no. End of story.

FAST FORWARD ▶▶

INTERVIEWER: You didn't find that the Nobel/Booker/Pulitzer/Goncourt inhibited your creativity in any way?

ME: On the contrary. I found it liberating. And the cheque was very welcome too (laughter).

REWIND ◀◀

I left Cardman's rooms and wandered out into the quad, holding my error-strewn chapter rolled up like a baton, like a truncheon, in my hand. The afternoon sun obliquely struck the venerable buildings, picking out the detailing of the stonework with admirable clarity. The razored lawn was immaculate, perfectly striped, unbadged by weed or daisy, almost indecently, absurdly green. I realized that I hated old buildings, hated honey-coloured crafted stone, hated scholarship, hated arrogant young dons with their superior ways. So much hate, I reflected, as I crossed Magdalen Bridge, can't be good for one. The leaves of my chapter helixed gently down on to the turbid brown waters of the Cherwell.

PLAY ▶

I walk through Felicia's neat, bright house trying to imagine myself here. Where would my things go? Where would my desk be? Everything is neat, neat, neat, everything is tidy and neat. Even the cuddly toys on her bedcover are neatly arranged in descending order of size. Predictably, I search her laundry basket for a pair of soiled knickers to masturbate into but find only tights, cut-off jeans and a rugby shirt – and somehow the auto-erotic moment is gone. Dutifully, I feed her dazzling, frondy fish, trying to analyse what I felt for Felicia, with her decency, her baffling, uncritical devotion, her compartmentalized mind, at once cutesy and clever, our fundamental incompatability . . . I could just about fit in here, I suppose, but where would baby go?

REWIND ◀◀

I was watching *Blade Runner* for about the thirtieth time when Felicia called.

'Hi. What is it?' I said.

'Just to let you know I landed safely.'

'Oh. Great. Where are you?'

'Singapore. K.L. tomorrow.'

'K.L.?'

'Kuala Lumpur.'

'Why don't people refer to San Francisco as S.F.? Always wondered about that? "Hey, let's go to S.F."'

'Are you all right, Edward?'

'What? Yeah. I think I'm going to abandon my thesis. Concentrate on the novel.'

'That's wonderful news. Look, I must dash, the car's waiting. Love you.'

'Bye.' I put the phone down. 'Love you.'

PLAY ▶

Claudia lights my cigarette for me, a gesture that, for some reason, always generates in me a little gut-spasm of lust, a little intestinal writhe.

'You must try some of our English beer,' I say. 'Old Fuddleston's Triple-Brewed Dog-Piss.'

'Oh yeah. I think I stay with vodka.'

'Very wise, Claudia, very wise indeed.'

We are sitting in a dark booth in a low-beamed smoky pub off Broad Street and I wonder whether I should kiss her now but decide to wait a bit – I'm quite enjoying the sexual sparring.

'So, Eduardo,' She plumes smoke at the ceiling. Then leans forward far enough so I can see the swell of her small breasts in the scoop of her t-shirt. 'You write novels. Can I read them?'

'You bet, Claudia. One day.'

FAST FORWARD ▶▶

INTERVIEWER: So why settle in BigSur/Sausalito/Arizona/Key West?

ME: Well, after the divorce, I needed to get out of Britain. I was with Cora-Lee by then and her father offered us the use of his villa/ beach hut/ranch. I was in rough shape emotionally and needed peace. Peace of mind. The most valuable commodity on the planet.

INTERVIEWER: Cora-Lee is substantially younger than you?

ME: That's true. But her wisdom is ageless.

SLOW MOTION ▮▶

Claudia's t-shirt comes off easily enough but I'm surprised to see her wearing a tough little sports bra thing with no clasp or hook I tug at a strap I am pretty fucking pissed we're both pretty fucking pissed all that beer and vodka Jesus how much did we drink I kick off a shoe and hear the zip on Claudia's jeans zing open she weaves away to the bathroom I haul the rest of my clothes off and slide under the duvet bollock naked I think bollock naked she comes in damn still in the bra thing blue panties not matching she whips the duvet back laughing and shouting at me in Italian *preservativa preservativa*.

PLAY ▶

As luck would have it, as filthy pigging stinking luck would have it, Prentist the dentist comes through the front door just as Claudia and I are crossing the hall. What sort of dentist comes to work at 7.45 a.m.? And why should I feel guilty? I'm a grown man renting a flat off another grown man. I introduce Claudia. The fact that I'm only in this flat because Felicia knows Prentice from the squash club is something I prefer not to contemplate right now.

Claudia looks at me in that way she has. 'Goodbye, Edward, I see you later.' I imagine that we must reek of sex – a pongy, spermy, sweaty, tangled sheets sort of exudation – filling the hallway like tear gas.

Claudia leaves.

Prentice turns to me. 'I don't know what she sees in you,' he says, his voice harsh.

'Claudia?'

'Felicia, you tragic bastard. I don't know why she wants to marry you.'

'Because she loves me, Prentist, that's why.'

'I want you out of here. End of the week.'

FAST FORWARD ▶▶

INTERVIEWER: Do you ever think of the future? Of death?

ME: Wasn't it Epicurus who said: 'Death is not our business'?

PLAY ▶

'Davidson, thoughtful, seemed to weigh the matter in his mind, and then murmured with placid sadness: "Nothing!"' I close the book. 'The end,' I say to Gianluca.

I walk down to the hall with him and we make our farewells. Gianluca thanks me, with some sincerity. I find myself wondering if Claudia has described to him how I look? I will miss Gianluca, and endless, interminable *Victory* – or will I? I know one thing for sure: I will never read a book by Joseph Conrad again. The mood is one of . . . of placid sadness. Saddish, but not unsettling, not unpleasant.

'Claudia say she will call you tonight.'

'I won't be here tonight,' I say. 'I'm moving out. I'll be staying with a friend. Tell Claudia . . . Just say goodbye from me.'

PAUSE ▐▐

'Let's get married,' I said to Felicia when she called to tell me when her plane was landing. It was strange to hear her crying all those thousands of miles away, her little choking noises, the sniffs. 'I mean, will you marry me?' I'm so happy, Edward, she said, I'm so incredibly happy.

PLAY ▶

I stand on the platform at Oxford station, a bunch of overpriced scarlet tulips in my hand, looking sympathetically across the rails at the commuters with their briefcases and newspapers. Felicia's train appears and slows to a halt, doors swinging open. I stand there waiting, not moving, and I see Felicia step down in her smart suit, lugging her suitcase (which contains, I know, a silk shirt for me), tucking her hair behind her ears, looking around for me, her future husband. I raise my bunch of overpriced scarlet tulips and wave.

FREEZE FRAME ■

Varengeville

Oliver frowned darkly and pushed his spectacles back up to the bridge of his nose, taking in his mother's suspiciously bright smile and trying to ignore Lucien's almost sneering, almost leering, grimace of pride and self-satisfaction. Lucien was his mother's 'friend': Oliver had decided he did not particularly like Lucien.

'What exactly is it?' Oliver said, playing for time.

'I believe people call it a bicycle,' Lucien said. Oliver noticed his mother thought this sally was amusing.

'I know that,' Oliver said, patiently, 'but why are *you* giving *me* a bicycle?'

'It's a present,' his mother said, 'it's a gift for you, you can go exploring. Say thank you to Uncle Lucien. Really, you're intolerably spoilt.'

'Thank you, Lucien,' Oliver said. 'You are most kind.'

The bicycle was solid, a little too big for him, black, with three gears and lights and possessed – Oliver admitted he was pleased by this gadget – a small folding-down support that allowed the bike to stand free when it was parked.

However, it did not take long for the real purpose of the gift to become evident. Oliver wondered if his mother thought he was really that stupid. Every time Lucien motored over from Deauville, always after lunch (always leaving before six), his mother would turn to Oliver and say, 'Oliver, darling, why don't you cycle into Varengeville and post this letter for me?' She would give him a hundred francs and tell him to have a *diabolo menthe* at the café in the square. 'Explore,' she would further enjoin, vaguely, waving her arms about. 'Wander here and there. Wonderful countryside, beaches, trees. The freedom of the open road. Fill your lungs, my darling, fill your lungs.'

And Oliver would wearily mount the big black bicycle and pedal off down the road to Varengeville, the letter tucked into his belt. He had a good idea what his mother and Lucien would be doing in his absence – he knew, in fact he was absolutely convinced, that it would involve a lot of kissing – and he was sure his father would not be pleased. He had discovered his mother and Lucien in a kiss on one occasion and had watched them silently, slightly disturbed at the violence, the audible suction with which their mouths fed on each other. Then they had broken apart and his mother had seen him watching. She took him at once into the next room and explained that Maman had been unhappy and Uncle Lucien was simply being kind and had been trying to cheer her up but that it would be best if he didn't tell Papa. They were both instantly aware – Oliver's eyes narrowing – that this explanation was laughably inept, that it did not even begin to undermine the blatant deceit. So she changed tactics and instead made him promise to her: she extracted one of her most severe and terrifying and implacable promises from him. Oliver knew he would never dare tell Papa.

Lucien came two or three times a week, always in the afternoon. Once he came with some other friends on a Sunday for lunch accompanied by a nervy, febrile woman with strange coppery hair who was introduced as his wife. It was early August and Oliver was beginning doggedly to count the days before he would go back to school in England, to count the days before he would see his father again, conscious all the while that the summer was only half done and that there would be many more cycle trips into Varengeville.

It was on his sixth or seventh journey into the village that he spotted the old painter. Oliver always took the same route: up the sloping drive to the gates, turning down the farm lane to the road; then there was an exhilarating swift downhill freewheel along the hedgerow to the D.75, then right along the cliff road towards Varengeville, with the brilliant ocean, restless and refulgent, on his left, his eyes screwed up behind his spectacle lenses, half-blinded by the glare of the afternoon sun.

It was the odd shape of the canvas that attracted his attention first: it was long and thin, almost like a short plank, screwed into a small easel. The old painter sat absolutely still on a collapsible canvas stool, his arms folded across his breast, staring out to sea, his brushes and paints resting on his knees. Oliver noticed his shock of completely white hair, neatly combed and, even though the man was sitting, he knew he must be tall and thin.

In Varengeville he posted his mother's letter and then went to the café for his *diabolo*. The café was always quiet in mid-afternoon and the surly young waiter, with a new downy moustache on his top lip, listened to his order, served him his drink, accepted his payment, tossed down the change, tore a corner off the receipt and wandered off, loudly straightening already straight chairs, without a word.

Oliver looked out at the little square and thought about things: his mother and Lucien, for a start, then the scab that was hardening nicely on his elbow; his desire to have a pet of some sort, mammal or reptile, he couldn't decide; the film that his father was making in London . . . Then he would observe, covertly but closely, the rare customers that came and went, and from time to time admire the perfect stolidity of his parked bicycle – canted over somewhat, but resolutely firm on its stand – and note how the slightly elliptical shadow version of it, angled flat on the pavement, shadow wheels touching real rubber wheels, was both absolutely exact and yet undeniably distorted. The phrase 'as faithful as a shadow' came into his head and he thought how true it was, but then wondered, where did your shadow go when the sun wasn't shining? . . . How could be something be faithful if you couldn't see it? . . . And then he found his thoughts were returning to his mother and Lucien and he decided he would cycle back as slowly as possible, hoping Lucien would be gone by the time he arrived home and he would not have to encounter him, mysteriously washed and perfumed, a permanent smile on his lips and full of an unfamiliar and repugnant affection for Oliver.

The old painter was still sitting motionless in his field, still staring out at the sea and the coastline. The afternoon had turned hazy, the sky full of spilt-milk clouds, but still glarey and dazzling. Coming from the other direction Oliver could now see what was on the canvas, and as he approached he was surprised to note that it seemed almost black, full of murky blues and dark greys. For an absurd second, as he glanced at the silvered sea with its vast backdrop of sunlit cloud, he wondered if the painter might be blind. And then he wondered if he might be dead. People could die like that suddenly, sitting up, just stiffen into a posture like that – they could, he'd read about it.

'Are you all right, Monsieur?' Oliver asked softly.

The painter turned slowly round. He had a big rectangular face, its features powerfully present – the nose, the eyes, the thin, wide mouth, the absolutely white hair – yet in no way distinctive or handsome, just a strong simple oblong face, Oliver thought, but somehow oddly memorable.

'But of course, young man,' the painter said. 'Many thanks for asking.'

Oliver had parked his bicycle and had climbed over the fence and approached the painter without seeing any movement in him, aware now that he wasn't in fact dead, of course, but curious about his impressive immobility.

'I thought,' Oliver began, 'because you weren't painting that –'

'No, I was just refreshing my memory,' the painter said. 'I just needed to come out here again, in case I had got something wrong.'

Oliver looked at the murky canvas, which showed, as far as he could tell, a ship washed up on a shore in the night. He looked up at the bleached, blinding sky and back at the dark, thin canvas.

'This happened a long time ago,' the painter said in explanation, pointing at his painting.

He began to ask Oliver polite questions: what is your name? –

Oliver Feverall – how old are you? – almost twelve – where do you live? – Château Les Pruniers, but just for the summer.

'You speak very good French, but you have an English name,' the painter observed. Oliver told him that his mother was French and his father was English. His mother was an actress, she had appeared in half a dozen films, perhaps he knew of her – Fabienne Farde? – the painter confessed he did not.

'Perhaps you've heard of my father, he's a famous film director, Denton Feverall?'

'I rarely go to the cinema,' the painter said, beginning to pack away his brushes and tubes. As far as Oliver could tell, he hadn't added a stroke of colour to his grimy canvas, just come outside and stared at it for a couple of hours.

They walked back to the gate that led to the coast road. The painter admired Oliver's bicycle, admired the efficacy of its folding-down stand. Oliver tried once more.

'It was given to me by a singer, a famous singer, he's in Deauville for the summer, at the Casino – Lucien Navarro.'

'Lucien Navarro, Lucien Navarro . . .' the painter repeated, holding his forefinger erect on his right hand as if calling for silence. Oliver waited. Then, after a while: 'No, never heard of him.' Oliver shrugged, wondering what kind of reclusive life this man led who had never heard of Fabienne Farde, Denton Feverall or Lucien Navarro.

They shook hands, formally, and the painter wished Oliver a good end to the afternoon and thanked him again for his solicitude. Oliver looked back as he cycled away and saw the old man striding down the road, his canvas and easel under one arm, the afternoon sun striking his silver hair, making it flame with light.

Lucien had a new car – a Lancia, whose roof came down. 'Lucien and his Lancia,' Oliver thought, a note of disgust colouring his reflections as he cycled off to Varengeville with his mother's letter, 'Lucien and his Lancia.'

Lucien had not visited for some six days and Oliver had noted his mother's moods steadily deteriorating. One morning she had not descended from her bedroom at all, only the maid was allowed access, bringing up all manner of curious drinks. Even Oliver's soft knock on her door in the afternoon produced only the moaned response 'Darling, Maman has one of her migraines' and he did not see her at all, he calculated, for a further thirty-seven hours.

And then Lucien was coming and she was alert and agitated, changing her clothes, shifting vases of flowers about the drawing room, her perfumes more noticeably pungent, her affection for Oliver overt, falling upon him suddenly, with brusque, sore hugs and alarming cannonades of kisses and caresses. Oliver looked impassively out of the library windows as Lucien's midnight blue Lancia crunched dustily to a halt and, for the first time, felt relieved he had to go to Varengeville and post a letter.

But in the village, standing in front of the pale yellow post box he felt a sudden flow of anger at his ritual banishment. He tore open the letter – always to his mother's sister in Paris – and, as he knew he would, discovered three perfectly blank sheets of paper. He folded them up, deliberately, slowly, and dropped them in a litter bin by a set of traffic lights. He cycled south out of Varengeville, towards the plateau, heading for Longeuil, not wanting a *diabolo menthe*, wondering how he was going to survive the two and a half weeks of August that were left, wondering how he could go through this pretence, this silly game, each time Lucien arrived. Why didn't she just say she wanted to be alone. He didn't care how long they kissed each other, or whatever else they got up to. He simply wanted summer to be over, he wanted to get back to school, he wanted his father to finish filming *Daughters of Dracula*.

The painter was walking along the road with his usual light burden of easel, folding stool and long, thin canvas. Oliver slowed to a halt and they greeted each other, Oliver noticing that, although the day was hot, the painter was wearing a tweed jacket with a shirt and tie and a curious knitted waistcoat. Old men felt the cold, Oliver remembered, even on the warmest days.

'Where are you going?' the painter asked. He gestured at the flat, baking landscape inland. In the enormous sky a fleet of huge, burly white clouds moved slowly along, northwards, pushed by a warm southern breeze. A heavy flight of crows crossed the stubble field beside them. 'It's hot out there,' the painter said.

'I'm not going anywhere in particular,' Oliver said, feeling unfamiliar tears sting his eyes.

'Is everything all right?'

'Yes, absolutely.'

'Come home with me,' the painter said. 'Have a cold drink.'

The painter showed Oliver into his studio: it was a large, tidy room with a Persian rug hanging on the wall. On an easel was a sizeable painting of a blue bird shape against a slate-grey sky. On tables and on the floor were rows of cleaned brushes laid on palettes, and others stuffed into ceramic pots. Small tables held neat rows of tubes of oil paint and on these tables were jars of flowers, many of them dried. Oliver was impressed.

'You must have hundreds of brushes,' he said. 'Thousands.'

'You may be right,' said the painter, smiling, placing his small canvas on an empty easel and stepping back to contemplate it. Oliver circled round to stare at it, glancing at the picture of the bird and thinking that he, Oliver Feverall, could paint a better-looking bird than that.

The small canvas looked like a sodden field beneath winter skies, three uneven stripes of brown, green and grey, the paint thickly smeared, but quite dry.

'I'm having real problems,' the painter said. 'I don't know what to do. I did one like this before and put a plough in it, and it seemed to work.'

'What about a man?'

'No. I don't want people in these pictures.'

'What about some crows?'

'It's an idea.'

★

As they were going outside to the terrace to have their cold drinks, Oliver heard a woman's voice call out 'Georges? Are you back?' The painter excused himself and went upstairs, returning a minute later.

'It's my wife,' he said. 'She thinks she's getting flu.'

They sat outside at a metal table under a small canvas awning which provided a neat square of shade and sipped at their cold drinks, fetched for them by a plump, smiley housekeeper. Oliver was introduced as 'Monsieur Oliver, my English friend,' and his hand was shaken. The painter drank mineral water, Oliver an Orangina, and they both sat there silently for a while in the relentless afternoon heat, staring out at the big, solid clouds steaming towards them, northwards. Oliver thought that the painter had a sad face and noticed how the lines that ran from his nose to his face were particularly marked, casting, even in this shade, dark sickle shadows.

'It's an interesting idea that,' the painter said, 'crows.' He turned to Oliver and continued, 'So, when's your birthday?'

'Next week. Wednesday.'

'Come by. We'll have another drink. I'll drink your health. No, I mean it, if you've nothing better to do.'

Oliver thanked him. Wednesday was usually a Lucien day – Wednesday and Friday.

They were silent again for a while, together.

'Do you know what a "love affair" is?' Oliver asked.

'Yes,' the painter said, 'I certainly do.'

'Do you think that if you're married you should have a love affair with someone else?'

'I don't know,' the painter said.

'Isn't it wrong?'

'It depends.' The painter sipped at his mineral water. He held up his glass as if to look at the sky through it. 'Sometimes water is the best drink in the world, isn't it?'

He walked Oliver to the road and watched him as he crouched to undo the padlock on the chain that Oliver had threaded through the rear wheel as an anti-theft device.

'Do you think someone will steal your bike?' the painter asked.

'You can't be too careful. In London I've had three bikes stolen.'

'But this is Varengeville, not London. Still it is a splendid machine, isn't it, wonderfully built.'

'I wish it had drop handlebars,' Oliver said. 'I think it looks a bit old-fashioned.' He kicked up the stand with his left shoe. 'I'd better get home,' he said, 'my mother will be waiting.'

'See you on Wednesday,' the painter said.

On his birthday his mother gave Oliver a very crumpled ten-pound note and promised him a proper treat when they returned home. Oliver said he was going to see a friend in Varengeville and set off up the drive a good half hour before Lucien was due.

The housekeeper was watering some pots of geraniums by the front door as Oliver approached.

'He's not here,' she said. 'They had to go back to Paris yesterday. Madame has bronchitis, we think.'

Oliver pursed his lips and pushed his spectacles up to the bridge of his nose. Damn, he thought, bloody damn. He looked about him, hands on his hips, wondering resentfully what he would do for the rest of the day – maybe he should just go to the beach.

'He's left a present for you,' the housekeeper said, disappearing back into the house and re-emerging with a long, thin brown paper parcel. 'He was very insistent you should have this.'

Oliver sat on the beach below the small cliff and took his shoes and socks off. He looked at his watch – he'd better stay here for a couple of hours at least, to allow Lucien time to leave. It was annoying that the painter had been obliged to go to Paris – he had been looking forward to the visit, it would have solved the problem of the day.

Oliver allowed himself an audible sigh and looked about him, idly. A stout, dark girl in a yellow bikini sunbathed some feet away, her small Yorkshire terrier at her side huddling under a bunched towel for shade. Further along a group of kids sat in a circle around a transistor radio. Toddlers studiously dug in the wet sand at the gentle surf's edge. Oliver thought about his birthday – what could he get for ten pounds? . . . Maybe Dad will call this evening. He's bound to give me ten pounds too, maybe more . . . He mentally totalled all the potential fiscal gifts that he might receive from his assorted relatives and came up with a satisfyingly large figure. Not such a bad birthday after all, he thought, and unwrapped the painter's present.

It was the wet fields painting, Oliver was not too surprised to discover – and just what was he supposed to do with it, he wondered? It wasn't particularly well painted, Oliver thought, and also the painter himself had seemed dissatisfied with it. He felt a slight surge of irritation that the painter had given him a picture that even he had been unable to finish properly. What it needed was something else in it, not just fields and sky. Maybe, Oliver thought, he should paint his bike in one of the corners, have it leaning over on its stand . . .

The sunbathing girl in the bikini turned over suddenly and rolled on to her small dog, which gave an anguished yelp of pain and surprise. No, Oliver thought, inspired, if he painted the sky blue then the field would look like a beach. Then he could paint the girl lying on the beach with her yellow bikini and her little dog. And then the painting would at least be finished – at least it would be about something. Oliver stared at the plump girl as she fussed and petted her discomfited dog. He found himself grinning, felt the laugh brim in his throat, and quickly covered his mouth with his hand in case she should see.

Notebook No. 9

[It had become his habit over the years, whenever he lunched alone, to take a small notebook with him, into which he jotted down his random thoughts and observations, preferring to disguise his solitariness by writing, rather than reading.]

No crab-cakes today, so I settled with bad grace for a pseudo-*salade niçoise* (no potatoes). This restaurant is renowned for its crab-cakes – this is why I and most of its clientèle come here – so why not supply crab-cakes on a daily basis? Just seen *Slang* – interesting thriller, because it all takes place during the course of one night. A clear *hommage* – which is to say rip-off – to Raupp's *Death Valley* but without its textures, its love of character. Defects: sudden shifts of mood from whimsy to hardboiled; silly plot contrivances (the lap-dancing scenes, the language school); *fantastic* coincidences – always a sign of waning inspiration. Raupp does this but it sort of works with him. Finally the film is just not *true* – and as Pierre-Henri Duprez, I think, once said somewhere, you can't hide anything from an audience. (Which is wrong, actually: look at the garbage in our cinemas that is avidly, unreflectingly, credulously consumed.)

I think Tanja would hate *Slang*. Positively loathe it.

I spotted bad looping, boom-mike shadow and a clumsily inserted repeat shot. I guess all directors have this tic – we can never be simple *cinéphiles*.

The lead girl, Michaela Wall, is beguiling (a blonder, rangier Tanja). Ultimately, any genre film is only as good as its characterization.

There is a woman sitting opposite me who smoked a cigarette in about ninety seconds: small puffs in sequences of three, then a beat, then another three quick small puffs. She didn't seem to inhale. One wonders what pleasure she derives from smoking.

Behind her, a mother and daughter with two screaming kids. The din! Quite middle-class too, judging by their accents. They just let the children wail, really – everyone in the café very pissed-off but not saying anything in true English fashion.

Tanja is forty-three minutes late.

Fascinating-looking girl serving in the Syndicate today. Russian? East-European certainly. Long ballet-dancer's back. Moley – mole on her cheek, moles on her neck. She's tall with a thin, patrician face, hair pulled back in a tight bun. What's she doing here? What's her story, her *parcours*? There's a sustained, slightly contemptuous expression on her face as she goes about her business serving drinks, clearing tables.

Just back from lunch at the Garrick with Leo Winteringham. Everyone in the place seemed to be over fifty, male – naturally – overweight, raddled-looking. Cigars and booze: the slightly *louche* end of the British establishment. Leo W. volunteered to fund any film I cared to direct – he must have made me that offer a dozen times, now. Strange figure, Leo: irreducibly American despite all his years in England. Lean, saurian, brusque – a curious player in this privileged English world (he was greeted warmly by everyone) admitted only because he has money.

As we were gossiping about the business (who's in, who's out, who's hot, who's cold) he mentioned that Tanja Baiocchi had left her husband. I managed to hide my massive shock and said that I didn't know she was married. Wasn't she in your last film, he asked? I said she was but there had never been any talk of a husband. Well, perhaps, not husband, he said – boyfriend, then, that French director, Duprez. Oh, I said, I know all about that, oh yes, and could confirm that the rupture, *entre nous*, was true – absolute and final.

3.30. The bar at the Syndicate is quiet but the people in it are still drinking steadily, as if reluctant to let the afternoon and the afternoon cafard begin. I should call Janet and see how the invitations are going for the cast and crew screening and get her to book me into the hotel in New York.

Drink: I had a glass of champagne before I went to the Garrick, a glass of white wine in the bar, two glasses w/wine at lunch and a port (Leo doesn't drink) and am now on my second glass of white wine at the Syndicate: effectively a bottle of wine. More than a bottle of wine: I must stop now. I never drink nearly as much when I'm with Tanja.

New York. Carlyle Hotel. Sitting here having my pre-pre-prandial drink (a bloody mary) – a new bad habit which is explained by the fact that I am just a few hours away from the screening of *The Sleep Thief*. I feel unusually apprehensive (this is my ninth film, for God's sake) and I know why: I'm expecting too much. Because I know the worth and merit of the film I'm expecting it to experience no problems – Cannes, a US distributor, a prize or two: no worries. I should just be patient – look at the slow burn of appreciation that delivered the success of *Escapade*. The film is finished, it is good work, we had fun, what more can you ask? (And I met Tanja, of course.) So let's see how the dice roll. Nothing may come of this screening – we may have to wait until Cannes, or even the UK release – we may have to wait longer, until Venice or Berlin.

I wish Tanja were arriving today so she could be here for the screening. Why does she have to come tomorrow?

Vague worries about the quality of the print, about the projector, about the sound level. But what can I do?

Sitting in F.O.O.D. on Lexington. Tanja has postponed her visit – another three days to wait. It would have been good if she'd made the screening (thin crowd – disappointing – but it seemed to go down all right. No offers yet. The print was appalling).

Two very groomed women sit beside me, talking to each other, with gratifying volume and clarity. Clearly they don't know each other very well.

'Where do you live?' one asks.

'Mexico.'

'Even further away than me – Vermont.'

Pause.

'Where in Mexico?'

'San Miguel. It's very beautiful.'

'Oh, there are a lot of expatriates, there.'

'There are a few of us.'

'I hear you can get a very cheap face-lift.'

'Cheap face-lifts, cheap domestic staff. It has its advantages.'

Men have more boring conversations than women, I find, speaking as a professional eavesdropper. Tanja was once in a movie shot in Mexico. She met Duprez there. I think.

'You may not have a drinking problem but I have a problem with your drinking.' Overheard in Bemelmans.

Bizarre sight in Going Loco (East Village). A young mother (twenty-one? twenty-two?), suckling her child in the corner of the café, receives a call on her cell-phone. She answers it, rises to her feet and walks to the window of the café chatting on the phone, the baby still at her breast. The unconcern, the utter absence of *pudeur* was entirely admirable – made me feel old, crabbed and confined by my upbringing and the received wisdom of my attitudes and values – as hard to remove as a tattoo. I like the atmosphere in this place – rackety, worldly – I am eating a pungent, garlicky gazpacho at the bar. Very smoky. Tanja flies in tomorrow.

4.00 p.m. Bemelmans. Drinking beer and eating cashew nuts. The place is full of older people: that generation of New Yorkers who like a cocktail mid-afternoon. There is a man beside me who has just ordered a second dry martini.

I lunched with Tanja. I went to her suite in the Plaza and to my astonishment there was a young boy there, about six or seven. 'This is Pascal,' she said as if his presence were the most natural thing in the world. Then Pascal said something to her in French and referred to her as '*Maman*'. What on earth does he mean by that? I asked. He's my son, she said, looking at me as if I were a crazy fool, that's what he calls me. A nanny came to take him away but I had lost my appetite. During lunch I managed to ask if Duprez was the father and Tanja reassured me he wasn't. Throughout our eight weeks of filming together on *The Sleep Thief* she never once referred to Pascal. Is this normal for a mother? Was she hiding the fact from me in case it interfered with our affair? Maybe she thought I knew and because I never brought his name up she felt it more discreet to do the same? She's coming to the hotel tonight once the boy has been put to bed.

Curious: I seem only to drink beer in France or the US. Never touch a drop in England.

In the pub, The Duke of Kent, Monday lunch. No food in the flat so I came here. An empty fridge in an empty apartment – how depressing is that? I was about to call Janet and have her order in a take-away when I remembered she was working on another film in Malta. Janet and my two assistants, gone. A film director, when a film is finally over, has to return to the unfamiliar state of actually doing mundane things for himself – like going to the bank, fetching clothes from the dry-cleaners, buying food and provisions. Strange to be self-reliant again, strange to be back in London after New York. Missing Tanja desperately, achingly – she flew to L.A. to meet her agent. She promised she would be in Cannes . . . I'm obsessed by her nervous, mobile beauty. She's never still – *agitée*, they would call her in France.

Opposite me three fat guys – heavy, enormous men. Eating pork sausage and mash, brown bread and butter. Two with pints of lager on the go, plus a bottle of red wine on the table between the three of them. I must start thinking about my next film, but I can't let *The Sleep Thief* go. While I still dream about Tanja all the time – the film, our film, lives on, as if we're playing out the lost, last reel. They've just ordered puddings and more beer. I try to imagine myself as Pascal's step-father: I have to come to terms with the fact that there would be three of us in any future arrangement. Perhaps we could find him a place in a boarding school. Benji and Max went away at his age and seemed perfectly happy all those years at Farnham Hall – which reminds me: where are they now? What're they doing? My salmon-caesar has arrived: scant sign of any salmon.

Café Méridien, Cannes. I ate here when I first came to Cannes with *Two-and-a-Half Grand*. I remember this little bistro so well, remember the surging, irrepressible confidence of my mood – my first film and selected for 'Un Certain Regard' – nothing could stop me. I remember walking past this place one early morning and pausing to watch as the patron hosed down the pavement and began setting out the tables. I saw a saturnine man performing the very same routine this morning and had the odd sensation of being aware that all those years ago I had stood on this exact spot and watched the same ritual – that here one's life had, for once, come a genuine full circle. Flash back: I was twenty-nine years old. Benji was two, Max was on the way . . . To think Annie and I were happy then . . .

Tanja called from Prague, where she's filming. They're over-running, she doesn't think she can make the screening. It's in her fucking contract, for Christ's sake: she has to be released for pub-licity. I have to call the studio: a screening of *The Sleep Thief* at the Cannes Film Festival and no Tanja Baiocchi – what's that going to look like? What signal will it send?

The little hotel I used to stay in is now called the Hotel Carlone. In a video-shop I found an old copy of *Dix-Mille Balles* (*Two-and-a-Half Grand*). I almost wept.

What colour is Tanja's hair? Caramel. Butterscotch. Fudge. Toffee . . . All edible, all sweets.

Idea for my next film, to be called *Blue on Blue* – the term used in the British Army for those occasions in warfare when you accidentally kill someone on your own side.

*

Meditation on the navel: a scar that every human being carries . . .
A baby's cry requires no translation . . . A scream has no accent . . .
A yawn is understood the world over . . . The banal truths of life
are no less true, despite their banality.

Saw Terry Mulvehey's new movie *The Last Rebel* (how did he
get into Director's Fortnight and not me?). Completely preposterous and yet beautiful film. The story of *Wings of a Dove* grafted on
to the American Civil War. No attempt to make the men's hairstyles
look remotely nineteenth-century. Mulvehey will sacrifice anything
if it will provide a beautiful shot – narrative plausibility, character
development, pace, suspense: everything yields to the lovely image.
Compositionally, the film is flawless, but as a real story about real
people – *rien*. Vanity and nullity. Tanja has not returned my calls
all week. I sent her a text-message demanding to know who was
Pascal's father. I worry, perhaps, that I've made a crucial error.

The Duke of Kent has been renamed The Flaming Terrapin in my
absence. Curious name for a pub, but what do I know? We now
have music (all but overwhelmed by the collective bellow of conversation), we now have mute televisions showing a rain-lashed golf
tournament between competing bright umbrellas. I push my char-
grilled Thai chicken around my plate and order another glass of
golden, sun-pervaded Australian Chardonnay (my third).

It is Friday lunchtime and you can sense the rowdy, burgeoning,
weekend release of appetites. These young people in their twenties
and thirties are eating and drinking and smoking as if their lives
depended on it. And they do of course: their lives depend on them
ceasing to eat, drink and smoke like this. Fuel Britannia. What is it
about us? On the evidence of the crowd in this pub we have become
a nation of careless, reckless trenchermen and trencherwomen.
Strapping girls drinking pints of stout and extra-strength lager;
young men with goatees and shaven heads bowed in front of
their heaped plates of carbohydrate, shovelling in the pies and the
burgers, the spare-ribs and the bangers, packing their pot-bellies
and pot-faces. I can't finish my Thai chicken.

I have just pushed through to the bar to fetch another brimming glass of wine. I now realize with some alarm that these are in fact 'large' glasses of wine that I've been drinking, which is to say one glass contains two normal glasses of wine. No wonder I feel suddenly a little flushed and unsteady.

How To Become A Successful Film Director: page one, paragraph one, line one. Don't fall in love with your leading lady.

A table of four dapper Japanese businessmen have just asked me to take a photograph of them and I have complied. Little do they know who framed that snapshot. Is there something odd in this image? Perhaps I should use it for the last moments of *Blue on Blue* – just put the four Japanese businessmen in the scene in the caff, before the hero shoots himself – in the background, taking photographs – make no comment. Cool.

Two foreign girls – nannies? tourists? – one German, one Belgian (?), talking in English beside me on the next table, unconcerned by my drinking and my proximity. I learn that one of them, the German, has finally established a good relationship with a man, which has now endured a full month. Her friend expresses genuine, unfeigned delight. (NB. The happiness of women when a girlfriend gets a man – not an emotion shared by the other half of the sexual divide.) These girls have both been eating green salads: one drinking water, one orange juice. This is lunch for them – astonishing – what would make them come to a heaving, honking, feeding-frenzy like this? These girls are the new internationalists, roving the world, speaking good but accented English to each other, a kind of flawless Euro-English: 'I am very bad with separation,' the German girl says as she stands up to leave. No true English speaker would express the idea in this way, but it is perfectly comprehensible.

Leo Winteringham has passed on *Blue on Blue*.

Is it fair to say that the only truths in the world you can really vouch for are those you yourself feel and can therefore verify? 'I am happy' is something only you can know to be the case, absolutely. All other interpretations of the world beyond yourself are therefore suspect – merely hunches and deductions. 'Tanja Baiocchi is an unbearably, impossibly beautiful woman', '*The Sleep Thief* is an exceptionally bad film' – I'm rambling – the rich Australian wine kicking in, taking its heavy toll. How does that line of Tennyson go? Man comes and tills the fields and lies beneath can you be too intelligent to live well Leo was my last hope and after many a summer dies the swan but I know nothing nothing not being sure about anything can be very stimulating creatively discuss what precisely do I know right now Tanja Baiocchi has returned to live with Pierre-Henri Duprez I am not happy I too am bad with separation the problem with me is that I never *[The notebook concludes here.]*

A Haunting

Part I. Los Angeles

'My name is Alexander Rief. My name is Alexander Rief. My name is Alexander Rief – and I think I may be going mad.'

I was sitting in the first-class cabin of a jumbo jet, en route for Los Angeles, when I wrote these words in my notebook, thinking – as I recall – that the simple reiteration of my name would give me some kind of hold on my fast-disappearing sanity. I had been looking at my sketches for the Demarco project in Pacific Pallisades and, feeling relatively fine, I had eaten and had drunk no alcohol because of the mild headache from which I was suffering. The headache started about an hour out of London; nothing so unusual in that – except that I rarely suffer from headaches – but I remember this one because it seemed almost physically to move round my head, almost as if something were crawling around the interior of my skull, starting at the nape of the neck and then shifting around the right side of my head to lodge itself in the centre of my forehead. I took two aspirin, and waited for the analgesic to do its stuff, but it seemed not to be working. The headache grew steadily in intensity so that it became impossible to ignore it. It was not blinding, it was not pulsing, but it was indubitably, naggingly there. I massaged my forehead with my fingertips, I rubbed my brow with the soothing gel that is provided in the complimentary first-class toilet bag and finally took out my work hoping that distraction would make it abate, or at least I would have something other to think about than the visions of blood clots, strokes and tumours that were beginning to nudge their way into my reasoning mind.

So I looked at my sketches for the Demarco terraces, the sweep of walkways down to the pool and its surrounding plantations, and I took out my pencil to add a little cross hatching to the row of cypresses I had decided to plant behind the pool house.

I began to shade in the leaf darkness and then, quite suddenly, I felt my arm growing cold as if there were a draught blowing on my right side. At the same time I noticed, but did not feel, that my grip upon the silver barrel of the pencil was strengthening, my nails flushed with blood, and a slight but discernible tremor of effort made the point of the pencil shimmer like a seismograph about to register a major eruption.

And then I began – or rather – then my *hand* began to make signs, big bold signs across my delicate drawing of the Demarco terraces. The signs looked like a form of elongated 'x', each of the four arms of the letter drawn out horizontally. My hand was lifting the pencil from the page in order for this sign to be properly drawn, and, as I finished one, my hand would immediately begin to draw another. Soon my sketch was covered and I flipped the page to allow the writing to continue. And so it did, deliberately, quite meticulous, all the 'x' shapes being drawn the same size, with nothing manic or frenzied about them.

I sat there, almost without breathing, as my right hand autonomously continued to mark the page. At one stage I reached over to place my left hand on top of my right fist, but I seemed incapable of exerting any force, the pencil continued to move, and soon I lifted my hand and watched as the mass of x's began to darken the page. I hunched over, to make it look as if I was writing, as the cabin staff passed up and down the aisle. By now I was sweating copiously and I was seized with a kind of terror which was unfamiliar to me. As my right hand moved across the page of its own volition I wondered if something had malfunctioned in my brain – as if the headache was the sign of the rupturing of some crucial blood vessels, or that some critical malfunction of my neurotransmitters had taken place, and I began to hear, in my inner ear, the sound of a silent wailing – a keening desperate bafflement – as if my soul, the soul of Alexander Rief, seemed to have lost control of the body it inhabited.

The 'seizure', the 'fit', seemed to last, I don't know, five minutes, ten minutes, I had not looked at my watch. Suddenly I felt my hand stop and the pencil point lay inert on the page. I felt my arm warm again as I touched it gently with the fingers of my left hand. I let the pencil fall and clenched and unclenched my fist. My brain seemed empty, suddenly quiet after the clamour of my inner misery and I exhaled slowly. Carefully I picked up the pencil, turned it in my fingers and I wrote down my name. 'My name is Alexander Rief. My name is Alexander Rief . . .' It was only after ten minutes or so, when I had finally calmed down somewhat, that I noticed my headache had disappeared.

'I sit in the gathering gloom of this Californian garden,' I wrote that night in my journal, 'and wonder what on earth I went through on the plane. Pressure of work? A mini nervous breakdown? These signs of aberrant behaviour can afflict the individual out of the blue in this manner, I know, but up until now I've lived a life entirely free of these stress crises, however stressful the situation I've found myself in. Now I feel tired, but entirely normal. I called Stella in London but decided to tell her nothing of what happened. Wise? Who knows? There seemed no point in worrying her unduly. Tomorrow to Demarco's and a walk through of the relandscaping plans. John-Jo flies in Tuesday.'

The rest of that evening passed unexceptionally: I called room service, ordered and ate a plate of angel-hair pasta and drank half a bottle of Chardonnay, trying to stay awake as long as possible, to mitigate the effects of jet-lag, to hoodwink my body clock, still functioning on London time. I walked through the cool, discreetly lit gardens of the hotel and thought again about what had happened to me on the plane, running through the sequence of events, seeing if further analysis provided any answers. No ready explanation came to hand. Back in my room I took out my notebook, looked at my defaced sketches for the Demarco house and pondered the dense clustering of cryptic signs that my hand had written across the pages. What were those elongated x's? What could they signify? I turned the page through ninety degrees and was none the wiser. Vertically they looked like schematic hour-glasses or egg-timers. They seemed to make no sense at all. I copied one on to the pad of hotel notepaper, suddenly wondering if this act might unleash new symptoms, but my hand was obeying my brain this time. What was it Hamlet had said to Horatio? 'There are more things in heaven and earth than are dreamt of in your philosophy . . .' I switched out the light and went – relatively swiftly – to sleep.

John-Jo Harrigan – my old friend and partner – ruffled his thinning gingery hair and screwed up his eyes as he shifted his gaze from the sea's blurry blue horizon and turned to stare at me, frankly baffled.

'Demarco's very worried,' he said. 'He liked your original drawings. Very much.'

'They were wrong. Everything was wrong. The shape of the pool was wrong.'

'He wants a rectangular pool. His wife is a compulsive swimmer. Likes to do her laps every day.'

'When he sees the new plans he'll change his mind. I don't know what I was thinking of. Wait till you see them, J-J.' I reached forward and patted his hand. 'The house will look sensational.'

'He says he won't brook any delay.' John-Jo lit one of his malodorous little cigars.

'I like that: "brook".'

'He's got a Ph.D. from Princeton. He's not a stupid billionaire.'

'We're not stupid architects. There will be no delay.'

We walked back along Malibu pier towards the beach.

'I think smoking's allowed on the pier,' I said.

'Actually, I think what really upset him,' John-Jo said, musingly, 'was that you hadn't shaved for the meeting.'

'I'm a landscape architect, not an accountant.'

'Are you growing a beard?' John-Jo chuckled, as if the notion was improbable.

I touched my spiky, raspy chin. 'Just haven't felt like shaving,' I said, frowning. 'California dreaming.'

'You're just a fucking hippy.' John-Jo laughed. 'I warned Stella, she wouldn't listen. I said, I remember: Stella, darling, you're marrying a goddam hippie.' He smiled at me. 'Let's have a drink,' he said, gesturing at a bar-restaurant that was just opening. 'Then I'll go and persuade Demarco you're a genius.'

I moved out of the elegant, impossible hotel with its dank, lush gardens in order to rework the plans for the Demarco landscaping in ideal solitude. I rented a one-room studio apartment in Venice, a block back from the beach, with a day bed, a shower room and a kitchenette. It was sparse and, after an afternoon's housework, as clean as it could be. I bought a large block of drawing paper, some pens, brushes and coloured inks and went to work. I knew I had to produce something instantly striking: my new plans were so dramatically different from the old that Demarco would have to fall in love with them at first sight – no amount of earnest persuasion would be likely to bring him round. I had one shot – so the drawings had to be as finished as I could make them, the audacity of the concept unmistakeably there, at once, immediate.

I had a phone but I decided to give no one my number. I arranged with the hotel to keep my messages and checked in with them a couple of times a day. I did not tell John-Jo or Stella I had moved. When I called it was as if I was still at the hotel – it was an easy subterfuge to maintain. Later it was to rebound devastatingly upon me.

'May 15th. Tuesday, I think. Good work the last two days, intense and concentrated. I could sell these drawings to a gallery. One curious event. My beard was growing; I hadn't shaved for the four days since my arrival and I was beginning to scratch and itch. I went to shave and found I could shave my jaw but not my upper lip. I placed the razor beneath my nose but I could not make my hand move. I tried my left hand but with similar lack of success – it was as if my muscles froze. Would not obey the command from my brain. Elsewhere on my jaw and chin I scraped away problem-free. I washed the soap off my face and saw there the beginnings of a fine, wide moustache, a moustache whose ends did not stop at the edge of my lips but whose bristles continued down and up on to the cheek in a vague handlebar swoop. Funnily enough, I liked what I saw. I reminded myself of old photographs of certain famous cowboys: Buffalo Bill, Wyatt Earp – very nine-teenth-century and, I thought to myself, due for a revival.'

Why was I so unperturbed? I had never grown a moustache in my life, so why now? I rationalized it as an unconscious desire to blend in in Venice, to become a denizen of this bizarre suburb on the sea, tucked in between respectable Santa Monica and the industrial wastelands around the airport.

I spent most of the day at home, working, made trips to the laundromat or the supermarket for provisions, slept soundly on my narrow bed and each morning when the sun rose went for a run on the beach. My moustache grew. I remember catching a glimpse of myself in a shop window as I wandered home clutching a brown bag of groceries – I was wearing jeans and a t-shirt, my greying hair was wild and uncombed – and for a brief second I did not recognize myself. A moustache can alter a familiar visage profoundly. I stopped, turned and stared: I liked what I saw. No one would know it was me, I remember smiling to myself as I wandered homeward. I called Demarco and fixed up an appointment for the next day – the drawings were ready to show.

That night I went to a bar, called 'Moon'. It was dark and preten-tiously decorated with a pronounced lunar theme – multicoloured moons were everywhere. The music was loud and harsh but, this being Venice, its clientèle was remarkably varied – all ages, all looks, the beautiful and the grotesque – so I felt quite at home. I sat myself at the bar and ordered a cocktail called, 'the Sea of Tranquility', blue in colour, strangely sour-sweet in taste – I was indifferent to its contents. I sipped my drink, my attention held absolutely by the girl behind the bar.

'May 19th. This girl was not pretty, she had a hardpinched face with soft uneven teeth and a pointed stud set in her bottom lip. Her right shoulder was darkly tattooed with some swirling kabbalistic sign. She wore a faded singlet, spandex cycling shorts and heavy mountaineering boots. After my third Sea of Tranquility and my third two-dollar tip she finally smiled at me and asked if I was celebrating. 'Tomorrow,' I said. 'Put the champagne on ice.' She had rings on all her fingers, including both her thumbs, I noticed. 'Big spender, huh?' she said, not impressed. 'Where are you from, anyways?' She swept the dollars away. I was drunk but I wanted her, wanted to feel that lip stud graze my body. So I told her who I was and where I was from and that I would be in tomorrow night for my champagne. She told me her name was Leandra.'

I walked down to the beach. It was a Sunday and the Sunday crowds had all but gone, leaving only the odd rollerblader or cyclist whizzing up and down the concrete paths. The Venetians were still out and about: the hawkers, the bodybuilders, the beggars, the tarot-card readers, the monologuists and various other lost muttering souls meandering up and down. I passed a guitarist (a double amputee as it happened) sitting in a barber's chair playing a slow sequence of chords and the combination of the music, my Seas of Tranquility, the unseen ocean with its wavecrash and the warm breeze stirred in me a profound and epiphanic moment of happiness. I felt that I had reached somewhere significant in my life – not a turning point or a watershed – just one of those markers, those milestones. A benign sense of ageing, perhaps, of the body clock sounding the hour.

'I can see you're a happy man,' a voice said. 'A successful man.'

I recognized the standard pitch of the fortune teller and turned to see a tall, lean man in a black fedora, sashed, fringed and beaded as if he were auditioning for the part of a gypsy soothsayer in a pantomime. He held out a bunch of white heather.

'Look,' he said. 'You're a Scotchman and I have white heather. I knew I'd meet a Scotchman today.'

Not a fortune teller, I thought, just another Venice nutter. 'I'm English,' I said. 'There's a big difference.'

'Oh no, you're a Scotchman. Buy my white heather for fifty dollars. It'll bring you luck.'

'No thank you.' I turned and walked away I didn't need his luck.

'Give it to Sarah.'

I stopped.

'Give it to your girl, Sarah. Sarah, the one you love.'

'I'm afraid you're all wrong. Look, it's getting embarrassing.'

'Your daughter Sarah, then.'

'I have two sons. Goodnight.'

I turned and left him, striding away, then slowed, trying to summon up the serenity I had so briefly experienced, but it did not re-occur. The fortune teller's absurd certainties had broken the mood, and, annoyingly, his words nagged at me as I walked home. White heather brought you luck – why? Who said it did? But I couldn't help thinking I should have bought his lucky charm.

Odell Demarco was waiting for me at the site, dressed in cream shirt and tan trousers and cream and tan correspondent shoes. Cement was being poured into the new foundations of the house that John-Jo had designed for him. In front of it and facing the sea lay a gently sloping seven-acre wasteland that I was meant to transform into his paradise garden. His smile was a little tense as we shook hands.

'Hey, Alex,' he said by way of hello. 'The moustache – like it, suits you.'

'Thank you, Odell,' I said. He hadn't given me permission to call him Odell but it was the Harrigan-Rief practice not to fawn on clients, however wealthy. If he wanted me to call him Mr Demarco then he would have to call me Mr Rief.

'Where's Yolanda?' I asked, Yolanda being the second, or perhaps the third, Mrs Demarco.

'Yolanda is kind of worried, if I may be candid,' Demarco said, candour shining worriedly from his eyes. 'She wanted me to take this meeting alone. But she did ask me to insist on the thirty-yard pool.'

'She should have been here,' I said, smiling. 'The pool is now sixty yards long.' I placed my sketchpad on the wide glossy bonnet of his car. 'Shall we go to work?'

That night in 'Moon' I ordered a bottle of vintage Krug from Leandra and insisted she have a glass. I heard the 'ting' of her lip stud hit its rim as she brought the glass to her mouth.

'Oh, I should have made a toast,' she said. 'What are we celebrating?'

I raised my glass. 'Death to all Philistines,' I said. Demarco had been remarkably firm and calm as he fired me that morning and I saw the billionaire in him, all of a sudden, all his magnate's ruthless self-assurance. He ordered me immediately to reinstate my original plans and I refused, politely. He ordered me to hand over the original plans – with their even terraces, their exact symmetries – and I again refused. He threatened a law-suit; I referred him to various clauses in our contract. He said he would halt work on the house and have a new one designed – so I in turn threatened a law-suit on behalf of Harrigan-Rief.

'You are free to accept or reject the design I propose,' I said. 'That is all.'

'But this is crazy. Where's the pool? What's this hill-thing you've put there? And what's that?'

'An acre of bamboo.'

'Are you out of your fucking mind? I'll be a laughing stock.'

'You've a chance to make your reputation as a man of extraordinary taste and foresight.'

We traded implicit insults for a little longer before he ordered me off the site and put in a call to John-Jo on his cell-phone.

In retrospect I think it was the transformation of the pool that most freaked him out – and the thought of Yolanda's potential response to my design. I had indeed proposed the shaping of an unevenly conic hill (instead of the neat descent of wide terraces) and around the base of the hill I had placed a pool in the shape of an ox-bow lake, irregularly curved, narrowing in the middle and forming a wide pool (with overflow) on the seaward side of the hill. There was not a straight line in sight and the paths I envisaged wound and meandered around gradients and through cut gullies, before losing themselves in the green darkness of the bamboo grove.

My drawings left nothing to the imagination: I had done two versions, one representing the immediate completion of planting and one as I imagined the place would look ten years hence. Nothing was ambiguous, everything was fixed and sure – exact. The gardens of the Demarco House in Pacific Pallisades would have been my crowning glory.

'May 23rd. I have not left my room for three days. Leandra brings food, drink and cigarettes when she comes back from the bar. We seem to have adopted the habit of making love in the morning – she says she's too tired after a night's work. I was disappointed to find that her tattoo is a solitary one and that she removes her lip stud to sleep. Her body is remarkably pale. If I'm not too hungover we make love before breakfast and she is happy to accept the hundred dollars I press on her. Tonight she says she is bringing me some pills – to "juice me up" she says.'

Leandra and I spent about a week together in this temporary coupledom before she grew tired of me. Or at least I supposed it was fatigue – it may have been sheer disappointment. When she didn't come back from the 'Moon' one night, I went there the next day to seek her out but she told me in no uncertain terms it was over. I offered her a two-hundred dollar fee and she called the manager.

'You're disgusting,' were her last words. 'Look at yourself. Take a bath. You stink.'

The subsequent days passed in something of a blur. I stopped keeping my journal and I took to serious and steady drinking. There was a girl who caught my eye in a 24-hour 7–11 where, driven out by hunger, I bought my snacks. She was Mexican, I think, and her name was Encarnacion. She had a friendly smile, was plump and had white-blonde streaks in her hair and many fine gold chains around her neck. I cleaned myself up and asked her to dinner. We ate Chinese in Santa Monica and wandered back to my studio. We were kissing in the middle of the floor when the door bell rang.

John-Jo Harrigan was standing there. I saw his eyes flick by me to Encarnacion, who was smoothing her rumpled blouse unconcernedly.

'Time to go home, Alex,' John-Jo said, softly.

Part II. London

'July 21st. London swelters in seasonal heat and torpor and I do not love my wife. I look at her, I see how attractive she is, I can summon up the memory of the love we once shared – and its intensity – but I realize I cannot live in the past. I am sharing the house with a concerned and congenial acquaintance who, apart from pointed remarks about my smoking, my drinking and my indolence, tolerates my presence – indeed, more than tolerates, she does everything she can to make me as comfortable as possible.'

But I could sense, even in my self-absorption, my absolute selfishness, that her patience and concern were finite. My sons Ben and Conor had left home – Ben was at university, now spending the summer with some girl in Cornwall, Conor was in Zimbabwe with

UNESCO – and we were more or less left to our own devices. Friends were discreet: the word was I had become unwell, needed time to recuperate. Only John-Jo was a regular visitor. On those stifling summer evenings I used to sit in the garden, my fist round a cold vodka, and watch Stella's tall figure move among the plants in the thickening light, pruning and deadheading, and be aware that my gaze was one of utter objectivity, noting merely the way she flicked back a wing of ashblonde hair, or the shape of her rump as she bent to pull a weed free, or her leggy stroll towards me on the terrace, and realized I could have been looking at anyone – at Leandra, even, or Encarnacion. And then with an urgent spasm of irritation and regret I would recall that I had gone no further with Encarnacion than one panting, tongue-tangling kiss and would blame – with adamantine illogic – Stella for that huge and abiding disappointment.

'July 25th. I worry for my future relationship with John-Jo. Yesterday I went out to the landfill site in Slough and the site manager would not let me in. So I called John-Jo and he said that my visit last week (when I had ordered the main valley we had constructed to be deepened) had cost the firm possibly tens of thousands of pounds as we would now not meet the deadline and the penalty clause payments would kick in. I said the landscaping was flawed. He said, and I quote, "It's just a fucking landfill, Alex." I said, "But my name goes on it." "*Our* name," he said, "we're partners, remember."'

I began to worry that the medication I was being given was affecting my mood – I felt either lethargic and surly or else irritable and wired-up. After John-Jo had flown me home to London I went to a clinic for a week's convalescence – apparently I was dehydrated and malnourished, my metabolism seriously out of kilter. I was tranquillized and slept for seventy-two hours. When I awoke, fuddled, but clean and relatively calm, I realized that while I had been asleep I had been bathed and shaved. On Stella's instructions my moustache had been shaved off. I missed it, my upper lip felt vulnerable and etiolated: I knew that I had to begin to grow it again immediately. I asked for cigarettes. I had not smoked for twenty years but for some reason had felt the craving begin in California – that smokeless zone – and was up to two packs a day before very long.

Sometimes I sensed Stella's covert stare on me and felt her sadness snaking out to enfold me. Even in my rare moments of lucidity, I resented her pity and incomprehension, resented her compassion. From time to time she tried to talk to me about it: what was happening? was I unhappy? why – in more fraught moments – was I trying to destroy our lives? She summoned Ben home for a weekend from Cornwall and we spent a tense few days. I found Ben suddenly gauche and unfunny, his undergraduate humour (my moustache was the subject of many a sally) became increasingly offensive. I saw that my coldness disturbed him, quite profoundly, and he decided to leave. I made no effort to see him off, though I noticed that Stella was red-eyed and teary all day – and I heard her later that evening talking urgently to Conor in Africa.

'August 2nd. I was in an optician's in Kensington High Street yesterday morning buying my third pair of sunglasses in three days from a sly-looking dark girl with a love-bite on her neck – whom I had just learned was called Megan – when a transformation occurred. It was as if I had shed something, or something had left me. For an instant I felt quite faint and shaky and drew a concerned inquiry from Megan. I breathed deeply and looked around me with suddenly clear eyes. I remembered I had come to this shop because I was becoming obsessed with this girl in the same way as I had with Leandra and Encarnacion. I apologized to her and left.

'I went home and apologized to Stella – the relief in her eyes was heartrending. We talked into the small hours, deciding that I must have been having some kind of breakdown, that perhaps the medication was finally beginning to work and some equilibrium was returning, finally, to our lives (I called Ben and apologized for my boorishness – poor lad). And yet, this morning, as I lathered my face with shaving cream and tried to shave off my moustache, my arms locked rigid once more. One step at a time, Stella said, easy does it. At least you're thinking straight.'

It was Petra Fairbrother, my psychiatrist, who encouraged me systematically to look at the evidence and lay out the clues. She was a fleshy, loose-lipped woman with large, soft hands that she flapped around a lot. She was also deeply intelligent but, like a lot of intelligent Englishwomen (and men, come to that) she took great pains to conceal her intellect beneath a fog of genial dilettantism. She would hear nothing of vague diagnoses like nervous breakdown, mid-life crisis, schizophrenia. 'Sounds, you know, more interesting than that – too, you know, sort of precise,' she said, pointing a pencil at me. She was particularly fascinated with the pages of my notebook where the elongated x's had been written, particularly intrigued by the fact that this sign-writing had never reappeared. She asked me to write the sign in front of her – which I did without pause.

'It triggers nothing?' she asked, disappointment tingeing her voice. 'Not a tremor, not a shiver?'

'Nothing,' I said, writing half a dozen more x's.

'I just feel it must be the key somehow,' she said, frowning, tugging on an earlobe and making popping noises with her lips.

'I think it's a sex thing,' I said, with some shame. 'Something buried in my psyche – to do with a certain type of woman.'

'But there was nothing sexual going on in the aeroplane, when it all started.'

I assured her there wasn't. Then I remembered about the headache.

'August 5th. Headache. Elongated x's. Moustache. Cigarettes. Sexual fantasy. Fantasies of prostitution. Women of lower class. Anomie. Lack of personal hygiene. Aggression. The Demarco garden. The landfill. Hostility to family. Alcoholism . . . Could the headache be the simple answer? Do I need a brainscan? I have had three days of normality – near normality. Stella shaved my upper lip last night. I felt nothing. We made love. Why do I feel this is some sort of phony peace, a false dawn?'

My worries were valid. I seemed to be fluctuating between a form of tense, watchful normality – family life restarted, I even went into the office – and moods that I only recognized were aberrant and dangerous in their aftermath.

One day, after leaving the practice in Notting Hill, I stopped to buy a newspaper and I saw a girl working in a butcher's shop (why do women who work as butchers or fishmongers wear so much make-up?). She was dark with a slightly prognathous jaw and a mass of dense, dry hair pulled back from her strong face in a bun the size of a cottage loaf. Her lips were cerise pink and her mascaraed eyes studied me beneath skyblue lids as I ordered enough meat to feed a platoon of soldiers. As she sliced rump steak, and bagged dozens of sausages I stared at her avidly – noting the bloom of dark hair on her forearms, her sturdy calves as she turned to reach for the cleaver, the hairbrush handle jutting from the pocket of her nylon overalls. I leant up against the glass of the counter feeling my erection flatten against the pane, wondering if this burly girl was the daughter of the small, bald man mincing veal along the counter, and what she or he would say if I asked her out for a drink. I paid for my meat with two fifty-pound notes – betokening immense wealth, I hoped – and said,

'I hope you don't mind my asking but I've just moved into this neighbourhood and I was wondering if there was a good pub around here – you know, one you'd recommend . . .'

She scratched her arm and frowned. 'What d' you think Frank?' she asked the veal-mincer. There was a short debate on the merits of the local pubs until one called the Duke of Clarence was elected as the most salubrious. I thanked them, smiled at her, my eyes full of messages, and left.

As I dropped my heavy bag of meat in the nearest litter bin a depressing wave of insight washed over me and I saw my sexual obsession in all its weaselly shame. But in the butcher's I had had only one thought in mind, all my snouty desire focused on this strapping girl with her rosy, bloodstained hands. I felt salt tears prick at my eyelids as I drove home to my long-suffering wife.

'August 9th. It seems I hit John-Jo yesterday morning in the office, swung a series of haymakers at him, one connecting with the side of his jaw, breaking the ring finger of my left hand. I remember nothing of it. Apparently I was incoherent with drink. For the third night running I had spent the evening in the Duke of Clarence waiting for my butcher-girl to show, in vain. So as the pub closed I bought a bottle of vodka and settled down in my car to drink it. I must have made my way to the office, somehow, the next morning. Stella says I accused John-Jo of betraying me, of systematically stealing my ideas over the years, taking credit where none was due . . . Then launched myself at him. Poor Stella.'

'It seems to be changing,' I said to Petra Fairbrother. 'It's not like California, where it was constant, now it comes and goes, as if something's being switched on and off.'

'Might I bum a ciggie off you?' Petra asked. She took one from my pack and I watched her light it awkwardly, as if it was the first time in her life she'd attempted such a thing, and then saw her inhale smoke deep into her lungs. 'Lovely,' she said, 'So, do you think the grip is weakening?'

'The grip?'

'Whatever has you in its power.'

'You sound like some sort of necromancer, witchdoctor.'

'I'm speaking metaphorically, Alex dear. But, then again, I suppose we could, not unreasonably, be seen as witchdoctors, modern ones,' she smiled, then plumed smoke out of the side of her mouth in a noisy gust, 'trying to drive your demons away.'

'Demons . . .' I repeated slowly. 'A demon.'

'A handy metaphor. But you are warring with demons, Alex, make no mistake.'

I frowned, thinking. 'All the girls are dark, and they all had jobs. I don't just want to buy sex, I'm sure.' I told her how I had stood in a London phone box, the glass sides darkened with dozens of prostitute's cards, illustrated with improbable nubile beauties of all races, plying for trade. 'I felt nothing. I could have called any one of them up. It's something to do with the type of girl, a working girl . . .' I looked at her helplessly. 'Maybe I should be hypnotized?'

'What happened to your hand?'

'I tried to beat up my oldest friend.'

'Christ. We'd better get to work.' She pursed her lips, rattled her fingertips on the desk top. 'Would you mind if I spoke to someone about your case? Just a hunch.'

'August 14th. The Rankin Hotel, Bloomsbury. I have moved out of the house and Stella has asked for a divorce. Crazily, stupidly, I took a girl home, a waitress called Katerina, Russian, I think, or Ukrainian. I said she could stay, be our lodger, as we had plenty of spare rooms. Stella came back as she was inspecting the guest bedroom in the basement. I never laid a finger on her (I was planning to, of course). In the fight that followed it transpired that John-Jo had told Stella about finding me with Encarnacion. Stella was convinced I was mired in some miserable, middle-aged fit of satyriasis – she had been prepared to suffer it for a while, but not any more. I disgusted her, she bawled at me, how could I bring a girl into our house? What was she meant to do? She had some dignity left. She ordered me out of the house and I meekly went. Tomorrow I go to Edinburgh, perhaps it's best I try to sort this out on my own.'

Part III. Edinburgh

Edinburgh in high summer was buffeted by gales and driving rain out of the north, interspersed with baffling periods of brilliant breezy sunshine, the wet streets drying before your eyes, umbrellas stowed, raincoats shrugged off, the terraced gardens beneath the dark, looming castle suddenly busy with half-naked sunbathers, before – inevitably – the slate-blue clouds gathered over Fife and the North Sea and bore down on the city again and the unrelenting drenching downpour resumed with all its former energy.

I had not been here for years and I had forgotten how the city in August surrendered itself to its annual invasion of Festival-goers, Princes Street and the Royal Mile loud with polyglot chatter, railings and billboards a patchwork collage of posters and advertisements. Yet beneath all this bright tat and cultural tourism, this cosmopolitan artfest, and the fizz and crackle in the atmosphere – almost palpable – of people set on indulging themselves, the old, dour, sooty reserve of the place appeared merely to be biding its time. These frivolous laughing folk will be gone in a week or so, seemed to be the message one read in the grim, impassive faces of the locals, and then we can get on with the serious business of living.

I was strongly conscious of this, of the old city and its implacable mores, as I walked along one of the gaunt, dark grey Georgian crescents of the New Town – the rain slanting down again, stinging my cheeks and brow – towards number 37 and noted the brass plaque (teared with icy drops) beside the bell-push which declared: 'The Royal Scottish Institute of Hydrodynamic Engineering', and, below that, the terse instruction, 'Tradesmen report to the rear of the building'.

A tiny grey-haired woman with supernaturally bright eyes opened the door and directed me to a seat in the wide, penumbrous hall, where I was surveyed by numerous varnished portraits of engineering worthies from the nineteenth century. 'Mr Auchinleck will be with you presently,' she said and scurried back to her office from where I could shortly hear – a rarer and rarer sound this – the noise of a manual typewriter tapping rapidly away.

It had been Petra Fairbrother who had unwittingly sent me north from my mean hotel in Bloomsbury. She tracked me down there and informed me by telephone, excitement colouring her voice, that she thought she had a 'lead' – though she had no idea what exactly it would portend.

She had shown my pages of 'automatic writing', as she termed it, to a friend of hers, a mathematics don at Cambridge University. He thought the signs – the elongated x's – were vaguely familiar and had promised to investigate. I fancifully imagined my pages being passed round the senior common rooms of various Cambridge colleges, grey heads nodding sagely at my hieroglyphs, learned speculation ensuing . . . But, whatever happened, he called back some few days later to say that the sign had been recognized by someone in the engineering department. There was every possibility, Petra Fairbrother related to me, that the sign I had written, 35,000 feet above the Atlantic, represented a concept evolved in hydrodynamic engineering known as a 'Saltire Wave'.

A few hours in a local library unearthed the key facts about the Saltire Wave. It was a phenomenon discovered by the Scottish engineer Findlay Smith Quarrie in 1834. One afternoon, riding his horse along the banks of the Union Canal near Edinburgh, he noticed that when a barge was suddenly halted, the body of water around it, after an initial violent agitation, calmed itself and then moved ahead independently in an even wave, as if the barge were still there and the displacement of the water caused by the barge's forward motion was still occurring. On this particular day, Quarrie had spurred his horse forward and had followed this wave along the canalside for several miles. The wave was miraculously real, but its cause seemed spectral. It was as if, Quarrie remarked in the paper he submitted to the Institute of Hydrodynamic Engineering – with due apologies for the anthropomorphic nature of his observation – 'the water was still *remembering* the effect of the barge'.

In the paper he proposed a mathematical symbol to represent this phenomenon: two parallel lines forced to cross as a result of an energy twist in the middle. He called it the Saltire Wave because the shape that ensued resembled an elongated version of the white 'x' on the blue ground of the Scottish flag – known familiarly as the 'Saltire Cross'.

I sat in the shadowy hall of the Institute, waiting for Mr Auchinleck, with an empty but open mind. I was not sure why I felt I had to come to Edinburgh, or of what I might achieve or discover, but at least I felt I was acting, doing something positive. Some strange enlightenment might arrive as a result of this visit and I had a sixth sense that it would be found in the long-defunct persona of Findlay Smith Quarrie.

There was the sound of squeaking rubber on the polished parquet of the Institute before Mr Auchinleck appeared. He was a young man in his thirties with a frizzy mass of wavy brown hair. He was wearing a grey suit and a plaid shirt with no tie. The squeaks had been produced by the crude sandals he was wearing, the soles apparently cut from auto tyres. I could not help looking down and was vaguely distressed to see his unduly long toenails extending through the sandal thongs like curved yellow talons.

Auchinleck – 'Call me Gilles,' he immediately invited – was a genial fellow and intrigued to learn I was on the trail of Findlay Smith Quarrie and his Saltire Wave.

'A fascinating man,' Auchinleck said. 'Sort of ahead of his time. I don't think, to be honest, he really knew what he had found with his Wave.' He grinned. 'Now we say everything's a wave, don't we? Atoms are both wave and particle,' he recited in a sing-song voice. 'Don't they claim that even thought is basically a wave phenomenon?'

'Is it?' I asked, intrigued.

'Well, so they say. Waves, waves everywhere. Do you want to see what he looked like?'

'Who?'

'Quarrie.'

Gilles Auchinleck led me upstairs to the Institute's original lecture room, purpose built, a semicircular bank of wooden pews facing a wooden dais that backed on to an enormous, crowded oil painting.

'1834,' he said. 'The founding members. There's Quarrie standing by his famous pump.'

I stepped forward, following the direction of his pointing finger to stare at the well-executed portrait of a plump rosy-faced figure, more like a country squire than one's idea of a Victorian engineer, his stomach straining at the buttons of his silk waistcoat.

'Quarrie made a fortune from that pump,' Auchinleck said. 'By the middle of the century it was in every coal mine in the world.'

He went on, but I wasn't listening, as my eye had been caught by a saturnine figure in the background – a man in a dark suit with a odd white silk stock at his neck. In one hand he held a burning cigar and his eyes seemed to stare directly out of the canvas. His face was slumped – his features haggard, through illness or debauchery one would have guessed – but what was most striking about him was his wide moustache, dark across his sallow face, its wings extending beyond the edge of his lips and curving upwards in a cropped, swooping handlebar shape on to the cheeks themselves.

'Who's that man?' I asked, pointing, 'the one at the back.'

'Good question,' Auchinleck said. 'If we go down to the library I'll be able to tell you exactly.'

'Edinburgh. August 17th. They say that on occasions the force of a person's gaze can be felt physically (maybe the "look" is a form of wave?) and if intent enough can make the object of that gaze turn round, yet the girl behind the bar – at whom I have been staring for the last five minutes – smokes on unconcernedly, looking everywhere except at me. She is dark, of course, young, with a small shading of acne at the corners of her wide mouth. When she poured me my fourth large scotch and water I noticed that her nails were bitten to the quick. She has a tall, boyish figure and her hair is spiky with gel. I sit here in the corner scribbling, and I feel the need I have for her like an ache in my gut. Like a dagger in my gut. I will drink on here until closing time and then ask her to come home with me to my hotel. There is a difference now: I seem to be able to step back from the seizure, the fit, the madness, or whatever it is – I seem to be able to acknowledge that it is underway. Is this a sign of its hold on me diminishing? Or merely that I am learning to live with it, as the invalid does with his chronic incontinence? But it is as if some corner of my brain remains my own . . . And yet I will not rise to my feet and leave this place.'

Wallace Kilmaron. Wallace Kilmaron. His name was Wallace Kilmaron – the man in the painting with the cigar and the moustache. Auchinleck had been able to identify him with the aid of a key to the painting's multitude of portraits (some thirty-three in all) and gave me a little information. Kilmaron had been an expert in drainage and irrigation systems and had done much of his work in Holland, where he was acknowledged as a nonpareil when it came to constructing floodwalls, canals and all the complex business of water displacement involved in land reclamation. His dates were 1796–1840. Auchinleck had no idea how he had died but it was clear that he had not reached any great age, even by the standards of the nineteenth century. More interestingly, he had resigned from the Institute in 1835 – hence the paucity of information they held. 'Most of the fellows lodged their archives with us,' Auchinleck explained, 'which was half the purpose of establishing the Institute in the first place. Something must have gone wrong there – we've nothing on Kilmaron, I'm afraid, apart from these few basic facts.' As if he were in some way responsible for this omission, Auchinleck obligingly put in a call to a friend at the National Library of Scotland and an appointment was arranged for me the next day, where everything the library had on Kilmaron would be made available.

I was early and went to a café to wait for the main doors to be opened. I felt a tension in me, born of a bizarre confidence that the answer to my problems lay within that solid grey sandstone building. I was hungover also, my night's drinking having only provoked a thin, mean headache, and I felt soured further by the residual sense of shame at my vain importuning of the girl behind the bar. She had barely been able to sum up the energy to dismiss me, as if this were an event that happened nightly – drunk, middle-aged men leeringly asking her home for a nightcap. But as I sat in the café, trying to forget the look of contempt in her eyes, trying to concentrate on the crossword in the *Scotsman* and idly watching the morning drizzle fill the gutters outside, I felt my right side growing cold as if from a draught and suddenly my hand began to move across the checkerboard squares of the crossword puzzle drawing a series of Saltire Wave symbols. I must have done a dozen or so elongated x's when suddenly I regained the power in my arm.

I looked at the page with no fear or panic this time – I saw it more as a form of communication from the – from the what? – from the shade of Wallace Kilmaron, I suppose, as if he were whispering 'congratulations' to me down through the decades. And across the street I saw the porter swing the heavy wooden doors of the library open.

Wallace Kilmaron died a bitter and frustrated man, aged forty-four, from an 'infection of the lung and belly' – in other words from causes unknown to contemporary medicine. In his life he had published a dozen or so scientific papers, mostly in learned journals, to do with his field of expertise. One small book, however, was lodged in the Library's archives, privately printed by a printer and bookseller in Leith, entitled: 'On a Phenomenon of Turbulent Water'. Its publication date was 1835 and a reading of it, combined with the three obituaries that had appeared on his death and an exchange of letters in the *Annals of Civil Engineering*, were enough to piece Wallace Kilmaron's story together.

In 1833 Wallace Kilmaron had been involved in a major project of land reclamation between the Waal river and the Lower Rhine in Holland, to which end a complex pattern of drainage channels had been dug over an area of some dozens of square miles. One day a narrow, flat-bottomed square-ended skiff (used for the transportation of dredged mud and sand) had sunk tight in one of the channels. During the efforts to refloat the boat (teams of horses and winches being employed) the confines of the narrow waterway, combined with the heaving and lowering of the stern and bow of the skiff, had set up a series of turbulent waves. Kilmaron, standing supervising on the bank, had noticed how these waves 'like the travelling hump of a whiplash' would speed down the water channel 'without change of form or diminution of velocity'. Intrigued, Kilmaron decided to follow one of these waves on its progress and recorded walking hundreds of yards alongside one of these 'surges', as he called them, likening them to a form of tidal bore, 'a rounded, distinct elevation of water'. He noted further that when the channel changed course the wave would seemingly diminish into wavelets and then, as the channel straightened, the wavelets would magically reform into the original surge as if 'somehow contained in the turbulence of the water was a memory of the surge's original identity'.

So fascinated was he by the discovery of this phenomenon that Kilmaron constructed a large wooden platform floating on the surface of the water which, by a clever distribution of weights, could be made to oscillate about a fixed axle, thereby creating regular surges – or Coherent Waves, as he now called them – to order. Weeks of experimentation allowed him to arrive at some understanding of the phenomenon, which he described in the scientific paper that he wrote as a form of resonance, rather than turbulence, representing order rather than chaos, and which was dependent on precise relationships of depth and width of water channel and degree of agitation if it was to occur. He proposed a mathematical symbol to designate these conditions which took the form of two whiplash humps superimposed, and which, when further simplified, resembled a curiously flattened and rounded 'x' shape. He submitted that this condition should be known hencefor-ward as the Kilmaron Wave, and he journeyed back from Holland to Edinburgh to read his paper – 'On a Phenomenon of Turbulent

Water' – and present his findings to the recently formed Institute of Hydrodynamic Engineering – only to discover that Findlay Smith Quarrie had beaten him to it by a matter of weeks and the small world of hydrodynamic engineering was loud with discussion about Quarrie's amazing 'Saltire Wave' and all that it implied.

'August 18th. Edinburgh. I am fully conscious of the dangerous illogic of what I am about to write, fully aware of what danger it places me in, of how it will alter the way I am perceived, but I know, I know for sure in my heart and head that everything that has happened to me since that day in May, when my hand began to scribble symbols on my notebook – that everything is to do with Wallace Kilmaron and his death in 1840.'

As I read and deduced what had occurred since his discovery of the Kilmaron Wave I knew that somehow – somehow – the events of over 150 years ago were systematically destroying my life. The final evidence came when I read at the end of one of his obituaries that six months before his death Wallace Kilmaron had married a parlourmaid in his household, one Sarah McBride, and left his estate to her. It was a union that was never recognized by Kilmaron's family, who later contested in court that the marriage and the rewriting of the will had occurred while Kilmaron was in a state of 'drunkenness and dementia'.

Part IV: Biarritz

Didier Visconti smiled, and placed his big, tanned hand briefly on my shoulder.

'Don't mention it, Alex,' he said. 'You paid for everything. Everybody's going to talk about it. I'll be famous. I should be grateful to you.'

For some reason I felt like weeping with gratitude, felt like hugging this cheery, burly Frenchman, felt like telling him he had saved my life. Instead, I said: 'I can't tell you why – or I could tell you why, but it would make no sense – you'd think I was crazy. Let's say it was something I had to do.'

Didier looked down at the sign, cast in metal and embedded in the turf at the edge of the fourteenth tee. I had had it rendered in six languages – French, English, German, Dutch, Italian, Spanish. It read: 'The water hazard on this hole is unique in golf. It is based on a phenomenon of turbulent water first discovered in 1834 by the Scottish engineer Wallace Kilmaron, a phenomenon known as the Kilmaron Wave.'

We followed a meandering foursome of middle-aged Swedish ladies down the fairway towards the fourteenth green. 'Les Cerisiers' was a new golf course owned and constructed by Didier Visconti, a wealthy builder, some few miles north of Biarritz, landscaped by Harrigan-Rief Associates some six years ago. In the course of the landscaping I had redirected a small stream into a narrow, deep-banked channel some hundreds of metres long that ran down the side of the fourteenth fairway and crossed in front of the fourteenth green – to act as a fiendish water hazard (any balls lost in it were irretrievable) – before vanishing underground to feed the artificial lake in front of the clubhouse (architect: John-Joseph Harrigan).

During the months of construction and landscaping I had formed a firm friendship with Didier Visconti and had become powerfully attracted to this section of the Atlantic coast. When I had proposed my alteration to the fourteenth hole water hazard, over the telephone from Edinburgh, Didier had instantly agreed and I had flown south with photocopies of the relevant pages from Kilmaron's book.

A local carpenter and blacksmith had managed to construct a mini-replica of Kilmaron's wave-producing platform (powered by a small petrol motor to make it tilt and level) and I had installed it where the stream was diverted into my man-made channel. It worked fairly well, producing a series of whiplash travelling wave-humps that continuously ran the length of the water hazard.

Didier and I stood in the evening sunshine looking at the Kilmaron Waves travelling down the length of the water channel as the Swedish ladies hacked and fluffed their balls up on to the green.

'Do you think the moving water will put them off?' Didier asked. 'Do you think it's too distracting?'

'That's why it's called a water hazard,' I said. 'I predict: in ten years you'll see these Kilmaron Wave hazards everywhere. The Americans will love it. It's new – and a bit of living history.'

'We must do a deal,' Didier said, his mind working quickly. 'I give you a royalty, yes?'

'The rights are all yours,' I said. 'Make a few more millions.'

Didier laughed and shook my hand, then drew me into a bearhug.

'Why are you doing this Alex?' he said, releasing me. 'Why are you giving this to me – you could be rich?'

I thought about this, watching the Kilmaron Waves roll steadily, effortlessly, by my feet.

'Let's just say . . .' I considered. 'It's for my peace of mind.'

Science is full of these bizarre coincidences, of two or three or more people making the same discovery, arriving at the same proof, the same axiom or theory, simultaneously. That two Scottish engineers in 1834 should have observed the same phenomenon of turbulent water some weeks apart and have both sought to claim the distinction for the discovery is – in the annals of scientific discovery – of little significance. By luck – by a matter of geographical placement – Quarrie arrived with the authentication first, and was able to christen it by the name he chose. Quarrie settled on the Saltire Wave – not the Quarrie Wave, significantly – and I am sure that here lies the source of Kilmaron's enduring bitterness. Quarrie was a wealthy man – his pump for mine workings was to make him a millionaire – and the Quarrie Pump was already familiar around the world. Wallace Kilmaron, working anonymously in the sodden fields of south-east Holland, thought he had found a way of making his name live for ever – of achieving a kind of immortality. But his hopes were abruptly dashed. For some natures, for more fragile temperaments, such disappointments are impossible to bear.

*

'September 2nd. Cap Ferret. I sit in the shade of this beach shack watching the breakers roll in. I am driving north from Biarritz up the Atlantic coast, slowly and with many halts such as this – apprehensive, waiting to see, testing, saying to myself that it is over, that I am my old self again.

Last night I telephoned Stella and told her I thought I was well again, that I wanted to return home. She said no – at once, brutally. She did not want to see me again, she had no desire for further humiliation. I told her about Kilmaron and she laughed. "You sad old man," she said. "If you think you can fool me with this nonsense." If anything, my story about Wallace Kilmaron and how I had exorcized his malign presence from my life appeared to make her even more enraged. "You're sick," she said, her voice harsh with disgust. "Seek help. But keep away from me and the boys."

The thought has struck me repeatedly – as I search for an answer to what has happened to me these last months – that perhaps the theory of the Kilmaron Wave has wider applications. Just as the Kilmaron Wave seems to be an enduring physical manifestation of the memory of the boat or turbulence that was its original cause, I find myself wondering if individuals too can provoke a similar wave effect – a wave effect that will pass through time.

Wallace Kilmaron died in a torment of bitter anger and dis-appointment, beaten to his small portion of enduring fame and intellectual immortality by Findlay Quarrie. Did that turbulence, that manic agitation of his mind, somehow continue after his death and travel on through time looking for its target? Nervous breakdown, mid-life crisis, mental disease – perhaps these are simply different names for the same phenomenon. It strikes me now that all of us who have suffered in this way may in fact have been similarly haunted – we may all be victims of Kilmaron Waves breaking upon us from the past? . . . An individual death has many consequences, touches us in many immediate ways, ways we can see and identify – grief, loss, sadness, sorrow. But what if it goes further than that? What if the turbulence caused by that sudden halt in life's progress sets up other forms of motion, other disturbances? . . . Just like the water in the canal "remembering" the effect of the moving barge, maybe the world and time remembers the turbulence of certain lives. And I wonder how many lives Wallace Kilmaron has damaged or destroyed since 1840 – and provoked similar incredulity and incomprehension – until, by luck, by wild chance, his wave broke upon me, another engineer . . .

I look at what I have written and see how it could be further evidence of my problem, my particular madness. Stella clearly thought it was the final desperate lie – a pathetic delusion attempting to explain my many betrayals and hurts. But I do feel a palpable difference in myself as I sit here on the Atlantic coast. I feel calm, I feel I have arrived at some kind of understanding. The Kilmaron Wave travels on without change of form or diminution of velocity. What was it Auchinleck had said? "Thought itself is a wave phenomenon." Wave motion dominates the world of sub-atomic particles, so why not our human lives? Or our human histories through time? Could this, I wonder, could this be the source of all our hauntings?

The sun hammers down and I sip my cold beer slowly, watching the green waves of the Atlantic roll endlessly in. The woman who runs this bar is playing Brazilian rock music. She has a slight and firmly muscled figure and is wearing a pale blue t-shirt, tight enough to reveal the precise shape of her small, unsupported breasts. Her hair is dyed blonde. She smiles over at me, holding up another beaded, chill bottle of beer. I shake my head. I note these details and feel nothing more. The beer I am drinking is ideally cold. A faint breeze comes off the ocean. And I wonder if I am finally free of Wallace Kilmaron at last.'

Fascination

It is six in the morning and I sit in my kitchen looking out at the garden, watching the sun slant obliquely past the old lime tree and across my lawn to reveal the dense silver mesh of spiders' webs linking the grass stems. For a few seconds, as the earth turns and the sun rises, my tufty rectangle of suburban lawn flashes in my fascinated eyes like a burnished shield – before becoming dull green grass again, my quotidian epiphany gone for ever. And I think: where and when had I seen that before? Which of the myriad interlocking memories woven through my life had fired there? Then my moment of transcendence becomes mundane: I say to myself, I really must have my mower repaired, soon – Felicia will want the lawn cut and it is my constant ambition to pre-empt her reproaches and complaints.

'And there among the grass fell down / By his own scythe the Mower mown.' 'Damon the Mower' by Andrew Marvell. I must stop thinking about poetry.

I'm the first of the household awake and dressed. Upstairs I can hear my wife, Felicia, moving about in the bathroom. My baby son, Gareth (I've never really liked that name – my father-in-law's), sleeps on. Has there ever been a more narcoleptic infant, I wonder? We wake him, late, and he becomes immediately fractious and angry – isn't it meant to be the other way round?

'Edward,' Felicia calls down, 'Could you make me a cup of tea, darling?'

You never liked the town, right from the start. When Dad and Mum parked the car on the front and Dad stepped out and began to run on the spot, doing his deep breathing exercises, and you heard Mum make her inevitable remark about the extra oxygen molecule in the ozone, you wandered off, embarrassed by Dad, and contemplated the shingle beach, the mouse-grey sea and the pier and the tawdry stucco of the hotels and the houses. You searched the idlers on the promenade, and the strollers by the surf's edge looking for a sign, some signal that living in this town would be all right, would provide some consolation. A modest quotidian epiphany would have sufficed (you'd been reading Joyce) – but your eyes remained unenlightened and your soul sagged again.

Felicia kisses me and I climb into our (her) Volvo. She's pleased that I'm writing these articles, back being a proper journalist again, albeit freelance, earning 'real money', as she calls it, secretly delighted that I have abandoned poetry. I spent three weeks on my piece for *revolver* and she couldn't believe I was doing it unpaid (she did not regard six complimentary offprints of the article as proper recompense). Spending all this time writing 'The Image of the Train in Contemporary British Poetry' was not gainful employ, in her opinion. I wanted to say: but your bank pays you six – no eight – times as much as I earn in a good year, so why shouldn't I do something I actually take pleasure in? But some residual shame at being a kept man made me ring Phil (at Felicia's urging, her wheedling) and to my surprise he gave me this commission. And so I kiss my wife goodbye, start the engine and drive off to research this, my third article on the new generation of women athletes (sportsbabes) for *Elite* magazine: first the fencer, then the cyclist, now the high jumper.

You were glad you had resisted Mum's urging – her wheedling – that you should find a hostel or a YMCA, and had insisted, instead, on a bedsit. It was above a bakery and the smell of warm bread coming through the floorboards seemed to reassure her as she poked around while you and Dad brought up the suitcases and the turntable, the amplifier and the speakers. The window looked out on the garden and Mum stood there identifying the shrubs and trees: forsythia, a laurel, sycamore and lime. Ash, Dad said. No, lime, Mum insisted. They stood around for a while, reluctant to let you go, reluctant to leave you to your freedom, but your set face, your pointed refusal to suggest a cup of tea or a final stroll eventually drove them away. 'Bye, Edward, darling,' Mum said, kissing you farewell, 'don't work too hard.' Dad remonstrated: 'Do work too hard, that's what he's here for.'

When they left you put up your posters – I remember the dark girl wrapped in clingfilm, and Aristide Bruant with his red scarf – and then went to find a pub – the Cornwallis – where you drank a pint of beer and smoked three cigarettes and wondered again how someone as manifestly intelligent as you had managed to fail, splendidly and unequivocally, his best subject at school: history.

I don't like the town at all, and not just because of the jets flying in low above it on their approach to Gatwick airport. Everything seems 'newish', which is worse than new, and everywhere (the tethered saplings, the themed roundabouts, the preponderance of road signs, the neatly planted verges) is evidence of the town planner's homogeneous hand. There is a historic centre to the place but I never even reach it (and so have to imagine its church with the fourth-highest steeple in Sussex, the remains of the Norman castle and the Georgian brewery) as the ring road directs me inexorably towards the football ground and the sports complex where I am to meet Juliana Lewkowitz and watch her train.

At the crammer, your tutor for History was a hard-faced woman called Mrs Franzler. Mrs Franzler asked you what university you had applied for and you told her it was Oxford. What do you want to read? she asked. History, you said. When she asked you why you had failed your History A-level you said you'd had a mini nervous breakdown – had stared at the paper for three hours and not written a word. Not a single word? Not even a mark. Her eyes narrowed with suspicious disbelief and she set you an essay of astonishing complexity on the 1813 Corn Laws. So let's see just how clever you are, then, she said. Outside the building, you leant against a tethered sapling and smoked a consoling cigarette. Then you went home to your bedsit to work and you saw the girl.

I walk across the stadium towards a small group of athletes in track suits, sitting on the grass listening to a taut, over-muscled man in white shorts and a white t-shirt who is reading from a clipboard. I'm looking for Juliana Lewkowitz, I say. The man ignores me and carries on talking – he's talking about food, about calories, proteins and carbohydrates. Excuse me, I say. Would you mind not interrupting? the man says coolly, finally looking at me. I'm from *Elite* magazine, I say, here to interview Juliana Lewkowitz. I suddenly obtain his full attention. We move away from the others and he introduces himself: Dale Auden he says, he's the club coach – Juliana's coach. Any relation to W.H., I ask? W.H. who? I must stop thinking about poetry. Juliana, it transpires, has a bit of a sniffle. He has sent her home.

You were unlocking your door when the girl came clumping carefully down the stairs from the bedsit above. Her eyes were on her very high heels as she descended sideways, stooped like an old person, fearful she'd fall. Her streaked blonde hair hung forward over her face and, as she reached your landing and safety, she straightened up and with both hands swept it back over her forehead. At that moment your heart felt taut, over-muscled, and you opened your mouth to gulp more oxygen. You smiled hello.
    'Just moved in?' she said.
    'Yes.'
    'Right. See you.'
    You sat for an hour trying to write something about the Corn Laws and failed. She had a scab on her left knee.

I call Felicia from the Tudor Lodge hotel and explain the Juliana situation: there is no point in driving all the way back to Oxford simply to turn round and drive back here the next day. Don't forget we've got dinner at Tim and Rosie Moreton's, tomorrow, Felicia reminds me. I have forgotten: I wanted to forget. Don't be back too late, she warns, gently. After I hang up I realize I've neglected to ask how Gareth is.

The Tudor Lodge hotel is just off the ring road, a mile from the sports complex. It is modern, newish, like everything else in this town. It has a gym and a small swimming pool, a pitch-and-putt mini golf course, a bar called the Portcullis and a restaurant called the Escutcheon. Soft porn films are available on a pay-per-view channel in the privacy of your own room. There is no need for me to leave its precincts.

You were trying to write another of Mrs Franzen's terrifying essays (on Palmerston's second government, 1859–65) when the girl knocked on your door. Did you by any chance have a screwdriver? she wanted to know. She needed to change a plug. You didn't have a screwdriver, *per se*, but you did have, to your vague embarrass-ment, a multi-function penknife that possessed a screwdriving component and which you were happy to lend to her. In the time it took her to change her plug you managed to tidy your room, boil a kettle and take down the poster of the dark girl in clingfilm.

'Thanks very much,' the girl said, handing back your penknife.

'Would you like a cup of coffee?' you managed to say. And she thought about it for a second and said, yes, why not? Wouldn't mind a cup of coffee.

Her name was Yvonne. She wanted to be a nurse. She was working as a cashier in a bookmaker's, trying to save money. She took three sugars. She had a boyfriend called Tony. The scab on her knee (her personal escutcheon) had disappeared. She had been born in Bedford. She declined your offer of a cigarette (she only smoked menthol). She had a pretty, small-featured, pouty, aggress-ive face – as if she couldn't make up her mind whether to sulk or be angry. She hated this town too but it was cheaper than London. Her blonde-streaked hair was thick and long. She asked you no questions about yourself. You wondered how you could arrange to let her know your name.

Dale Auden has instructed me to be at the stadium early, at seven, and I arrive as requested, with a mild hangover (three post-prandial brandies in the Portcullis while I read Elizabeth Bishop for my next *revolver* article: 'The Impossibility of Desire in the Poetry of Elizabeth Bishop'). To my vague irritation I am the first person and the stadium is locked. A bus pulls up at the nearby bus stop and a tall girl descends, carrying a navy blue grip, and she comes over towards me. She's wearing jeans and a multi-pocketed cerise wind-cheater, her dark hair is pulled back from her strong Slavic face in a pony tail. She's a good two inches taller than me and I am five foot eleven (all right, five foot ten).

She smiles, showing her white, uneven teeth.

'Hi,' she says, 'Dale not here yet? Typical.'

I say, my breath suddenly short: 'You must be Juliana.'

'Edward,' Yvonne said when you opened the door (who told her your name?). 'Can you drive?'

'Yes,' you said. 'Why?'

'Couldn't do me an enormous favour, could you?'

Yvonne handed you the keys of a cerise Ford Fiesta parked outside the baker's.

'This your car?'

'Tony's,' she said with uncommon vehemence. You couldn't help noticing she seemed agitated. 'He was meant to be here an hour ago.'

'Tony?'

'Bastard.'

In the car, Yvonne offered you one of her menthol cigarettes. You declined.

'I really appreciate this, Edward,' she said, blowing smoke at the windscreen. 'But it's, you know, kind of like really important.'

You said you were glad to help. In fact you were excited to be sitting with this girl in her boyfriend's car, pleased to be leaving your half-finished essay behind (on the decline of villeinage in fourteenth-century England) and you couldn't help noticing as you reached to switch on the headlamps how Yvonne's denim skirt had ridden really quite far up her thin, pale thighs.

'Where are we off to?' you asked.

'Kent,' she said. 'Then Gatwick airport.'

Dale Auden and I watch Juliana Lewkowitz warm up with a few fifty-metre sprints and continue watching as she strips off. I half listen to Dale drone on (about pylometric exercises, about arm drive and leg plants) as I take in the lanky, lethargic grace of this girl as she bends and stretches. Everything is in proportion but longer, somehow, like an El Greco or a Klimt. I like this notion and decide to open my article with the concept of a Klimt nude made modern athletic flesh. Or maybe Egon Schiele, I reconsider, as I look at Juliana's thin, pale thighs, her arms, her wrists, her fingers. Her minute shorts and vest are made of a stretchy, clinging quasi-fabric that reveals the jut of her pelvic bones and flattens her small breasts on her ribcage.

Dale sets the bar of the high jump at what seems to be my height and Juliana paces out her run. Dale, rather like a drill instructor, yaps out instructions ('Lateral lean!' 'Leg loading!' 'Mass transfer!') as Juliana tightens her pony tail and then begins to rock to and fro as she contemplates her first jump of the day. Then, in a flattening arc, she runs, she lopes, she bounds up to the jump and throws herself up, twisting on to her back, arms and head first, over the bar, straightening her legs as she sails over to land on the inflated mattress – which gives a wheeze and a gasp (of astonishment?) as this flying girl falls backwards on to it.

Juliana climbs off, wincing with displeasure at her successful jump, one finger freeing the seam of her tiny shorts from the cleft of her buttocks.

'Crap,' Dale shouts at her. 'Absolute crap.'

*

You sat in the Fiesta with Yvonne, parked in a picnic area off a country road. All around you in the darkness lay the county of Kent. Yvonne continued to smoke and fiddled with the radio, searching the airwaves for a station that pleased her. Little contemporary rock music seemed to her taste. She winced with displeasure and switched the radio off.

'What are we actually doing here?' you asked.

'Waiting for someone.'

'Oh. Can't you drive?'

'I've been banned. Breathalysed – over the limit.'

'Right.'

She looked at you. 'What're you doing at that college?'

'The crammer? History. I failed my A-level, you see. Retaking the exam.'

'Do you want to be a historian?'

You thought about this. 'No.'

'Why are you doing history, then?'

'It's my best subject.'

'But you failed it.'

It was a fair point – then somebody opened the rear door of the car and jumped in.

Dale Auden will not leave me alone with Juliana.

'She's two centimetres under the UK national record. Going to go next season, isn't it, Juliana?'

'I'll give it my best shot, Dale.'

'That's my girl. Oslo here we come.'

Juliana is sitting on the running track knotting the laces in her trainers. She stands up, unfolding herself, undoes her pony tail and shakes her dark glossy hair free. The gestures have a naturalness, an innocence, that unmans me. Dale finally goes away to talk to some hurdlers.

'Would you like to have dinner tonight?' I ask. 'I feel I haven't really had a chance to have a proper conversation.'

She glances over at Dale – why?

'I don't know,' she says.

I tell her I'm staying at the Tudor Lodge, tell her that *Elite* likes its profiles to concentrate on the personal as well as the professional, offer to pick her up from home, have a taxi drive her back. I am very persuasive.

'See you tonight then, Mr Scully.'

'Call me Edward, please.'

You turned round in your seat to gain a better view of the small man who had entered the car.

'Who the hell's he?' the small man said, staring at you angrily.

'He's called Edward. Bastard Tony never showed.'

'Oh . . .' He seemed to relax and smiled. 'Very grateful, Edward. I'm Tommy.'

'He's my big brother,' Yvonne said and she laughed, with a sudden naturalness, an innocence, as if everything was now explained entirely to your satisfaction.

'We'd better get a move on,' Tommy said. 'That plane leaves in a couple of hours.'

Somehow – oddly – Juliana looks younger in her makeup. She is wearing a dress and shoes with low heels that give her a four-inch height advantage over me. Walking into the Escutcheon with this extremely tall, slim girl seems as bizarre and surreal an event as I've ever experienced. And, feeling this strange and dissociated, I manage only to eat half my sirloin steak – I have no appetite, I only want to drink. Juliana doesn't drink and so I have the bottle of Châteauneuf du Pape all to myself, which is just as well, as I was quite shaken by Felicia's cold anger when I told her that circumstances beyond my control were going to prevent me making the Moreton dinner.

Juliana, in the absence of any questions from me about her highjumping, asks me many questions about my writing. I tell her about my first published novel, *Morbid Anatomy*, and my second, *Aztecs*, still uncompleted after all these years. I tell her that what I really like to write about is poetry and for the first time the glaze of polite interest disappears from her expression and she looks at me with genuine curiosity. She says she loves poetry. I look into her eyes and say I do too. And then one of those adult silences falls between us, as if a policeman has stepped up behind her and laid his heavy hand on her shoulder: she now knows I want to make love to her, a prospect she had never considered until this moment. She colours and bends her head to cut a piece off her lasagne. Something about the pressure and angularities of her long fingers on the knife and fork, the conspicuous bump of the bones on her wrists make me suddenly want to weep.

'For Juliana comes,' I whisper, 'and she what I do to the grass, does to my thoughts and me.'

'Pardon?'

'*The Mower's Song* by Andrew Marvell. How old are you?'

'Ah . . . Nineteen.'

I'm nearly twice her age. I could be her father.

You stood with Yvonne in a cafeteria in Terminal One at Gatwick and watched Tommy argue with his wife. It was a quarter to midnight. There had been an announcement: the plane to Palma, Majorca had been delayed three hours.

'That's Irene's plane,' Yvonne said. 'It'll buy us some time.'

'I should really be thinking about going,' you said, remembering your essay on villeinage that had to be completed by nine o'clock the next morning.

'We have to take Tommy back,' Yvonne said.

'Back where?'

'To the prison. It's an open prison, don't worry. As long as he's back before seven they'll never know he's been gone.'

'Right.'

Yvonne could tell from your expression that aiding and abetting even the temporary escape of a prisoner was not something you'd planned on doing in your life. So she explained that Tommy was in for embezzlement, a victimless crime.

You asked about the purpose of this visit to Gatwick and Yvonne said that Irene, Tommy's wife, was going to Spain to be with Tommy's ex-partner. Tommy had to persuade her to stay, for the sake of the kids, hence the midnight rush to Gatwick.

'The kids?'

'They have two kids.'

Irene and Tommy came over to the coffee bar and Irene was introduced. She was a small, buxom woman with a knowing look to her eye, dressed scantily and brightly for the Spanish sun. Tommy asked Yvonne if he could have a word and left you and Irene alone. You bought her a coffee and she accepted one of your cigarettes.

'I hear the plane's delayed,' you said.

'Charters.'

'Nightmare.'

'So,' she said, looking at you shrewdly, 'are you and Yvonne . . . ?'

'No. No, I live in the bedsit under hers.'

When she drew on her cigarette small deep furrows appeared in her upper lip. She smoothed the lapels of her short-sleeved jacket, adjusted the lie of her cleavage, unclipped and reclipped an earring.

'Ever been to Majorca, Stephen?'

'Edward.'

'Edward.'

'No, but I've been to Barcelona.'

'Never been to Barcelona. Las Palmas?'

'Ah, the Canaries.'

'*Las Islas Canarias.*'

'Never been there.'

Tommy and Yvonne returned, Tommy unable to keep the smile off his face with news that the charter flight to Majorca had now been cancelled. Irene didn't believe him and even when an announcement followed quickly she still insisted you accompanied her to the desk to confirm that this was so. It was as if your presence would thwart any dark plot by Tommy. The plane was indeed cancelled: there was an air traffic controllers' strike in France

affecting most European flights. To your consternation tears began
to brim in Irene's eyes.

'This is what happens to me, Edward. I can never be happy. Just
when I think my life's going OK, and finally I'm going to be happy,
this sort of thing always happens to me.'

'Maybe it's fate,' you said. 'You never know. Think of the kids.
Maybe you're not meant to go.'

She ran a knuckle under each eye as she considered this, then
she reached for your hand and squeezed it. You felt her long nails
bite into your palm.

'Thanks, Ed. Truly. Thanks.'

In the foyer of the Tudor Lodge hotel I stand with Juliana waiting
for her taxi. I feel a form of panic stirring in me, like a skittish
animal. I can't let this girl go.

'Juliana,' I say, 'If you come up to my room I can show you that
poem.'

'What poem?'

'The Juliana poem.'

'I'd better get back.'

'I'd like to write a book about you. A book of your life.'

'There's my taxi.'

I want to kiss her but I realize I will have to stretch my neck and
stand slightly on my toes to do so. I step towards her and she
freezes. The Impossibility of Desire in the Poetry of . . . Juliana's
height suddenly makes me ridiculous. She stands there looking at
me, wary, unsure – unhappy maybe: maybe I've spoiled something.
She thanks me for the supper and I watch her leave through the
thick plate glass of the Tudor Lodge hotel's front door. As she
bends into the taxi she turns and gives me a brisk, brief, final wave.

It was dawn by the time you parked the cerise Fiesta outside the
bakery.

'What a night,' Yvonne said. 'I can't believe Irene's staying. What
did you say to her?'

'I don't really know,' you said. Irene and Tommy had had a few words and then Irene had taken a taxi back to her mother's, where she'd left her children. On the return journey to the open prison Tommy had been reflective, asking you several times to repeat the exchange you'd had with Irene. Tommy patted you gratefully on the shoulder, kissed Yvonne and slipped out of the car and into the night.

'It's just across the fields,' Yvonne said. 'They come and go all the time, Tommy says.'

'Don't they have guards at this prison?' you asked.

'Of course. But they trust the prisoners. That's why it's called an open prison.'

You followed Yvonne up the stairs, your eyes on the pale blue veins showing on the backs of her knees, at that moment you wanted to do nothing more than reach out and run your hand over her flexing calf muscle. You felt desire stir in you like a skittish animal.

You paused on the landing, fished in your pocket for the key.

'Do you want a cup of coffee, or anything?' you asked. You could see yourself in your narrow bed with Yvonne, belly to belly; you could smell her, feel her thick hair drag across your chest.

'Better get some sleep. Got work in three hours.'

She backed away, slumped like a marionette for a moment to feign extreme exhaustion, straightened with a smile and blew you a kiss. As evanescent as a blown kiss, you thought. What could be more insubstantial?

'Thanks a million, Ed. See you later, maybe.'

I tell Dale Auden I don't like his tone. Don't like his implications.

'And I don't like you, full stop,' he says.

We are in the carpark. I throw my grip into the back of the Volvo and turn to face him. He jabs his finger at me.

'You asked her up to your room.'

'To continue the interview.'

'Bloody pervert.'

I try to punch him in the face but he raises his arm and I strike his shoulder instead, hard. With astonishing speed he immobilizes me with some kind of double arm lock and hisses threats and obscenities into my ear. Then he pushes me brusquely away and I career into a shrub – twigs snap . . .

'I'm going to call your editor,' he says. 'Pervert.'

'Get a life,' I shout at him. He laughs at that and wanders off. I flex my fingers: my hand hurts. Get a life.

You found the continued clattering and tramping up and down the stairs an irritation and eventually looked out of your room. Yvonne and a guy in a leather coat were coming down from her bedsit, Yvonne carrying a suitcase, the guy lugging a cardboard box.

'Hi,' you said, surprised. 'Want a hand?'

'No thanks, we're fine, thanks. This is Tony.'

Tony nodded and grinned hello at you above his cardboard box.

'Moving out?' you said, suddenly realizing.

'Yeah. Going to Penzance.'

'Cornwall? My God. Never been to Cornwall.'

'Come and see us,' Yvonne said.

Five minutes later, she came back up the stairs and knocked on your door.

'I forgot to tell you,' she said, 'Irene went to Majorca. Yesterday. Took the kids with her this time.'

'God.'

'Just goes to show.'

You tried to understand this news, wondering if in some way you were responsible.

'How's Tommy?'

'He's a bit cut up. Not surprising, really.'

'Yeah.'

You stood there in your room with Yvonne and you both thought about that night you had shared, silent for a few seconds. Then you looked at each other. You flexed your fingers.

'I'll send you a change of address card,' she said, softly.

'Don't forget,' you said, but you knew she would.

Then she stepped forward, took your head in her hands and kissed you hard, with a small clash of teeth, and her tongue was in your mouth, squirming, flickering. But before you could grab her she was gone, backing out of the room, with a wicked, half-suppressed smile on her face, and Tony was honking the horn of the cerise Fiesta in the street below. You heard her heels rapping the stairs.

You went and sat at your desk, trying to stay calm, thinking about Yvonne and the way she had kissed you. You knew it would be something you would never forget, that it would become one of those events that shaped and defined you as a person, a key link in the chain mail of memories woven through your life. As you looked out of the window you noticed that a slanting ray of the morning sun had squeezed between two houses and touched the higher branches of the lime tree at the bottom of the garden, turning its dusty, tired summer leaves into shimmering coins of lemon-green, making the tree seem young again, and making you think of spring.

When I arrive at the house I find it empty. Felicia will have taken Gareth out in his stroller. The day is mild and breezy, the clouds swift in the blue sky. It's only three o'clock in the afternoon but I pour myself two inches of vodka and fill the glass with ice cubes and brace myself for the row that will surely come.

I sip my drink, feeling my lips numb slowly, and look out of the window. The clouds move and a sudden angle of afternoon sun slanting over the top of the next-door house touches the uppermost branches of the old lime tree at the end of the garden. For a moment a thick wand of sun turns its tired summer leaves into refulgent coins of lemony green, making the tree seem young again and making me think of spring.

Beulah Berlin, an A–Z

Angst, ennui, weltschmerz, cafard, taedium vitae, anomie . . .
Curious how oddly beguiling these words are. I almost don't mind
suffering from the conditions they describe. Some of the so-called
'beautiful diseases', perhaps. But I exaggerate: for most of my life
everything was normal – I only realized I was in trouble when
I went to Berlin.

Berlin gave me my name and was the making of me. Before
Berlin everything was conventionally straightforward: I was born,
I became a child, I went to school then college (media studies), then
film school – nothing about my life was particularly interesting.
In film school I wanted to be an editor (I yearned for control),
but then changed my mind after a year and decided to become an
art director (I was good at drawing). How do you know when
your life is intrinsically uninteresting? You just do. Some people
live quietly, unhappily, with this knowledge, others do something
about it.

At a film festival in Hamburg, where a short film I had art-directed
was being screened, I met my first husband, Georg. He was an
artist and, after the festival, I suddenly, spontaneously, went with
him to Berlin. I was twenty-two years old and I think I knew that
this would be the beginning of everything. A month later we were
married.

A man has just walked by leading a Great Dane and a Dachshund.
How peculiar. (I am writing this in Amsterdam.)

Georg and some of his friends staged an exhibition called 'Stunk'
(it should be pronounced with a German accent). They rented a
floor of an office building for a month on the something-strasse
and it became their art gallery. (Stunk-Kunst.) Georg asked me to

contribute and that was how 'The Transparent Wardrobe' happened, how Beulah Berlin came into being. After being Beulah McTurk for twenty-two years I knew that Beulah Berlin was bound to be more intriguing, altogether cooler.

Colour dominated my wardrobe in those days. I wore the brightest clothes – as camouflage. Now I wear only black, white and grey. At the 'Stunk' show I hung my garish clothes on chrome rails and wore nothing but a black brassière and panties. People then selected a combination of items from my wardrobe, wrote the request on a piece of paper and I wore whatever they had suggested for an hour. Black stiletto and a brown hiking boot; a leather jacket and a bikini bottom; a straw sombrero and pyjama trousers. I took a polaroid photograph of the combination and pinned it on a giant pinboard. I have to say that without Beulah Berlin and her transparent wardrobe the 'Stunk' show would be completely forgotten. Ninety-nine per cent of the press coverage was about me and my tireless transformations. By the time the lease ran out I had over a thousand photographs: the pinboard was a multi-coloured collage of various Beulah Berlins. Georg never really forgave me, I now see in retrospect, and from then on our relationship went steadily to the dogs.

Dogs are wonderful animals and it's a source of endless regret to me that I've never been able to have one as a pet – because of my allergies. Who was it who said, 'The more I see of men the more I come to value dogs'? Matthew Arnold, Nietszche? Somebody. Certainly I place dogs higher in my estimation than my ex-husbands. Well, my first and second exes, definitely, not necessarily my soon-to-be third ex.

'Exudations' was the name of Georg's next show. We were still married, just, and I agreed to participate again. If 'Stunk' made me famous, 'Exudations' made me notorious. Georg's plan was to remain indoors in our apartment for a year and to collect and preserve everything his body exuded. Everything, yes – I don't need to go into every detail – for instance, he strained his shaving water through muslin to recover the bristles. These 'exudations', bottled and boxed, hermetically sealed and carefully labelled, would then form the basis of a touring exhibition, the idea being that they provided an idiosyncratic but perfect historical record of his body over one year. I managed to last three weeks before I fell seriously ill with some gastro-bacteriological infection. Georg refused to leave the flat – his work was still in progress, he argued, and moreover he was in perfect health – and eventually the police had to break the doors down (neighbours were complaining also). Disinfection and fumigation followed, and 'Exudations' was no more than a brief footnote in the history of contemporary German art. I sued Georg for my medical bills (I was uninsured and he refused any contribution, claiming I had betrayed him) and, of course, our marriage didn't survive. Georg went to live in a shack in Ibiza. I haven't seen him since. I now realize that Georg was an accident waiting to happen, a faulty missile they forgot to test-fire.

'Fire one!' Cornelius exclaims each time he has his orgasm. Cornelius is my secret boyfriend – my U-boat captain. I used to think this was funny but it's beginning to irritate me (Otto knows nothing about Cornelius). In fact fire warmed and illuminated my early life – or, should I say, fires. Our home was in Eastbourne, on England's south coast. My father's business was the fitting and installation of gas and electric fires. I once asked him why he liked Eastbourne so.

'I hate it,' he said.

'But the people are nice.'

'I hate them.'

When he became ill I blamed it on this lifelong hatred festering in him. He should have moved away, especially after he and my mother divorced. It was the place's fault, this overcrowded south-east section of our small island. The place's fault, England's.

Glands, my father later claimed, were the root cause of his lassitude and weight loss. He was in no pain but it was clear something was seriously, profoundly wrong with him. He started taking all manner of self-prescribed vitamin and health food combinations to battle his 'gland' problem. Ginseng and cod-liver oil. Nettle tea and royal jelly. Huge amounts of vitamin E and strange seaweed stews. He munched sunflower seeds all day. When I told Cornelius about my father's habits he laughed. When I asked him why he said they were a perfect example of the humorous tragedy of existence.

I took the urn with my father's ashes across the Channel to France and scattered them on the battlefields of the Somme. I thought he would appreciate being abroad, away from Eastbourne. I wandered about the meadows – it was summer – taking a pinch of ash from time to time and allowing it to fall from my fingers, carried away by the breeze. The air was full of the scent of freshly cut hay.

Hay fever suggests summer. Mowers in the thickening meadows and the pollens taking to the air as the grasses fall to the advancing scythe. Not in my case: for me hay fever is a spring phenomenon. Now I know why T. S. Eliot said 'April is the cruellest month' – he too must have suffered from early-season pollen allergies. But now my allergies are with me all year long. I open a newspaper and my nose begins to run; a woman passes me and her perfume causes my throat to contract. I cough and cough. (Why do these women douse themselves in so much scent? Why this love of chemical odours?) At night I lie in bed and my hip-bones ache as if I have arthritis. I'm not alone, I know, we're all becoming slowly poisoned, over-sensitized. We are all, in our own ways, ill.

Illness casts a bright light, the rest of life retreats into the shadows beyond its refulgent glare. When my father was ill, no matter where I was, or what I was doing, I seemed to think about him a dozen times an hour. Eventually, there was nothing for it, and I moved back to Eastbourne to a bed and breakfast in the same street. He never went to hospital, district nurses used to visit him throughout the day, while I provided him with increasingly deliquescent then entirely liquid meals. Soon all he wanted was beef consommé. 'Ah,' he would say, as I bought him the steaming bowl, 'soupe du jour.'

Journal-keeping has sustained me since I was twelve. Over the last few years, however, I've refined the process. When I wake I write the first thing down that occurs to me and before I go to bed I write down the last thing on my mind. You should try it: it is astonishingly meaningful. Those two sentences define and plot your life in the most random yet illuminating way. I look back to 14 April 1999. Morning: 'Gianluca is a pure unreconstructed bastard.' Night: 'I drank champagne all day today – not a bite to eat. I've never felt better.' 22 November 1996. Morning: 'Wintry sunlight makes my room look dirty'. Night: 'Edith Wharton is good but boring, must resist the temptation to skip.'

Kipling, Rudyard Kipling, wrote a book called *Stalky and Co*. In it there is a character called M'Turk, which I suppose is a form of McTurk (though the apostrophe is something I have never seen before). It is the only evidence I've been able to find of a McTurk in literature.

My own name 'Beulah' comes out of a book, a book that my mother was reading before I was born. *The Knights of the Golden Horseshoe*, by William Alexander Carruthers, set in the antebellum Deep South. My mother was on a Deep South craze at the time, she loved everything about the romanticized vision of the place. I suppose it took her away from Eastbourne and my father's shop of fire. 'The Land of Beulah,' she used to sigh, and thus I was named. But Beulah McTurk is all wrong. It suggests to me a plump and heavy woman, yet I am tall and very, very slim. Consequently, I was happy to become Beulah Berlin, to be named after a city. It suggests something steely, tougher, as if I surround myself with a protective forcefield, a non-stick coat of shellac, say, or teflon.

London: too weird and wired, these days. New York: too busy.

San Francisco: too healthy. Paris: too self-conscious. All these cities I have known well, or as well as any one person can know a city. There are times in your life, though, when relaxation is what you crave and I had to leave London, felt the panicked urge to flee. So where else would I go but Amsterdam? It drew me as a candle flame draws a moth.

Mother disapproved of my name change. She disapproved of my life as an artist, of Georg, my first husband and, I suspect, Otto, my third. I never told her about my second. But I have a feeling she would like Cornelius, my secret boyfriend: he is handsome, selfish and raffish, like a beau in a Carruthers novel.

Otto, my third husband, is English despite his Germanic christian name. He's called Otto Carlyle and he repairs computers. He declines to use common terms of endearment like 'darling' and 'sweetheart' and calls me instead things like 'my pragmatic monad', or 'my ambrosial liquor'. I rise to the challenge. When he leaves on his trips or when we speak on the phone we sign off like this:

Otto: 'Goodbye, my fish and chips.'

Me: 'Goodbye, bird with the coppery, keen claws.'

Otto: 'All love to the slender gymnast.'

Me: 'See you soon, windmill of my mind.'

Otto is very tall and after my father's death I wanted, for some vague reason, to be with a tall man. He is six feet four, I am five feet nine.

Nineteen sixty-nine. The year of my birth. 27 March 1969. That week, the first Concorde was undergoing its test flights. John Lennon and Yoko Ono were doing their lie-in for peace at the Amsterdam Hilton. I am, just, a child of the sixties, and it seems to me only apt that I should now be back in Amsterdam. Full circle, after a fashion. A near-perfect O.

Otto has just called from Dakar. Whenever he's abroad and he calls I place a photograph of him in front of me. It was taken at a beach café in Antibes when we were staying with my then gallerist, Clive Count (the 'o' is silent, I used to say later, after he dropped me). Otto is wearing surfing trunks and a baggy t-shirt, his hair is wet and sticks up in spikes – he looks like an impossibly lanky waif. I've come to hate a disembodied voice, I hate talking on the telephone, but it's never so bad when you're looking at a photo.

Photography is the art form I practise these days – I took it up seriously after I stopped touring with 'The Transparent Wardrobe', in fact. Then I taught film studies at a private university in San Francisco for two years before I began to photograph people's feet.

Of all our body parts the foot is the one we treat the most harshly. No other part of our body – faces included – shows with such brutal candour our individual ageing process. We stuff our feet into unsuitable shoes, we walk for miles, we barely minister to them, occasionally cutting toenails, occasionally painting said toenails. But the calluses, corns, chilblains, veruccae and steady deformations alter them year on year in the most visible way. I have twenty-five subjects (friends and acquaintances, young and old) and every six months I take a photograph of their faces and feet, juxtaposed. Already two have asked to drop out; they find it too distressing, they say, as if the ticking clock of their own mortality is manifest there at the end of their legs, hidden in their shoes. Perhaps you saw my exhibition in Ghent, or Basle, or the one in East Gallery East in London? Some people's feet look like vegetarian growths, others like eroded landscapes. The exhibitions were great successes. Every morning before the doors opened there would be a substantial queue.

Qwertyuiop, that's what I'm going to call my child, male or female, whenever I have him or her. He or she can then make any name they want out of that combination of letters. Trey. Opi. Yute. Power. I don't care. I'm not sure, however, if I want Otto to be the father. I told him it was all over between us but he has followed me to Amsterdam and, somehow, is living in this flat I have rented on the Kaisersgracht. He says that Schiphol airport is the perfect hub for his business, and I suppose it's true. (The computers he fixes are huge and usually abroad: airports, hospitals, government departments, he was even hired by the Pentagon for two months.) In his spare time he's writing a novel called *Garden Airplane Trap* (after the painting by Max Ernst. I think Ernst has the best titles in modern art). Otto's often away doing his mysterious job and, even though that's when I see Cornelius, I find I miss him. Then, when he returns, I resent him. I want his presence and also his absence. When he's not at work he spends most of his time writing his novel and reading.

Reading is my great solace. I read a lot, but some years ago I decided, faced by the millions of books I hadn't read, to make my reading systematic. So every year I chose a theme and only read books that fall into the specific category. For example in 1995 I only read books whose titles were women's names. I read *Emma*, *Madame Bovary*, *Thérèse Raquin*, *Aunt Julia and the Scriptwriter*, *Clarissa*, and some others I can't remember. In 1998 I moved on to animals. I read *Kangaroo*, *Birdy*, *The Sandpiper*, *The White Monkey*, *The Pope's Rhinoceros*, *Travels with a Donkey*. This year I'm on cities: *Goodbye to Berlin*, *London Fields*, *L.A. Confidential*, *Last Exit to Brooklyn*, *Is Paris Burning?*, *The Viceroy of Ouidah*. Next year it'll be abstract nouns, I have *Persuasion* and *Chaos* lined up ready to go on January 1st. More and more I find I like this way of giving your random, haphazard progress through time some sort of hidden organizing factor, known only to you, only understood by you, a personal encryption. It looks normal – somebody reading a book – but underneath you alone know the significance – your life's private palimpsest.

Sestina, villanelle, sonnet. My favourite poetic forms in order of preference. It must be because I like the imposed shape: the rules, the order, the poetic matrix. I recently read a good poem about tins washed up on a beach and last weekend went out to the dunes at Kennemerduinen and collected a dozen or so of these drift-tins. I imagine a show – the sand-scoured, sun-bleached, wave-washed, storm-tossed tins and beside them the pristine, primary-coloured supermarket version. It could be very moving. The life of tins; their slow death by water. I like to smoke a cigarette when I read poetry, I don't know why – I don't smoke a lot – but, with poetry, I just like to.

Tobacco is a strange drug, when you think about it. Alcohol seems more natural – we all have to drink after all – and my favourite drink is champagne. But drawing smoke into your lungs is not an instinctive process in any way. I like the smell of wood smoke, but if I see a bonfire I don't rush over to it and start inhaling the fumes. My father took up smoking in the last month of his life as an act of simple defiance, he said, a rebuke to his draining vitality. We would smoke together all evening as I read him poetry. I understand his position better now, see things from his point of view.

U-turns define life's progress, it seems to me, better than the traditional image of forking paths. How often in our life can its significant events be described as a U-turn? Falling out of love, for example, is a major emotional U-turn, rather than a bifurcation on life's highway. This sojourn in Amsterdam is a U-turn. I had to get out of London after my father died. Coming here is not a step forward but rather an urge to turn back down life's road. Otto is a bit of a U-turn too. I fell out of love, we were going to split, and now we're back together. Two U-turns, there. Now I'm turning away from him again towards Cornelius – it's confusing. Cornelius hoards food – I found thirty tins of sliced peaches in a cupboard. He has four kilos of butter in his fridge. A warning sign? Maybe, to use a film image, my life is a series of jump-cuts. The continuity is illusory, imprecise, we just jump-cut from one sequence to another. Very *nouvelle vague*.

Vague ambitions are to be encouraged. Life should be full of half-thought-out plans for what you might like to do but haven't got the real desire, or the energy or the time or just enough money. I vaguely want to go to Russia. I vaguely want to learn Spanish. I vaguely want to read the novels of Ronald Firbank. I vaguely want to tattoo myself somewhere risqué . . . Cornelius has a tattoo (a twirly fleur-de-lys) on his coccyx. I cherish these vague ambitions because they seem to presuppose another existence – another life for myself – in which they might actually come about. The more vague ambitions you have the more potential lives you could lead. I explained all this once at great length to a psychiatrist (just after Georg and I had divorced) who was keen to put me on Valium. I don't think he thought I was very well.

*W*eltverbesserungswahn. How I love these German words. That's what my psychiatrist (he was German) said was wrong with me, what I suffered from (along with various other mental maladies). It must have been the foetid, daily trauma of the 'Exudations' period, then my hospitalization, then Georg leaving me that made me marry this man, this maniac. On the rebound in a singularly disastrous way. What was I thinking of? I left him after two weeks and have never mentioned his name again, and never will. The single legacy of our relationship is this diagnosis, *Weltverbesserungswahn*: the conviction that the world could be better. My psychiatrist husband said it was a delusion, not a conviction, and that my refusal to acknowledge it as a delusion was proof that I was deluded. You see why I had to go. The only thing that was satisfactory during my two weeks' marriage to this man was the sex.

*X*anadu is the name of the bar I work in three nights a week in Jordaan. Cornelius is the manager. He has a small apartment at the top of the building where we make love when Otto is away. He's just bought a thousand tins of sardines. I asked him if he liked sardines and he said no, but they were at a bargain price and you could never tell when your tastes might change. I promised myself I'd stop seeing him as soon as my book is ready (I think my tin idea is a book, now, not a show) – but I think he's in love with me, dammit. What's wrong with these men? I met a publisher last week here in Amsterdam, and he said almost immediately that, all things being equal (what can he mean? Curious expression), he could publish my book next year.

Years go by. I see myself as an old lady living in an apartment block by the sea (not Eastbourne, not Ibiza). I keep the curtains drawn day and night, all year round. Qwertyuiop visits regularly. When he/she arrives he/she takes his/her shoes and socks off and I photograph his/her feet. He's/she's a good boy/girl, Qwert (is he/she Cornelius's?), and he/she shows concern.

'What's the weather like?' I ask.

'Open the curtains, Mum,' he/she says. 'See for yourself.'

'No,' I say. 'It's more interesting if you tell me.'

And so he/she does his/her best: sunny, scudding clouds, threat of rain later in the day. In my dark apartment I prefer to use my imagination. I like this fantasy of my future, but what will the reality be? Some old bag living off cigarettes and booze.

Zoos consoled me after my father died. And the zoo in Amsterdam is one of the world's best, so I'm told. I used to watch the chimps but they depressed me. Too human: sitting around showing off their hard-ons, hurling shit at each other. And the pacing cats were terrifying – to-and-fro, to-and-fro – all that charged, energetic resentment at their captivity. So I looked for animals that seemed content with their zoo life and more and more I found I was watching the rhinos. I came to love their massiveness, their heft and their effortless charisma. In my worst moments (when Cornelius begged me to leave Otto and live with him; when Otto asked me to come on his next trip – to California) I longed to be a rhino with my rhino armour. And so I would calm myself, watching them, imagining I was a rhino in a zoo, my day an ordered round of eating, defecating and sleeping. In a zoo, but free somehow. Free from the world and its noisy demands. Free, finally, from angst.

The Woman on the Beach with a Dog

'Every person lives his real, most interesting life under the cover
of secrecy.'
Anton Chekhov

For some reason Garrett Rising decided, when he was twenty miles
out of Boston and heading for New York, that he had to see the
ocean: he needed that far horizon, he needed the sound of surf
breaking, he felt, more than anything. He knew it would calm him,
so he turned off the highway and headed east for the beckoning
finger of Cape Cod.

He had been to Cape Cod as a child, when he was ten or eleven,
he thought, when the Rising family had spent three weeks of one
summer in a rented house in Provincetown. He had dim memories:
a mustard yellow house, windows that jammed, his father's unceas-
ing anger, the placid bay facing the town and the tumultuous ocean
on the other side of the dunes.

When he stopped for gas in Orleans he felt a small tremor of
excitement squirm through him. In the face of his problems, in
the face of this new disappointment, he was doing something
spontaneous – and something stupid too, no doubt – but he didn't
care, and besides he couldn't see what harm it would do to anyone.
All he knew was that he couldn't go back to New York just yet –
he needed the solace of the waves.

Garrett Rising was a tall, limber man with broad shoulders; he
had a small belly on him but, he argued, he was forty-one, after all,
as old as the century, and there wasn't much he could do about
that. He had fair hair shot with grey and his nose was small and
fine with a pronounced flare to the nostrils. Many women had told

him that it was his small, fine nose that made them look at him a second time.

'Great movie,' the attendant said handing him his change and inclining his head at the cinema across the street: The Rio, it was called, written in a cursive cerise neon script across the cinema's façade. The film that was playing was *Scarlet Autumn*.

'Yeah?' Garrett said. 'I must try and catch it, one of these days.'

'You won't regret it.'

Garrett drove on. He had passed through South Wellfleet when he began to feel tired and saw the sign: 'Pamet River Inn, next right, Ocean View, Deluxe Rooms'. He turned and bumped down a rutted road towards a large white clapboard two-storey building with a *porte cochère* and a gravelled turning circle and, on either side, a wing of individual wooden chalets linked by a sheltered walkway. The inn was protected from the Atlantic winds by a grassy hill that rose up from the shore beyond, and in the lee of the hill was a small copse of scrub pines. As Garrett stepped out of his car and heaved his suitcase from the trunk, he could hear the reassuring wash and rumble of the surf and off to the south saw the early afternoon sun glinting hard and silver on the restless ocean.

He checked in and a boy carried his suitcase to the furthest of the 'cottages', as he knew they were now called, and showed him in. It was a Friday in April, the boy reminded him, the hotel was quiet, just three guests – and the restaurant only opened on Saturday night and Sunday lunchtime, until the holidays started. Garrett gave him five dollars and asked him to fetch a pint of whisky. He wandered round the room and pulled back the drapes to let the clear marine light fill the space more. There was a neat kitchen with a stove, a sink and an icebox, a bathroom and the main room had, as well as its double bed, two armchairs and a coffee table. The walls were white and unadorned except for an old print of some gaunt-looking Puritans discovering a cache of corncobs hidden beneath an Indian blanket in the undergrowth. You could live here, Garrett thought, comfortably and easily: everything a person required to live a simple, uncomplicated life was here, and the fantasy excited him once again. He was glad he had come: but he wouldn't call home with the change of plan until the whisky arrived.

He picked up yesterday's *Globe*, which someone had left on the coffee table, and saw the headline about the Nazi bombing raids on London, hundreds dead and wounded. He remembered his only visit to London, in '32, when he had been on his way to Hamburg, when Sean Kavanaugh had sent him to Germany to buy the two Reiner-Hoffman printers at rock-bottom prices. He had been a rich man in Germany with his American dollars, he remembered; he'd never felt so rich since. In London on the way back he had stayed in the Hyde Park Hotel, and he wondered vaguely if it had been hit by the bombs. He remembered the girl he had taken to his room. One pound, ten shillings she charged him. What was that? Ten dollars? Sweet girl – what was her name? Kitty? Mary? Hotel rooms always made him think of sex, which was not that surprising, he reminded himself with a brief, warm flare of shame, as the only sex he experienced these days tended to take place in hotel rooms.

The whisky came, he drank some and called his wife in New York and told her plans had changed and he was obliged to stay over.

'Did you get the contract?' Laura asked.

'We're almost there,' he lied. 'Just a few details to confirm.'

'Thank God. Did you call Daddy?'

'I'll call him this weekend. He's retired, you know.'

'He likes to be informed, he still likes to –'

'So I'm staying over. Tell him I'm staying to sort out the details.'

'How long?' Laura could not prevent the suspicion colouring her voice.

'I'll be back tomorrow.'

'Where're you staying?'

'I don't know yet. I'm at a pay phone. I'll find somewhere.'

'Nowhere expensive. We can't afford to –'

'How's Joanna?'

'Joanna's got another headache. I've called the doctor. She has no appetite.'

Garrett listened to his daughter's various symptoms, said good-bye and hung up. His daughter was eighteen and she seemed to have been ill from one thing or another since she was born. How could someone be so unhealthy and no doctor find a reason? Her mother fussed too much, had always fussed needlessly, endlessly, over her: too much fussing made you sickly. Garrett checked these thoughts – he could feel the anger build in him again. He picked up his hat: time to hear the noise of the sea.

The beach was empty and the clouds had hidden the sun – the light had turned grey and monotone making the sea-grass on the dunes dull like moss. The wind whipped his tie and he had to turn his body and cup his hands tightly around the match as he lit his cigarette. He thought about old Mr Foley and the way he had broken the news: he had been fair – couldn't argue about that – gave him three months' notice. 'Foley and McBride won't be renewing the contract, Garrett, I'm so very sorry.'

Garrett stared unseeingly at the horizon as he tried to compute the effect this would have on the company. He calculated: seventy per cent of their business was involved in printing Foley and McBride guidebooks – they'd run off 30,000 copies of the Los Angeles guide alone. Fifteen years they'd been Foley and McBride's printers. There would have to be lay-offs: Pauly, Tom Reed, Tom Harbinger . . .

He heard a shrill annoying yapping and looked round to see a small white dog with an erect, arced tail and a thick ruff of fur around its neck nosing at a coil of sea-wrack at the surf's edge. The dog's lead trailed behind it. Then came another shout, more distant, and Garrett looked down the curving beach to see a figure waving its arms and shouting something. He only caught the words 'Mister, please –' before the wind carried the rest away.

Garret wandered over to the dog and picked up its lead. The dog snapped and growled at him. What kind of a dog is that, he wondered? Pissant little white dog.

The figure approached, wearing a rust-red windcheater and beige canvas trousers, short in the leg. It was a woman.

'Thank you, so much,' she said. Her thick brown hair was dragged back in a loose pony tail. She had a strong bony face and a deep voice, a voice that was full of confidence, the confidence of money, he thought, as she thanked him, profusely, sincerely, for catching her dog, her naughty, ill-disciplined, spoilt brat of a dog. There were gold rings with coloured stones on her hands, he saw, as he gave her the dog's lead. Hard to tell her age, a bit younger than he was. Mustn't stare so.

'What kind of a dog is that?' he asked.

'It's a Pomeranian.'

'Oh, right.'

'Have you a cigarette you could spare me? I'd kill for a cigarette.'

He offered his pack, she took one and they manoeuvred around against the wind to light it, their shoulders brushing once or twice.

She looked at him and smiled.

'I couldn't believe it when I saw a man in a hat and a three-piece flannel suit standing on the beach. Is that a mirage, I thought, a chimera?'

'I'm staying at the hotel.'

'The Pamet? God, am I that far down? How are the rooms?'

They walked back to the inn together, the woman explaining that she was going to phone for her car to be driven down from Truro to fetch her. Her naughty dog was called Euclid, she said, though she realized she should never have given her stupid mutt such an intelligent name.

'My name's Garrett Rising,' he said, offering his hand.

She shook it. 'My name's Anna . . .' She paused and then said a name that he couldn't quite catch. Demonserian? Staufferman? He thought it would be rude to ask her to repeat it, so, instead, he offered her the chance of using the phone in his room.

After she called her home, she wandered around his little cottage, curious. She laughed at the print, unzipped her windcheater and unreflectingly picked some wool-balls off the soft front of her cream jersey, dropping them carefully in the wastebasket as she nosed around. Euclid settled down on a mat by the bed, completely docile.

'You've got everything a man could need, here,' she said, walking into the kitchen.

Except a woman, Garrett thought, automatically, and in that moment, having acknowledged his need for a woman, Garrett desired *this* woman, this Anna-woman, this tall, handsome, confident woman, more than he had desired anyone or anything in years. And in the way that this kind of mental recognition seems to transfer itself automatically and instinctively from man to woman, from woman to man, he saw Anna pause, close the icebox and turn to look at him. He knew from the small, amused frown on her face, from the merest narrowing of her eyes that she had registered what he was thinking, had noted the tiny significant change in the atmosphere. Garrett relaxed: like it or not, signals had been exchanged.

'May I offer you a drink?'

He poured out two glasses of whisky – 'Just cover the bottom,' she said – and as they chinked the rims she thanked him again for catching Euclid. Garrett relished the burn of the whisky in his throat, the small fire in his belly, and, emboldened, asked her if he could buy her dinner.

'Never on a Friday,' she said, not perturbed. 'Friday night we go to the movies in Orleans. Rain or shine. Oh, there's my car.'

'We?' Garrett said.

'My husband.' She smiled, apologetically, Garrett thought, as if she'd liked the beginning of this adventure – its erotic potential.

'But . . . he's out of town. Thank you so much, Mr Rising. Euclid and I are for ever in your debt.' Now she looked like she was about to laugh. 'Come on Euclid, let's go home.'

'My pleasure.'

Garrett watched her lead the dog along the boardwalk towards a large, glossy Packard. The man driving opened the door for her, picked up Euclid, and placed him on the front seat. The woman looked back and waved, just a flick of the hand. Garrett closed the door.

In Orleans, that evening, at the Rio, Garrett watched *Sacred Autumn* with only half a mind, the other half on Anna and, inevitably, on the future of Kavanaugh-Rising Inc. When the lights went up suddenly, he sat for a moment baffled, wondering why the actress had been so tearful at the end, what had happened to make life bear down on her so. He stood up and placed his hat on his head and strolled up the aisle. Anna was sitting in the back row.

'Hi,' he said.

'Drive me home?'

In the car, just as they passed through Wellfleet, she reached over and felt the hard ridge of his penis through the flannel of his pants.

'Good,' she said, 'I thought so.'

When he woke he was first aware of a refulgent big rhomboid of lemon light on the wall facing him. The shape of the sun on the wall blinding his eyes, as if he had woken to a different, simpler world where there was only light and empty walls. He turned and noticed the drapes were parted wide and the low, early sun was filling the room. He sat up in bed and saw that Anna was dressing. She stepped briskly into her skirt and zipped it up.

'Morning,' he said. 'What time is it?'

'Early.'

'Come back to bed.'

'I have to go.'

He dressed quickly and together they walked down through the dunes to the beach. She slipped off her shoes and turned to him.

'I'll be home in no time,' she said. 'Thank you, Garrett.'

He kissed her and she thrust her tongue deep into his mouth, holding him hard to her. Then she buried her face in his neck and he heard her draw her breath in hard as if she were filling her lungs with the smell of him. 'It was nice,' she said softly into his collar. 'What a word, my God.'

'When can I see you?'

'This is crazy.' She punched him gently on the arm. 'No, no, no.

It would all be too complicated. It's over – we had our adventure.'

She touched his lips with her two fingers to stop him saying any more and turned and walked away from him, not looking back, striding up the beach to – where? – to Truro, she had said. Can't be a big place, Truro, he thought – you'll be easy to find.

Tom Harbinger held the new sheets out to him. Garrett was staring across the street into an office where he could see the receptionist through the plate glass window. The summer sun angling in painted a lucent green rectangle on the dark green walls and lit the girl as she talked on the phone. She looked a bit like Anna, he thought, younger, hair shorter, but that kind of angular face with prominent cheekbones. He remembered Anna on the phone, calling for her car, how she tucked the phone under her chin and spun the rings on her finger as she talked. She –

'What do you think?' Tom Harbinger said. 'Garrett?'

'What? Oh sure, they look great.'

He signed the docket and Tom took the sheets away. Funny how things happen, Garrett reflected, for maybe the thousandth time: we lose Foley and McBride and we get Trans-American Airlines a week later. He had thought he was lost and yet he was saved. True, airline timetables weren't as interesting as guide books, but what did he care? He was a printer – and they needed new timetables four times a year.

He went into his office and called Laura. The doctor thought that Joanna was suffering from nerves, she told him, there was a clinic he recommended she go to. Of course, he said, whatever it costs: Trans-American Airlines had made him prosperous again. He had a sudden image of Anna shucking off her brassière to reveal her white, uptilted breasts and he felt his bowels slacken. These images came to him spontaneously and with absolute clarity, absolute palpability, as if they were memories of events that had happened yesterday. Over four months now, and not a day, not a waking hour had gone by without his thinking about her.

Listen Laura, he said, I have to go back up to Boston today. But it's Friday. I know, I know, but old man Foley called – he wants to see me urgently – Christ, I think he may give me the guide books back. Tell him to fuck himself, Laura said, vehemently. I've got to go, Garrett said: fifteen years of business and all – I owe him. You're a weak man, Garrett, she said. Sure, he said, weak as they come.

The film playing at the Rio was called *The Golden Stranger*, starring Dalton Paul and Jayne Callot. Garrett had arrived early and for a while sat alone in the cinema with only the bored usherette for company. Slowly the seats filled and the lights eventually went down. He had a good view of the entrance but he hadn't seen Anna come in. When the movie began he thought about leaving and laughed at the idea that a woman like Anna would go to the movies every Friday night like some kind of ordinary housewife. He hadn't been able to book a room at the Pamet Inn and had found a kind of guest house in Orleans which was clean but basic. Now he thought about it, how could he take Anna back there, a woman like her? Ridiculous, he thought, and tried to concentrate on the film but he had missed key plot developments and the fellow he thought was the bad guy turned out to be good.

He came out of the men's room and saw her standing alone in the lobby smoking a cigarette. It was raining outside and cerise rain slanted down through the neon areola of the sign. She wore a light coat and her hair was down. It was shorter than the last time he had been with her, he thought, as he went up behind her and touched her elbow, softly.

'Hi.'

She turned and the look on her face, the instant, pure joy in her face only lasted a second until it turned hard and panicky.

'What're you doing here? For God's sake!'

He kept his voice low and his face expressionless. 'I had to see you. I'm going crazy. I think about you all the time.' He smiled. 'It's pathetic. All the time, all day – I think about you. I can't help myself.'

She dropped her voice and dropped her gaze. 'I know,' she said.

'Me too.' Then she looked up and her face brightened falsely. 'Hi, honey,' she said. 'Look who's here.'

Garrett turned and saw the man he'd been pissing next to in the men's room. A tall, stooped, bald man with a slack face who looked about twenty years older than Anna.

'This is Mr Rising – the man who saved Euclid.'

'And may you suffer eternal punishment,' the bald man said, his grin showing his good, even teeth. 'Euclid is my *bête noire*.'

'Charlie, don't be cruel. You love Euclid, you know you do.'

'Like my own kin. Live in Orleans, Mr Rising?'

'Just visiting.'

'Next time you see Euclid, pass by on the other side, I'd appreciate it. I'll get the car, hon. Nice to meet you.'

They shook hands and Charlie, the husband, left.

Anna looked as if she were about to cry.

'You see, you fool! What're you playing at? What do you think this is?'

'Come to New York,' he said, taking out his card and scribbling on the back. 'My office is downtown, Greene Street. There'll be a room booked in your name at the Hamilton hotel on Sixth Avenue and Houston for one month. Come to New York and call me.'

'No.'

'We have to see each other again. At least once.'

'No. Go away. It's finished.'

'At least once.'

There was the sound of a car horn tooting outside. She gave him an angry, flying, hopeless look and left.

After they had made love, Garrett pulled on his shirt and trousers and ordered room service – two club sandwiches and two beers. When he took the tray at the door he pretended not to see the bellboy's smirk.

They ate their sandwiches and talked quietly about each other, how they felt about each other and how they realized that the day they had met on the beach had changed their lives.

'Fate,' she said.

'Euclid,' he said, and they laughed at that.

'It's hopeless, you know,' she said, after a while. 'I can't leave him.'

'And I can't leave her.'

'There, it's hopeless.'

'We can meet here.'

'What kind of a life is that?'

'It's better than a life of not meeting.'

'But what's the point?'

'What's the point otherwise? We'll see each other, that's the only thing that's important.'

She gave a little cry of frustration and despair, rolled over in the bed to face the wall, and Garrett stared at the carpet. The motif in the weave was of knights on prancing chargers; pennants flew from their upraised lances. The taste of beer was sour in his mouth. Perhaps they could go abroad, steal a holiday somewhere – surely they could think of some way of prolonging this, of eking out a life together. Moments together were surely better than a lifetime of separation. The thought of not seeing her was worse than death. He felt her hand searching for his and he took it.

'We have to do something,' she said

'We will, I promise.'

'What're we going to do?'

He felt a small lifting of his spirits now he knew she was ready to try it with him, this life of moments – moments of happiness.

'I'll think of something.'

'What?'

'I don't know,' he said, staring at the knights on their prancing chargers. 'I don't know.'

The View from Yves Hill

Where was I? Yes, it was a calculation I made to while away an idle moment in a busy week, just the other day, in fact. As a man, an elderly man, a man who – I say this without vanity – could be considered to be in his mid-sixties (though I am in fact seventy-five), I thought this was an interesting figure to quantify. I consulted my journals, my engagement diaries, my address books and I calculated that I had 'known', in the biblical sense, some forty-eight women. Not counting prostitutes, of course. You might deduce from this that I had a reasonable understanding of the fair sex. Not a bit of it.

The name is Hill. Yves Ivan Hill. English father, Russian mother with a fondness for French novels. Profession: man of letters.

I went out today, one of my ever rarer excursions, and took a stroll in the park (Hyde Park – I live to the north of that distended stretch of urban countryside). I bought a newspaper – *The Times* – and sat on a bench to read it. However, my mind began to wander, thinking of new plot lines for my movie scenario and after a while I stood up and wandered off: perambulation stimulates the imagination, I find. I hadn't moved twenty paces when I remembered my news-paper and retraced my steps. Another man, young, shabbily dressed, was sitting on the same bench reading my *Times*. 'That's my newspaper,' I told him. 'I left it there.' I almost added a 'sorry' but thought instantly: what do I have to apologize for? 'That's not your newspaper, mate,' he said. 'You left it behind – so it's England's now.' I told him both where and when I had purchased it and explained politely how I had come to leave it on the bench. 'You can have it when I've finished,' the young man said. Now I am not an angry person but I felt a pure form of anger sluice through my body. I walked away, turned and pointed at him. 'When you next have some bad luck,' I said, 'remember me. Because I'll be thinking of you.' I stared at him then strode on, ordering myself to calm down. Moments later I heard his footsteps behind me. 'Here, take your newspaper,' he said. I demurred, saying that it was no longer my newspaper, that it was England's, now. 'Take your fucking paper!' he yelled and threw it at me. It missed, of course, and flapped to the ground. We both left it there and went our separate ways.

Corless is the caretaker/porter of 'Swinburne House', the block of flats in which I reside. I prefer to think of him as a *concierge* and maintain a bourgeois Parisian's chill reserve in my dealings with him. I don't care for him or his rebarbative wife. When I came in the other day with my tins of mandarin oranges (forty in all) he nodded at me, with an insincere smile on his face (no offer to help, naturally) scarcely breaking off his conversation with some tradesman. I ignored him. At the lift, out of his view, I distinctly heard him say, 'Nice enough old bloke, Mr Hill, but he's not exactly Manchester United, is he?' The tradesman concurred. This categorization has been bothering me since I heard it uttered. I must ask Maria if she can throw some light on it.

Maria left me a note, which I here transcribe: 'I see, My dear Boss, that you have been and broken a plate – you are a bad, bad, naughty man!!! Your maid of all work, Maria O'Rourke.' She calls me 'boss', which I don't like, but in the nearly ten years she's been working for me I have been unable to persuade her to call me plain Mr Hill. 'You are my boss,' she says, 'whereupon I am the boss of the boss.' She says that because she works for a writer she must learn to exploit the full richness of the English language. 'Nevertheless' is her favourite word; she also loves (and cruelly misuses) 'whence' and 'hence'.

What is the point of rising early? I congratulate myself if I'm out of bed before midday. After my bath (a bath is not a bath if it lasts less than an hour) I lunch on a sandwich and a glass of pale ale. I write in the afternoon in my study. Maria comes, cleans the flat, runs errands if I require anything and prepares an evening meal for both of us. She will read to me from whatever trash magazine she happens to have in her huge handbag. We dine together in the kitchen at around seven. I then conduct a symphony (Beethoven or Brahms at the moment). Maria tends to leave after the first movement. Before I go to bed I smoke a cigarette and drink my own invented cocktail – a 'rumry'. Rum, sherry, warm milk and a spoonful of honey. I sleep like a baby.

The movie scenario I'm writing is entitled *Sex and Violence*. Its motivation is simple: every single scene is either sexy or violent. I had the idea in my bath one morning and I knew instantly I couldn't fail. However, the thing is harder to manage than I had imagined. Does it not seem strange, I wonder rhetorically, that a man such as myself, who was born in the nineteenth century when Queen Victoria was on the throne should, seventy-five years later, be exercising his imagination on such a project? No, I reply, it's not strange because everything in life is strange. It was strange being born in Tokyo; my late mother and father were strange people, spreading marmalade on toast is strange. Writing *Sex and Violence* is no stranger than entrusting a letter to a letterbox.

Maria's urge for constant reassurance is a little enervating. Boss, she says, do you like me? Of course I like you. Do you think I'm pretty? I think you're very pretty, Maria. Would you say, nevertheless, I was your pretty, dark-eyed Irish colleen? I would indeed. And so she goes about her cleaning singing pop songs all day. In fact she is an ordinary-looking woman in her late thirties with her short dark hair worn in a fringe. She dresses in an unexceptional, nondescript style – blouse, skirt, dark coat. She lives with her aged parents, and there is a brother who emigrated to Australia. Other human beings, however well you may think you know them, are utterly opaque, utterly mysterious.

*

Bills, bills, bills. Bills descend on me like seagulls round a fishing boat, squawking, importuning, pecking. I mine a little meagre ore from the bedrock of my capital and once again bless my dear mother's small legacy. But if the cost of living doesn't level off soon I won't be able to afford a maid. I told this to Maria one day when I was irritated with her and she said she would work for her bestest boss for nothing, if necessary. I said she should get married, find a decent 'boyo' she could look after. How could she get married when she worked for me, she said, tears welling, hurt written all over her face. I had to spend an hour complimenting her beauty and talent.

Christmas 1969. My fantasy of celebrating Christmas is to stay in bed asleep for five days. What would Jesus Christ make of this commercial bacchanalia established in his name? Corless came to the door with his present: a nauseating brass matchbox holder with 'Swinburne House' stamped on its base. He lingered creepily, hoping for a tip, but I offered him a cup of tea knowing he would refuse. We pay enough of a maintenance charge as it is. I threw the matchbox holder in the bin. Maria found it and roundly berated me for my lack of charity. I said she could take it home to Kilburn, give it to her mother and father.

New year. I saw 1970 in through a mist of rumry and cigarette smoke. Maria called and said she wouldn't be coming as she had to go for a 'test'. To spite her I spent two hours cleaning the telephone – it was filthy. I then soaked all my change in hot water and Dettol and cut my hair.

As I'm slowly sinking in a quagmire of debt, I've started to fill in the football pools. Corless cuts me these days since my refusal to pay out his Christmas perquisite. The man's not fit to lace my boots. Robert Donat, I remembered, was at one stage very interested in making a film based on my novel *The Parsley Tree*. I met him a few times before the war (the second one). I thought I might write to him and ask him if he knew of any young producers who might be interested in *Sex and Violence*. Turns out he died in 1958.

The few weeks after Alice Durrell said she would marry me were my happiest, I would say. I was back from the war, unscathed (the first war, that is) and I looked ridiculously handsome in my naval uniform. Bell & Winter had paid me £100 for my first novel, *The Trembling Needle*. I look back on that period as if they were part of the history of another person – with absolutely nothing to do with the man I am today. But that happiness must have paid me a dividend that I can draw on now – unless the subsequent bitterness over the break-up with Alice cancelled it out . . . It seems wrong somehow that the glow dies, that remembered happiness doesn't do the same trick as experienced happiness. I had too much then, overflowing with the stuff. It would be a fine thing if you could store your happiness in a happiness bank, and make the odd withdrawal when life becomes hard – like a bee and its honey, or a squirrel with its store of nuts. Now Maria's in hospital the life I lead is of a tedium never known on land or sea.

I hadn't left the flat for eight days and had kept the curtains drawn all day. I thought I needed a bit of weather and walked out into the park. It was so cold I had to go back for my hat, my coat with the fur collar and my white scarf. I walked down to the Serpentine and a man accosted me. 'Are you Yves Hill?' I said I was and he said we had been colleagues at the BBC during the war. 'I knew it was you because of the hat and the fur-collared coat,' he said. 'You were always very . . . exotic, dashing.' He told me his name but I couldn't remember him. He was very polite but then everyone at the BBC in those days was paralysingly polite – in fact that was one reason I had to leave. I couldn't exist in that regime of permanent good manners and solicitude. I began to think people were mocking me with their 'good mornings' and 'how are yous' and 'looking very wells'. In fact now I think I was suffering from a form of persecution mania. Then my dear mother died and that gave me the where-withal to set myself up in the flat in Swinburne House. 'Where-withal' – a new word for Maria. The BBC man asked me what I was up to so I told him I was writing a movie scenario. 'Lucky man,' he said. 'What wouldn't I give to lead your life.' It showed me again – not that I needed showing: perception of another is a fiction constructed by the perceiver.

A letter from Maria telling me about her operation and apologizing for still being in hospital: 'As you know my dearest dear boss my only dream is to be back in Swinners washing your telephone for the third time in a week!!! No but seriously you are the grandest sweetest man in the world. Don't miss your meals as I do worry about you not being able to cope nevertheless you must concentrate on your writing as that is what makes you tick as they say. Whence I only want to be back in Swinners as you can imagine I'm so ruddy fed up being sick. I just want to look after my sweet boss for alway's and alway's.'

A young woman came today from some provincial university to interview me. She is writing a book about the 'interwar' English novel. She almost said – I could see her forming the words as she set out her tape recorder – that she couldn't believe how lucky she was having tracked me down because ('I thought you were dead') . . . because, ah, because many writers guarded their privacy and she could quite understand that. I saw her looking round the living room trying to make an inventory, wondering why there should be five large cartons of Carr's Water Biscuits in the corner, stacked tins of pilchards in tomato sauce, several hundred toilet rolls. 'I tend to buy in bulk,' I explained to her, 'whenever I see a bargain, or whenever anything is significantly discounted.' I offered her a glass of rum, sherry or pale ale. She asked instead for a cup of tea. I don't drink tea, I said, and I would counsel you not to. Why, she asked. Have you ever looked at the inside of a teapot, I replied. Think what's happening to your innards. She switched on her machine and we talked of writers I had known. She was good enough to mention some of my novels, which she appeared to have read, singling out for modest praise *The Astonished Soul*, *Oblong* and *A Voice, Crying*. I told her about Robert Donat and *The Parsley Tree* but she claimed not to know any film producers. Her hair could have done with a wash, I noticed as she left. She was wearing jeans and a sheepskin-style coat with fur trim that gave off a distinct and unpleasant smell, as if it had not been properly cured. 'It was a real pleasure to meet you, Mr Hill,' she said. 'I shall go back and reread your books.' After she'd gone it struck me that this young woman was probably my only reader; even more – that perhaps I had just met the very last reader of Yves Hill. My ultimate reader. It was not a consoling thought.

A complex and difficult tube and bus journey to Tooting Bec to find the hospital Maria was in. I felt like an anthropologist mingling with undiscovered tribes as I voyaged south through London. Some pretty girls, though, caught my wandering eye. Then it took me half an hour to find the ward – corridors stretching for miles, signs everywhere that seemed only to lead you deeper into the labyrinth. Maria looked pale and pinched, a maroon nylon turban-thing on her head drawing off what little colour was left in her face. I had brought the usual propitiatory fruit and a copy of *Sex and Violence* for her to read. She was tearfully grateful. She wanted to know if I had moved any furniture, changed anything in the flat, insisted I itemize my meals, expressed concern about my absence of routine. 'I shall sort you out, boss, just you see, when I get back.' I assured her no crockery or glasses had been broken. To make conversation I told her about the interviewer with the stinking coat and she was most put out. 'How dare she?' she said. 'How dare she come into our spotless flat bringing smells?' I bussed home through the gathering dusk not wanting to descend into the commuter underworld again. I dined off pilchards and mashed potato, then mandarin oranges drenched in condensed milk, all washed down with a double rumry. *Quel régal!* Conducted the entire Mahler's Fifth, blubbing all the way through the adagietto. The ineffable sadness of that music.

*

I waited in all day for something I'd ordered from *Exchange & Mart* – possibly the most wonderful publication in the world – and was not disappointed when it arrived. What I'd ordered was a chair, a simple wooden chair, that can be easily transformed by the application of a few levers and bolts into either a work-table (for joinery or that sort of thing) or a step-ladder. I can spend a day leafing through *Exchange & Mart* and not notice time passing: the bargains, the enticing gadgets are extraordinary. I've ordered a dozen nylon astro-turf doormats that I intend to lay from the front door to the kitchen – the route where there is most traffic of feet. Then a perplexing phone call in the evening from a man with an Irish brogue telling me that Maria had to have another operation and that they were hoping for the best. 'And to whom am I talking?' I inquired. 'Are you Mr O'Rourke?' No, he replied, he was Maria's fiancé, Desmond.

I heard a tapping at my window this morning (I am on the third floor) and pulled back the curtains to be dazzled by an oblique winter sun. A bird, a blackbird, was pecking at the glass. I shooed it away. I realize now that it is the utter inadequacy of human contacts that makes us turn to art. I know why I became a novelist: only in fiction is everything about other people explained. Only in our fictions is everything sure and certain.

'He could sometimes be seen walking in Hyde Park. A tall man in his seventies, a little portly. His hair, quite grey, was thinning and as he was self-conscious about his baldness he often wore a hat, an increasingly unfashionable accessory in this day and age. He had known considerable success as a novelist in the 1920s and '30s but his reputation had declined. All his books were out of print but he managed to live comfortably enough on a small, carefully managed legacy that his mother, a Russian aristocrat, had left him on her death. He was regarded by those who encountered him as difficult and stand-offish, or else eccentric and scatterbrained. In actual fact he looked on the world and its denizens with a curious and not unkind eye. Most things he saw amused him.'

Lunch

DATE: Monday.

VENUE: Le Truc Interessant, Lexington Street, Soho.

PRESENT: Me, Gerald Vere, Melanie Swartz, Peter (somebody) from Svenska Bank, Barry Freeman, Diane Skinner (account exec. from S.L.L.& L.), Eddie Kroll (left before pudding).

MEAL: Tabouleh chinois, roulade de foie de veau farcie, millefeuille de fruits d'hiver.

WINE: Two Moet & Chandon non-vintage, two Sancerre, an '83 Pichon Longueville, a big Provençal red called Mas Jullien. Port, brandy (eau de vie de prune for Diane S.).

BILL: £878, service not included.

EXTRAS: Romeo y Julietas for Vere and Freeman, t-shirt and condiments set for Melanie. Twenty Silk Cut for Diane S.

COMMENTS: No piped music. Tabouleh chinois an orthodox tabouleh with sliced lychees mixed in. Unusual. Roulade de foie exquisite, served on a little purée of celeriac. Diane S. barely touched her food, 'saving up for dessert'. Millefeuille – eight out of ten for the pastry. Fruits bland. Diane S. picked up tab. Taxied me back too. Thank you Swabold, Lang, Laing and Longmuir. Thank you very much.

DATE: Tuesday.

VENUE: Eurotel Palace, Heathrow Airport.

PRESENT: Me, Diane S.

MEAL: Insalata Tricolore, Dover sole, tarte aux pommes.

WINE: G & T in bar, Merry Dale Chardonnay, House champagne with pud.

BILL: £96 (service incl.).

EXTRAS: Irish coffee served in our room. £5.50 each. Twenty Silk Cut.

COMMENTS: Almost inaudible classical muzak. Rubbery mozzarella. When will the British stop serving 'A selection of vegetables'? Tasteless carrots, watery broccoli, some kind of swede. Tarte aux pommes a simple apple pie, not flattered by translation. House champagne surprisingly good – small bubbles, buttery, cidery. Undrunk Irish coffee – waste.

DATE: Wednesday.

VENUE: Chairman's dining 'set', sixth floor. Pale oak panelling. Silver. Good paintings – a small, perfect Sutherland, Alan Reynolds, two Craxtons.

PRESENT: Me, Sir Torquil, Gerald Vere, Barry Freeman, Blake Ginsberg (new m.d.), some senior suit from Finance (introduced as 'you know Lucy' – can't be his first name, surely? Very foreign looking).

MEAL: Vegetable terrine, lamb chops with new potatoes, raspberries with crème fraiche. Stilton.

WINE: Hipflask in loo downstairs, then Vodkatini (could have been colder), a perfectly good Chablis, followed by a '78 Domaine de Chevalier (stunning). Port (Taylor's, missed date).

BILL: A heavy price to pay.

EXTRAS: At least I saw the Sutherland.

COMMENTS: Apart from the vegetable terrine (always a total waste of time) this was superior corporate catering. Sensible. Lamb nicely pink. Superb wine. They had the grace to wait until the cheese. The condemned man had eaten a hearty meal. Fucking heartless cold fucking swine.

DATE: Thursday.

VENUE: La Casa del' Luigi, Fulham Road.

PRESENT: Me, Diane, (later) Jennifer.

MEAL: Minestrone, spaghetti bolognese, tiramisu.

WINE: G & Ts, Valpolicella, replaced by a Chianti Classico when spilt. Large grappa after Jennifer's arrival and departure.

BILL: £73 rounded up to £90. Scant gratitude.

EXTRAS: Twenty Silk Cut. Three glasses, two plates. Dry cleaning to be notified.

COMMENTS: Minestrone was tinned, I'd swear. Alfredo's spag. bog. amazingly authentic as ever (why can't one ever achieve this at home?). He refuses to divulge his secret, but I'm convinced it's the chicken livers in the ragú. Which must simmer for days, also. Watery, ancient tiramisu. Big mistake to eat so close to home. HUGE mistake. Jennifer would have walked right past. What bastard waiter called her in?

DATE: Friday.

VENUE: Montrose Dining Club, Lincoln's Inn. Basement, large overlit room, long central table. Staffed by very old ex-college porters and very young monoglot girls who appear to be from Eastern Europe.

PRESENT: Me, Alisdair Lockhart.

MEAL: Potted shrimps and toast, duck à l'orange, treacle tart (!).

WINE: G & Ts, club claret, club brandy.

BILL: £28. (I paid. Astonishing value. Alisdair said he could add it to his bill but I insisted.)

EXTRAS: About £5000 if I know Alisdair.

COMMENTS: Time travel. Back to school. This was English cuisine until quite recently, we have forgotten that this was how we all used to eat. Potted shrimps like consuming cold butter, limp toast. Duck cooked to extinction, repulsive cloying sauce. I ordered treacle tart for nostalgia's sake. (Alisdair has appalling dandruff for a comparatively young man.) I said Jennifer was being very difficult, thus far. He was not sanguine. Asked if this had happened before so I told him of Jennifer's ultimatum. Spoke briefly about custody of Toby. He left early as he had to get to court. Depressing. Drank whiskey in an Irish pub.

DATE: Saturday.

PLACE: My kitchen, Rostrevor Road, Fulham.

PRESENT: Me and (intermittently) Birgitte, the au pair.

MEAL: Raided fridge – cottage cheese and crispbread, remains of Thursday's shepherd's pie, some of Toby's little yoghurt things, cheese triangles. Birgitte sent out for a pizza but I couldn't be bothered waiting.

WINE: 'Three goes of gin, a lemon slice and a ten-ounce tonic . . .' Who said that? Then two glasses of Pinot Grigio, before I went down to the basement and rooted out the Ducru-Beaucaillou. Fuck it. I gave some to Birgitte, who made a face. She preferred to drink her own beer. She gave me a can when I'd finished the Beaucaillou. Strong stuff. Slept in the afternoon.

BILL: The Human Condition.

EXTRAS: I miss Toby and Jennifer. I miss our usual Saturday lunch. Best lunch of the week.

COMMENTS: Music – Brahms Horn Trio initially, but it made me want to weep. Birgitte played something rhythmic, ethnic. She gave me a tape of ocean waves breaking on a shore. 'For calming' she said. Big, big-hearted girl. Why would anybody eat cottage cheese? What, in terms of taste and texture, could possibly recommend it? Jennifer and her silly, perpetual diets. Perfectly slim, perfectly . . . The cheese triangles were unbelievably tasty, ate a whole wheel's worth as I drank the Beaucaillou.

DATE: Sunday. Cold, low, packed clouds, a flat, sullen light.

VENUE: Somewhere in eastern England on the 11.45 to Norwich. Writing this in the bar. On my way to Mother and Sunday lunch.

PRESENT: Me, three soldiers, a fat woman, and a thin, weaselly man with a mobile phone.

MEAL: Started with a Jimmyburger on the station concourse, then a couple of Scotch eggs in the bar. On the train I had a bag of salt 'n' vinegar crisps and an egg and cress sandwich from the steward with the trolley. In the buffet thus far I have had a pork pie, a sausage roll, something called a 'Ploughman's Bap' and a Mars bar. There is a solitary mushroom and salami omelette wrapped in cellophane that they will do in a microwave. Why am I still hungry?

WINE: Large vodka and orange in the station bar – vague, very temporary desire to keep my breath alcohol free. Two cans of gin and Italian vermouth in the train before I wandered buffetwards. Started drinking lager: 'Speyhawk Special Strength'. Notice the squaddies are drinking the same. They do quarter bottles of wine in here, I see. I've now bought a couple, having ordered the omelette. It is labelled 'Red Wine'. No country of origin. Tart, pungent, raw. I worry it will stain my lips. Mother will serve, as usual, Moselle and call it hock.

BILL: I refuse to spend more than £20.

EXTRAS: A lot of cigarette smoke, everyone is smoking including, covertly, the steward behind the bar. Smoke seeps between the fingers of his loosely clenched fist resting on his buttocks. The fat woman is smoking. The man on the mobile phone is smoking as he mutters into his little plastic box. I have a metallic taste in my mouth, and am seized by a sudden, embittering image of Diane S. – naked, laughing.

COMMENTS: The English countryside has never looked so drained and dead under this oppressive pewter sky. The barman beckons . . . Now I have my mushroom and salami omelette, a piebald yellow with brown patches, steaming suspiciously, a curious, gamey but undeniably foodlike smell seems suddenly to have pervaded the entire carriage, obliterating all other odours. Everyone is looking at me. I screw the top off my 'Red Wine' and fill my glass as we hurtle across Norfolk. Gastric juices squirt. I'm starving, how is this possible? My mother will have the archetype of an English Sunday lunch waiting for me. A roast, cooked grey, potatoes and two or three vegetables, a lake of gravy, cheese and biscuits, her special trifle. I look out of the window at the miles of sombre green. Rain is spitting on the glass and the soldiers have started to sing. Time for my omelette. I know what I am doing but it is a bad sign, this, the beginning of the end. I am deliberately setting out to ruin (because, let's face it, you cannot, before lunch, lunch) lunch.

Loose Continuity

I am standing on the corner of Westwood and Wilshire, just down from the Mobilgas station, waiting. There is a coolish breeze just managing to blow from somewhere, and I am glad of it. Nine o'clock in the morning and it's going to be another hot one, for sure. For the third or fourth time I needlessly go over and inspect the concrete foundation, note again that the powerlines have been properly installed and the extra bolts I have requested are duly there. Where is everybody? I look at my watch, light another cigarette and begin to grow vaguely worried: have I picked the wrong day? Has my accent confused Mr Koenig (he is always asking me to repeat myself)? . . .

A bright curtain – blues and ochres – boils and billows from an apartment window across the street. It sets a forgotten corner of my mind working – who had drapes like that, once? Who owned a skirt that was similar, or perhaps a tie? –

A claxon honks down Wilshire and I look up to see Spencer driving the crane, pulling slowly across two lanes of traffic and coming to a halt at the kerb.

He swings himself down from the cab and takes off his cap. His hair is getting longer, losing that army crop.

'Sorry I'm late, Miss Velk, the depot was, you know, crazy, impossible.'

'Doesn't matter, it's not here anyway.'

'Yeah, right.' Spencer moves over and crouches down at the concrete plinth checking the powerline connection, touching and jiggling the bolts and their brackets. He goes round the back of the crane and sets out the wooden 'Men at Work' signs, then reaches into his pockct and hands me a crumpled sheet of flimsy.

'The permit,' he explains. 'We got 'til noon.'

'Even on a Sunday?'

'Even on a Sunday. Even in Los Angeles.' He shrugs. 'Even in 1945. Don't worry, Miss Velk. We got plenty of time.'

I turn away, a little exasperated. 'As long as it gets here,' I say with futile determination, as if I had the power to threaten. The drape streams out of the window suddenly, like a banner, and catches the sun. Then I remember: like the wall hanging Utta had done. The one that Jochen bought.

Spencer asks me if he should go phone the factory but I say give them an extra half hour. I am remembering another Sunday morning, sunny like this one, but not as hot, and half the world away, and I can see myself walking up Grillparzerstrasse, taking the shortcut from the station, my suitcase heavy in my hand, and hoping, wondering, now that I have managed to catch the early train from Sorau, if Jochen will be able to find some time to see me alone that afternoon . . .

Gudrun Velk walked slowly up Grillparzerstrasse, enjoying the sun, her body canted over to counterbalance the weight of her suitcase. She was wearing . . . (What was I wearing?) She was wearing baggy cotton trousers with the elasticated cuffs at the ankles, a sky blue blouse and the embroidered felt jacket with the motif of jousters and strutting chargers. Her fair hair was down and she wore no makeup; she was thinking about Jochen, and whether they might see each other that day, and whether they might make love. Thinking about Utta, if she would be up by now. Thinking about the two thick skeins of still damp blue wool in her suitcase, wool that she had dyed herself late the night before at the mill in Sorau and that she felt sure would finish her rug perfectly, and, most importantly, in a manner that would please Paul.

Paul looked in on the weaving workshop often. Small, with dull olive skin and large eyes below a high forehead, eyes seemingly brimming with unshed tears. He quietly moved from loom to loom and the weavers would slip out of their seats to let him have an unobstructed view. Gudrun had started her big knotted rug, she remembered, and he stood in front of it for some minutes, silently contemplating the first squares and circles. She waited: sometimes he looked, said nothing and moved on. Now, though, he said: 'I like the shapes but the yellow is wrong, it needs more lemon, especially set beside that peach colour.' He shrugged, adding, 'In my opinion.' That was when she bought his book and started to go to his classes on colour theory – and she had unpicked the work she had done and began again. She told him: 'I'm weaving my rug based on your chromatic principles.' He was pleased, she thought. He said politely that in that case he would follow its progress with particular interest.

He was not happy at the Institute, she knew; since Meyer took over, the mood had changed, was turning against Paul and the other painters. Meyer was against them, she had been told, they smacked of Weimar, the bad old days. Jochen was the same: 'Bogus-advertising-theatricalism,' he would state, 'we should've left all that behind.' What the painters did was 'decorative', need one say more? So Paul was gratified to find someone who responded to his theories intead of mocking them, and in any case the mood in the weaving workshops was different, what with all the young women. There was a joke in the Institute that the women revered him, called him 'the dear Lord'. He did enjoy the time he spent there, he told Gudrun later, of all the workshops it was the weavers he would miss most, he said, if the day came for him to leave – all the girls, all the bright young women.

Spencer leans against the pole that holds the powerlines. The sleeve of his check shirt falls back to reveal more of his burned arm. It looks pink and new and oddly, finely ridged, like bark or like the skin you get on cooling hot milk. He taps a rhythm on the creosoted pole with his thumb and the two remaining fingers on his left hand. I know the burn goes the length of his arm and then some more, but the hand has taken the full brunt.

He turns and sees me staring.

'How's the arm?' I say.

'I've got another graft next week. We're getting there, slow but sure.'

'What about this heat? Does it make it worse?'

'It doesn't help, but . . . I'd rather be here than Okinawa,' he says. 'Damn right.'

'Of course,' I say, 'of course.'

'Yeah.' He exhales and seems on the point of saying something – he is talking more about the war, these days – when his eye is caught. He straightens.

'Uh-oh,' He says. 'Looks like Mr Koenig is here.'

Utta Benrath had dark orange hair, strongly hennaed, which, with her green eyes, made her look foreign to Gudrun, but excitingly so. As if she were a half-breed of some impossible sort – Irish and Malay, Swedish and Peruvian. She was small and wiry and used her hands expressively when she spoke, fists unclenching slowly like a flower opening, thrusting, palming movements, her fingers always flexing. Her voice was deep and she had a throaty, man's chuckle, like a hint of wicked fun. Gudrun met her when she had answered the advertisement Utta had placed on the notice-board in the students' canteen: 'Room to rent, share facilities and expenses.'

When Gudrun began her affair with Jochen she realized she had to move out of the hostel she was staying in. The room in Utta's apartment was cheap and not just because the apartment was small and had no bathroom: it was inconvenient as well. Utta, it turned out, lived a brisk forty-five-minute walk from the Institute. The apartment was on the top floor of a tenement block on Grenz Weg, out in Jonitz with a distant view of a turgid loop of the Mulde from the kitchen window. It was clean and simply furnished. On the walls hung brightly coloured designs for stained glass windows that Utta had drawn in Weimar. Here in Dessau she was an assistant in the mural-painting workshop. She was older than Gudrun, in her early thirties, Gudrun guessed, but her unusual colouring made her age seem almost an irrelevance: she looked so unlike anyone

Gudrun had seen before that age seemed to have little or nothing to do with the impression she made.

There were two bedrooms in the apartment on Grenz Weg, a small kitchen with a stove and a surprisingly generous hall where they would eat their meals around a square, scrubbed pine table. They washed in the kitchen, standing on a towel in front of the sink. They carried their chamber pots down four flights of stairs and emptied them in the night soil cistern at the rear of the small yard behind the apartment building. Gudrun developed a strong affection for their four rooms: her bedroom was the first of her own outside of her parents' house; the flat was the first proper home of her adult life. Most evenings, she and Utta prepared their meal – sausage, nine times out of ten, with potatoes or turnip – and then, if they were not going out, they would sit on the bed in Utta's room and listen to music on her phonograph. Utta would read or write – she was studying architecture by correspondence course – and they would talk. Utta's concentration, Gudrun soon noticed, her need for further qualifications, her ambitions, were motivated by a pessimism about her position in the Institute to which all talk inevitably returned. She was convinced that the mural-painting workshop was to be closed and she would have to leave. She adduced evidence, clues, hints that she was sure proved that this was the authorities' intention. Look what had happened to stained glass, she said, to the wood- and stone-carving workshops. The struggle it had taken to transfer had almost finished her off. That's why she wanted to be an architect: everything had to be practical these days, manufactured. Productivity was the new god. But it took so long, and if they closed the mural-painting workshop . . . Nothing Gudrun said could reassure her. All her energies were devoted to finding a way to stay on.

'I've heard that Marianne Brandt hates Meyer,' she reported one night, with excitement, almost glee. 'No, I mean really hates him. She detests him. She's going to resign, I know it.'

'Maybe Meyer will go first,' Gudrun said. 'He's so unpopular. It can't be nice for him.'

Utta laughed. And laughed again. 'Sweet Gudrun,' she said and reached out and patted her foot. 'Never change.'

'But why should it affect you?' Gudrun asked. 'Marianne runs the metal workshop.'

'Exactly,' Utta said, with a small smile. 'Don't you see? That means there'll be a vacancy, won't there?'

Mr Koenig steps out of his car and wrinkles his eyes at the sun. Mrs Koenig waits patiently until he comes round and opens the door for her. Everyone shakes hands.

'Bet you're glad you're not in Okinawa, eh, Spence?' Mr Koenig says.

'Fire from heaven, I hear,' Spencer says with some emotion.

'Oh, yeah? Sure sounds that way.' Mr Koenig turns to me. 'How're we doing, Miss Velk?'

'Running a bit late,' I say. 'Maybe in one hour, if you come back?'

He looks at his watch, then at his wife. 'What do you say to some breakfast, Mrs Koenig?'

Jochen liked to be naked. He liked to move around his house doing ordinary things, naked. Once when his wife was away he had cooked Gudrun a meal and asked her to eat it with him, naked. They had thick slices of smoked ham, she remembered, with a pungent radish sauce. They sat in his dining room and ate and chatted as if all was perfectly normal. Gudrun realized that it sexually aroused him, that it was a prelude to love-making, but she began to feel cold and before he served the salad she asked if she could go and put on her sweater.

Jochen Henzi was one of the three Masters of Form who ran the architecture workshop. He was a big burly man who would run seriously to fat in a few years, Gudrun realized. His body was covered with a pelt of fine, dark hair, almost like an animal, it grew thickly on his chest and belly and, curiously, in the small of his back, but his whole body – his buttocks, his shoulders – was covered with this fine, glossy fur. At first she thought she would find it repugnant, but it was soft, not wiry, and now when they were in bed she often discovered herself absentmindedly stroking him, as if he were a great cat or a bear, as if he were a rug she could pull round her.

They met at the New Year party in 1928, where the theme was 'white'. Jochen had gone as a grotesque, padded pierrot, a white cone on his head, his face a mask of white pancake. Gudrun had been a colonialist, in a man's white suit with a white shirt and tie and her hair up under a solar topee. By the party's end, well into January 1st, she had gone into an upstairs lavatory to untie her tight bun, vaguely hoping that loosening her hair would ease her headache.

Her hair was longer then, falling to her shoulders, and as she came down the stairs to the main hall she saw, sitting on a landing, Jochen – a large, rumpled, clearly drunken pierrot, smoking a dark, knobbled cigar. He watched her descend, a little amazed, it seemed, blinking as if to clear some obstruction to his vision.

She stepped over his leg, she knew who he was.

'Hey, you,' he shouted after her. 'I didn't know you were a woman.' His tone was affronted, aggressive, almost as if she had deliberately misled him. She did not look round.

The day the new term began he came to the weaving workshop to find her.

I take my last cigarette from the pack and light it. I sit on the step below the cab of Spencer's crane, where there's some shade. I see Spencer coming briskly along the sidewalk from the pay phone. He's a stocky man, with the stocky man's vigorous rolling stride, as if the air is crowding him and he's shouldering it away, forcing his passage through.

'They say it left an hour ago.' He shrugged. 'Must be some problem on the highway.'

'Wonderful.' I blow smoke into the sky, loudly, to show my exasperation.

'Can I bum one of those off of you?'

I show him the empty pack.

'Lucky Strike.' He shrugs, 'I don't like them, anyway.'

'I like the name. That's why I smoke them.'

He looks at me. 'Yeah, where do they get the names for those packs? Who makes them up? I ask you.'

'Camel.'

'Yeah,' he says. 'Why a camel? Do camels smoke? Why not a . . . a hippo? I ask you.'

I laugh. 'A pack of Hippos, please.'

He grins and cuffs the headlamp nacelle. He makes a *tsssss* sound, and shakes his head, incredulously. He looks back at me.

'Goddam factory. Must be something on the highway.'

'Can I buy you some breakfast, Spencer?'

Paul met Jochen only once in Gudrun's company. It was during one afternoon at four o'clock when the workshops closed. The weavers worked four hours in the morning, two in the afternoon. The workshop was empty. The big rug was half done, pinned up on an easel in the middle of the room. Paul stood in front of it, the fingers of his right hand slowly stroking his chin, looking, thinking. From time to time he would cover his left eye with his left palm.

'I like it, Gudrun,' he said, finally. 'I like its warmth and clarity. The colour penetration, the orangey-pinks, the lemons . . . What's going to happen in the bottom?'

'I think I am going to shade into green and blue.'

'What's that black?'

'I'm going to have some bars, some vertical, one horizontal, with the cold colours.'

He nodded and stepped back. Gudrun, who had been standing behind him, moved to one side to allow him a longer view. As she turned, she saw Jochen had come into the room and was watching them. Jochen sauntered over and greeted Paul coolly and with formality.

'I came to admire the rug,' Paul said. 'It's splendid, no?'

Jochen glanced at it. 'Very decorative,' he said. 'You should be

designing wallpaper, Miss Velk, not wasting your time with this.'
He turned to Paul. 'Don't you agree?'

'Ah. Popular necessities before elitist luxuries,' Paul said, wagging
a warning finger at her, briefly. The sarcasm sounded most strange
coming from him, Gudrun thought.

'It's a way of putting it,' Jochen said. 'Indeed.'

We sit in a window of a coffee shop in Westwood Village. I've
ordered a coffee and Danish but Spencer has decided to go for
something more substantial: a rib-eye steak with fried egg.

'I hope the Koenigs don't come back,' Spencer says. 'Maybe I
shouldn't have ordered the steak.'

I press my cheek against the warm glass of the window. I can
just see the back end of Spencer's crane.

'I'll spot them,' I say. 'And I'll see the truck from the factory.
You eat up.'

Spencer runs his finger along the curved aluminium beading that
finishes the table edge.

'I want you to know, Miss Velk, how grateful I am for the work
you've put my way.' He looks me in the eye. 'More than grateful.'

'No, it is I who am grateful to you.' I smiled. 'It's not easy to find
someone more reliable.'

'Well, I appreciate what you –'

His steak comes and puts an end to what I'm sure would have
been long protestations of mutual gratitude. It's too hot to eat
pastry so I push my Danish aside and wonder where I can buy
some more cigarettes. Spencer, holding his fork like a dagger in his
injured left hand, stabs it into his steak to keep it steady on the
plate, and, with the knife in his right, sets about trying to saw the
meat into pieces. He is having difficulty: his thumb and two fingers
can't keep a good grip on the fork handle, and he saws awkwardly
with the knife.

'Damn thing is I'm left-handed,' he says, sensing me watching.
He works off a small corner, pops it in his mouth and then sets
about the whole pinioning, slicing operation again. The plate slides

across the shiny table top and collides with my coffee mug. A small splash flips out.

'Sorry,' he says.

'Could I do that for you?' I say. 'Would it bother you?'

He says nothing and I reach out and gently take the knife and fork from him. I cut the steak into cubes and hand back the knife and fork.

'Thank you, Miss Velk.'

'Please call me Gudrun,' I say.

'Thank you, Gudrun.'

'Gudrun! Gudrun, over here.' Utta was beckoning from the doorway of Jochen's kitchen. Gudrun moved with difficulty through the crowd, finding a gap here, skirting round an expansive gesture there. Utta drew her into the kitchen, where there was still quite a mob, too, and refilled Gudrun's glass with punch and then her own. They clinked glasses.

'I give you Marianne Brandt,' Utta said, quietly. She smiled.

'What do you mean?'

'She did resign.'

'How do you know? Who told you?'

Utta discreetly inclined her head towards the window. 'Marlene,' she said. Standing by the sink talking to three young men was Marlene Henzi, Jochen's wife. Gudrun had not seen her there. She had arrived at the party late, uneasy at the thought of being in Jochen's house with his wife and other guests. Jochen had assured her that Marlene knew nothing, Marlene was ignorance personified, he said, the quintessence of ignorance. Utta carried on talking – some business of amalgamation, of metal, joinery and mural-painting all being coordinated into a new workshop of interior design – while Gudrun covertly scrutinized her hostess. Marlene did not look to her like an ignorant woman, she thought, she looked like a woman brimfull of knowledge. ' – I told you it would happen. Arndt's going to run it. But Marianne's refused to continue . . .' Utta was saying but Gudrun did not listen further. Marlene Henzi was tall and thin, she had a sharp, long face with hooded, sleepy eyes and wore a loose black gown that seemed oddly Eastern in design. To Gudrun she appeared almost ugly and yet she seemed to have gathered within her a languid, self-confident calm and serenity. The students laughed at something she said, and with a flick of her wrist, which made them laugh again, she left them, picking up a plate of canapés and beginning to offer to the other guests standing and chatting in the kitchen. She drifted towards Utta and Gudrun, closer, a smile and a word for everyone.

'I have to go,' Gudrun said, and left.

Utta caught up with her in the hall, where she was putting on her coat.

'What's happening? Where are you going?'

'Home. I don't feel well.'

'But I want you to talk to Jochen, find out more. They need a new assistant now. If Jochen could mention my name, Meyer would listen to him . . .'

Gudrun felt a genuine nausea and simultaneously, inexplicably, infuriatingly, an urge to cry.

Spencer frowns worriedly at me. I look at my watch, Mr Koenig looks at his watch also, and simultaneously the truck from the factory in Oxnard rumbles up Wilshire. Apologies are offered, the delays on the highway blamed – who would have thought there could be so much traffic on a Sunday? – and Spencer manoeuvres the crane into position.

Jochen ran his fingertips down her back to the cleft in her buttocks. 'So smooth,' he said, wonderingly. He turned her over and nuzzled her breasts, taking her hand and pulling it down to his groin.

'Utta will be home soon,' she said.

Jochen groaned. He heaved himself up on his elbows and looked down at her. 'I can't stand this,' he said. 'You have to get a place of your own. And not so damn far away.'

'Oh yes, of course,' Gudrun said. 'I'll get a little apartment on Kavalierstrasse. So convenient and so reasonable.'

'I'm going to miss you,' he said. 'What am I going to do? Dear Christ.'

Gudrun had told him about the dyeing course she was going to take at Sorau. They met regularly now, almost as a matter of routine, three, sometimes four times a week in the afternoon at the apartment on Grenz Weg. The weaving workshop closed earlier than the other departments in the Institute and between half past four and half past six in the afternoons they had the place to themselves. Utta would obligingly stop for a coffee or shop on her way home – dawdling for the sake of love, as she described it – and usually Jochen was gone by the time she returned. On the occasions they met he seemed quite indifferent, quite unperturbed at being seen.

'Now, if Utta was the new head of the metal workshop,' Gudrun said, 'I'm sure she'd be much more busy than –'

'– don't start that again.' Jochen said. 'I've spoken to Meyer. Arndt has his own candidates. You know she has a fair chance. A more than fair chance.' He put his arms around her and squeezed her strongly to him. 'Gudrun, my Gudrun,' he exclaimed, as if mystified by this emotion within him. 'Why do I want you so? Why?'

They heard the rattle of Utta's key in the lock, her steps as she crossed the hall into the kitchen.

When Jochen left, Utta came immediately to Gudrun's room. She was dressing, but the bed was still a mess of rumpled sheets, which for some reason made Gudrun embarrassed. To her the room seemed to reek of Jochen. She pulled the blanket up to the pillow.

'Did he see you when he left?' Gudrun asked.

'No, I was in my room. Did he say anything?'

'The same as usual. No, 'a more than fair chance', he said. But he said Arndt has his own candidates.'

'Of course, but a "more than fair chance". That's something. Yes . . .'

'Utta, I can't do anything more. I think I should stop asking. Why don't you see Meyer yourself?'

'No, no. It's not the way it works here, you don't understand. It never has. You have to play it differently. And you must never give up. Never.'

Spencer checks that the canvas webbing is properly secured under the base, jumps down from the truck and climbs up to the small control platform beside the crane.

I explain to Mr Koenig: 'It's manufactured in three parts. The whole thing can be assembled amazingly quickly. It's painted, finished. We connect the power supply and you're in business.'

Mr Koenig was visibly moved. 'It's incredible,' he said. 'Just like that.'

I turn to Spencer and give him a thumbs up. There's a thin puff of bluey-grey smoke and the crane's motor chugs into life.

Jochen sat on the edge of his desk, one leg swinging. He reached out to take Gudrun's hand and gently pulled her into the V of his thighs. He kissed her neck and inhaled, smelling her skin, her hair, as if he were trying to draw her essence deep into his lungs.

'I want us to go away for a weekend,' he said. 'Let's go to Berlin.' She kissed him. 'I can't afford it.'

'I'll pay,' he said. 'I'll think of something, some crucial meeting.' She felt his hands on her buttocks; his thighs gently clamped hers. Through the wall of his office she could hear male voices from one of the drafting rooms. She pushed herself away from him and strolled over to the angled drawing table that was set before the window.

'A weekend in Berlin . . .' she said. 'I like the sound of that, I must –'

She turned as the door opened and Marlene Henzi walked in.

'Jochen, we're late,' she said, glancing at Gudrun with a faint smile.
Jochen sat on, one leg swinging slightly.

'You know Miss Velk, don't you?'

'I don't think so. How are you?'

Somehow Gudrun managed to extend her arm; she felt the slight pressure of dry, cool fingers.

'A pleasure.'

'She was at the party,' Jochen said. 'Surely you met.'

'Darling, there were a hundred people at the party.'

'I won't disturb you any further,' Gudrun said, moving to the door. 'Very good to meet you.'

'Oh, Miss Velk.' Jochen's call stopped her, she turned carefully to see Marlene bent over the drawing table scrutinizing the blueprint there. 'Don't forget our appointment. 4.30 again?' He smiled at her, glanced over to make sure his wife was not observing and blew her a kiss.

At the edge of a wood of silver birches behind the Institute was a small meadow where, in summer, the students would go and sunbathe. And at the meadow's edge a stream ran, thick with willows and alders. The pastoral mood was regularly dispelled, however – and Gudrun wondered if this was why it was so popular with the students – by the roaring noise of aero engines. The tri-motors which were tested at the Junkers Flugplatz, just beyond the pine trees to the west, would bank round and fly low over the meadow as they made their landing approaches. In the summer the pilots would wave to the sunbathing students below.

Gudrun walked down the path through the birch wood, still trembling, still hot from the memory of Jochen's audacity, his huge composure. She was surprised to see Paul coming up from the meadow. He was carrying a pair of binoculars in his hand. He saw her and waved.

'I like to look at the aeroplanes,' he said. 'In the war I used to work at an aerodrome, you know, painting camouflage. Wonderful machines.'

She had a flask of coffee with her and spontaneously offered to share it with him. She needed some company, she felt, some genial distraction. They found a place by the stream and she poured coffee into the tin cup that doubled as the flask's top. She had some bread and two hard-boiled eggs, which she ate as Paul drank the coffee. Then he filled his pipe and smoked, while she told him about the dyeing course at Sorau. He said he thought she needed a more intense blue to finish her rug, something hard and metallic, and suggested she might be able to concoct the right colour at the dyeworks.

'With Jochen,' he said suddenly, to her surprise, 'when you're with Jochen, are you happy?'

He waved aside her denials and queries. Everyone knew about it, he told her, such a thing could not be done discreetly in a place like the Institute. She need not answer if she did not want to, but he was curious. Yes, she said, she was very happy with Jochen. They were both happy. She said boldly that she thought she was in love with him. Paul listened. He told her that Jochen was a powerful figure in the architecture school, that all power in the Institute emanated finally from the architecture workshop. He would not be surprised, he said, if one day Jochen ended up running the whole place.

He rose to his feet, tapped out his pipe on the trunk of a willow and they wandered back through the birch wood.

'I just wanted you to be aware about this,' he said, 'about Jochen.' He smiled at her. 'He's an intriguing man.' His features were small beneath his wide pale brow, as if crushed and squashed slightly by its weight. There were bags under his eyes, she noticed; he looked tired.

'You're like a meteor,' he said. 'Suddenly you're attracted by the earth and are drawn into its atmosphere. At this moment you become a shooting star, incandescent and beautiful. There are two options available: to be tied to the earth's atmosphere and plummet, or to escape, moving back out into space' – she was baffled at first, but then remembered he was quoting from his own book, something she had heard in his class – 'where you slowly cool down and eventually extinguish. The point is you need not plummet,' he said, carefully. 'There are different laws in different atmospheres, freer movements, freer dynamics. It need not be rigid.'

'Loose continuity,' she said. 'I remember.'

'Precisely,' he said, with a smile. 'There's a choice. Rigid continuity or loose.' He tapped her arm lightly. 'Do you know, I think I may be interested in buying your rug.'

Spencer tightens the final bolt and crosses the street to join us on the opposite sidewalk. Mr Koenig, Mrs Koenig, Spencer and me. It is almost midday, and the sun is almost insupportably bright. I put on my sunglasses and through their green glass I stare at the Koenig's mini-diner.

Mr Koenig turns away and takes a few paces, his finger held under his nose as if he is about to sneeze. He comes back to us.

'I love it, Miss Velk,' he says after apologizing for the few private moments he has needed. 'I just . . . It's so . . . The way you've done those jutting-out bits. My God, it even looks like a sandwich – the roll, the meat . . . so clever, so new. How it curves like that, that style –'

' – Streamline moderne, we call it.'

'May I?'

He puts his hands on my shoulders and leans forward and up (I am a little taller) and he gives me a swift kiss on the cheek.

'I don't normally kiss architects –'

I try not to smile as I contemplate my personal refutation of everything the Institute stood for. 'Oh, I'm not an architect,' I say. 'I'm just a designer. It was a challenge.'

Gudrun never really knew what happened as the stories changed so often in the telling, and there were lies and half lies all the time. The truth made both guilty parties more guilty and they thought to absolve themselves by pleading spontaneity, and helpless instinct, but they had no time to compare notes and the discrepancies hinted at quite another version of reality.

Gudrun climbed the last block from the station and quietly opened the door of the apartment on Grenz Weg. It must have been a little before eight o'clock in the morning. She took a few steps into the hall when she heard a sound in the kitchen. She pushed open the door and Jochen stood there, naked, with two cups of steaming coffee in his hands.

His look of awful incomprehension changing to awful comprehension lasted no more than a second. He smiled, set down the cups said, 'Gudrun –' and was interrupted by Utta's call from her bedroom. 'Jochen, where's that coffee, for heaven's sake?'

Gudrun picked up a coffee cup and walked into Utta's room. She wanted Utta to see, there was to be no evasion of responsibility. Utta was sitting up in her bed, pillows plumped behind her, the sheet to her waist. Jochen's clothes were piled untidily on a wooden chair. She made a kind of sick, choking noise when Gudrun came in. For a moment Gudrun thought of throwing the hot coffee at her, but at that stage she knew there were only seconds before she herself was going to break, so, after a moment of standing there to make Utta see, to make her know, she dropped the cup on the floor and left the apartment.

Two days later Jochen asked Gudrun to marry him. He said he had gone to the apartment on Saturday night (his wife was away) thinking that was the day Gudrun was returning from Sorau. Why would he think that? she asked, they had talked about a Sunday reunion so many times. Once in his stream of protestations he had inadvertently referred to a note – 'I mean, what would you think? a note like that' – and then, when questioned – 'What note? Who sent you a note?' – said he was becoming confused – no, there was no note, he had meant to say she *should* have sent him a note from Sorau, not relied on him to remember, how could he remember everything, for God's sweet sake?

Utta. Utta had written to him, Gudrun surmised, perhaps in her name, the better to lure him: 'Darling Jochen, I'm coming home a day early, meet me at the apartment on Saturday night. Your own Gudrun . . .' It would work easily. Utta there, surprised to see him. Come in, sit down, now you're here, come all this way. Something to drink, some wine, some schnapps, maybe? And Jochen's vanity, Jochen's opportunity and Jochen's weakness would do the rest. Now, darling Jochen, this question of Marianne Brandt's resignation . . .

In weary moments, though, other possibilities presented themselves to her. Older duplicities, histories and motives she could never have known about and wouldn't want to contemplate. Her own theory was easier to live with.

Utta wrote her a letter: '. . . no idea how it happened . . . some madness that can infect us all . . . an act of no meaning, of momentary release.' Gudrun was sad to lose Utta as a friend, but not so sad to turn down Jochen's proposal of marriage.

I say goodbye to Spencer as he sits in the cab of his crane looking down at me. 'See you tomorrow, Gudrun,' he says with a smile, to my vague surprise, until I remember I had asked him to call me Gudrun. He drives away and I rejoin Mr Koenig.

'I got one question,' he says. 'I mean, I love the lettering, don't get me wrong – "sandwiches, salads, hot dogs" – but why no capital letters?'

'Well,' I say, without thinking, 'why write with capitals when we don't speak with capitals?'

Mr Koenig frowns. 'What? . . . yeah, it's a fair point. Never thought of it that way . . . Yeah.'

My mind begins to wander again, as Mr Koenig starts to put a proposition to me. Who said that about typography? Was it Albers? Paul? . . . No, Moholy Nagy, László in his red overalls with his lumpy boxer's face and his intellectual's spectacles. He is in Chicago, now. We've all gone, I think to myself, all scattered.

Mr Koenig is telling me that there are fifteen Koenig mini-diners in the Los Angeles area and he would like, he hopes, he wonders if it would be possible for me to redesign them – all of them – in this streamlined, modern streamline sort of style.

All scattered. Freer. Freer movements, freer dynamics. I remember, and smile to myself. I had never imagined a future designing hot-dog stands in a city on the West Coast of America. It is a kind of continuity, I suppose. We need not plummet. Paul would approve of me and what I have done, I think, as a vindication of his principle.

I hear myself accepting Mr Koenig's offer and allow him to kiss me on the cheek once more – but my mind is off once again, a continent and an ocean away in drab and misty Dessau. Gudrun Velk is trudging up the gentle slope of Grillparzerstrasse, her suitcase heavy in her hand, taking the shortcut from the station, heading back to the small apartment on Grenz Weg which she shares with her friend Utta Benrath and hoping, wondering, now that she has managed to catch an early train from Sorau, if Jochen would have some time to see her alone that afternoon.

Incandescence

ALEXANDER TOBIAS. The burning lake. That's what comes to me first about that weekend – the image of the sun on the lake, blinding me. The lake seemed on fire, as if it was burning with a low, sulphurous heat. It was a hot lemon colour – the water, I mean – and wraiths of steam were weaving from the surface. I stopped the car – it was that arresting – and stepped out to check that I wasn't hallucinating. I know now that it was a trick of the weather: a cold, overcast day suddenly turned hot and cloudless by some passing front – and then the angle of the sun on the water and my arriving at that bend in the drive at that precise moment – but for a moment or two the serene landscaped park at Marchmont suddenly seemed apocalyptic. I should have recognized it then for what it was: an omen.

LADY MARCHMONT. Yes, I invited Alex Tobias down for the weekend. I bumped into him in London, in the food hall at Harrods, of all places. I hadn't seen him for three or four years but of course I knew him very well. He was always down at Marchmont when he and Anna were, well, not so much engaged, but very close. He was very much in love with Anna, I always knew that. I saw him, went up to him and we got talking. He told me he'd been in the Far East – Japan or Hong Kong or some such place. He'd done very well – pots of money – but I felt sorry for him, suddenly. I can't explain why. I sensed a kind of sadness in him and so I said why don't you come down to Marchmont for the weekend, it'll be lovely to see you again – everyone would love to see you again. I told Anna and Rory and they didn't seem to mind at all. In fact Rory was very pleased, I remember. There was no animosity or jealousy – not a shred, not a whit. Everyone seemed delighted at the idea Alex would be coming. I was always very fond of Alex.

ALEXANDER TOBIAS. I motored on through the park towards the house, memories crowding in on me. How many times had I come up this drive? Through the south gates, past the lodge, the lake, the deer park with its huge dying oaks and then that turn around the stand of beech trees and there the house lies before you. I was a bit shocked, I confess, when I saw the scaffolding on the west wing. You can tell when scaffolding has been up for ever: it ages, like everything else. The place looked neglected, ramshackle. It had been four years since I had seen it and I couldn't believe how short a time it took for a grand ancient house to degenerate and decline into something forlorn and moribund. I parked and had a quick wander around. Nobody was working on the wing – nobody had been working there for weeks – there was a bucket on a rope filled with solid cement. The gravelled turning circle was badged with weeds. Buddleia was growing in the gutters. It was nothing like the old Marchmont.

ANNA MONTROSE. When Mamma told me she'd asked Alex down I felt genuinely happy: I so wanted to see him again. It was only later that I wondered if it was such a good idea. But Rory put me at ease. Don't be silly, he said, what's he going to do: kidnap you? Steal you away? I like meeting my wife's old boyfriends, anyway – they can tell they can't match the competition. Rory can make you laugh at anything. If you were on the deck of the *Titanic* as it was sliding beneath the waves he'd make you laugh. That's why I married him, I suppose. That's why I love him . . . As soon as Rory said it was fine I relaxed. And I began to look forward to seeing Alex again. In fact we were all looking forward to that weekend.

PENELOPE MARCHMONT. I was *really* looking forward to seeing Alex again. I remembered him from when I was about ten or eleven. He was part of the family: always there with Anna, always around. It was just after my fifteenth birthday when he and Anna split up. In fact it was the day after, that's why I remember it so well. I cried and cried, and to tell the truth I still don't understand why they broke up. One of those silly things that escalates, gets out of control and explodes – like a car bomb, wounding everyone. Anna didn't want to go to Hong Kong, or something. And so they had a fight and Alex went and he never came back. Then Anna met Rory and a year later she was Mrs Montrose. Richard says Alex has made a fortune on the Hong Kong stock exchange. He's very clever, Alex: I always knew he'd make a pile.

LADY MARCHMONT. We put Alex in the Rose Room. He always used to have the Blue, but I thought it would have been tactless to put him in his and Anna's old room. Also it's just under Rory and Anna's apartment. So: not a good idea. Alex was on good form, just like his old self. He had ever such a smart motor car. Richard would know what type it was – I'm hopeless with cars.

ALEXANDER TOBIAS. Lady M. put me in the Rose Room to 'spare my feelings'. She needn't have worried as I felt quite relaxed. I really wanted to see Anna again for all the usual reasons but also because I wanted her to see how I'd changed. It's funny: sometimes you only start to grow up in your late twenties. I'm a late-maturer. I was perfectly calm, I'd talked to myself. Anna was an old friend, pure and simple. She was a married woman. What was past was past. No lasting regrets. I felt absolutely confident I would be able to see her again, calmly, maturely, openly.

ANNA MONTROSE. He looked so much older. His haircut was different, combed off his forehead. That was my first thought: you've changed the way you comb your hair. In fact it was very slightly greying at the temples. He was, what, thirty-one? When I kissed him on the cheeks I rested my hands on his shoulders and I felt the material of his jacket. It must have been cashmere, I suppose. Some incredibly rare super-cashmere: I've never felt anything so soft. It just seemed to whisper: moneyyyyyy – Then I saw his car. This boy has clearly done well, I thought. He was very sweet but I could see he was nervous. He thought he was covering it up being all polished and debonair. But remember I knew him so incredibly well. I *know* him so well. Funnily enough, I think I know Alex better than I know Rory. I suppose I shouldn't say such a thing, but Alex was, in the years we were together, always completely transparent to me. I always knew what he was thinking.

LADY MARCHMONT. It was as if they had seen each other last week. I thought it was marvellous, marvellous. I felt so good seeing how relaxed they instantly were with each other. I thought: now, we're going to have fun, a wonderful weekend.

ALEXANDER TOBIAS. And then she came in. When she came in, for a second I thought I might vomit. She was just as beautiful. More beautiful, perhaps, because she looked so natural and ungroomed. Jeans, a v-neck sweater: I can't recall. Her hair was longer, I think. I had forgotten how clear her eyes were: the absolute trusting candour of her gaze. When she kissed me I thought I would pass out. Because I smelt her – that lavender trace of perfume, the shampoo smell of her hair. The touch of her hands on my shoulders was an almost physical pain. It overwhelmed me. All my planned polite reserve, all my prized composure and maturity gone. I wanted to get in my car and drive back to London. It was quite simple, really. When I saw Anna again I knew I loved her still. That I had never stopped loving her and that I would never stop loving her. And suddenly I felt a kind of grief for my life. It's a terrible thing, this, when you know your life has gone irrevocably wrong, and that, every day, until the day you die, you will be confronted with the idea of an alternative life that you could have, should have, lived. There were moments, that weekend, when I felt suicidal. I felt that I should end my life now rather than live on with the torment of what-might-have-been.

RICHARD MARCHMONT. We'd all gone out to a pub for lunch, that's right: Penny, Rory, me and Lucy, Rory's friend. That's right: we met her off the train at Tunbridge Wells and then went to a pub.

She's South African, Lucy, and she said she wanted a proper English pub lunch. You know, pork pies, bangers and mustard, ploughman's lunch, a pint of Old Ruddles genuine cask-stewed premium bitter sort of thing. And we found this pub – can't remember where – and I had too much to drink, as per. I think I was quite pissed when we got back to Marchmont. And Alex was there already. I saw this fucking amazing Merc parked outside. Penny screamed: it's Alex! And raced inside. Rory said he had to check something with Peter so Lucy and I wandered in and there was old Alex. Smooth bastard, tanned. And I realized I'd never really liked Alex, hadn't missed him at all. But I went up and hugged him. I was definitely pissed.

LUCY DE VRIES. They said this Alex Tobias had been an old boyfriend of Anna's. Very nice, I thought. Tasty. But after a bit I thought: another young English guy with a stick up his arse. He couldn't take his eyes off Anna.

PENELOPE MARCHMONT. He hadn't changed at all. So sweet, so nice looking. I like Rory but I could never understand how or why Anna had let Alex go, why she didn't fight more. Alex didn't seem to know me at first. You know that slightly panicky look in someone's eyes when they've forgotten your name. Of course I'd only been fifteen when he left. I wasn't even in a training bra. I said: Alex, bloody hell, it's me, Penny. And he laughed – with relief. And he said all the usual lovely Alex things – how I'd changed, how incredibly, amazingly beautiful I was, how I suited my hair like that, couldn't believe it. Then Rory came in and it was amazing – like a shock, like an earth tremor. Something happened in the room for a second. And then it was over.

RICHARD MARCHMONT. I distinctly heard Alex say, to himself, when Rory came in – 'Frank?'. I was right beside him. Then Anna went over and said, 'Alex, this is Rory,' and they smiled at each other and shook hands and we got some champagne out. But he definitely said 'Frank'. I wasn't that drunk.

ANNA MONTROSE. When I introduced them I could tell Alex was in a strange and terrible state – but he was charming.

LADY MARCHMONT. What did we talk about? We talked about the house, and Rory's plans for the lake – the fishing. It was lovely: lots of young people. I was so happy I pinched one of Penny's cigarettes.

ALEXANDER TOBIAS. I saw Frank Montrose come in. And my first thought was: good lord, what's that scumbag doing here? And then – you know how your brain works like the fastest computer – within a millisecond, before Anna had even taken a step towards him I knew this was 'Rory'. And the thunder of simultaneous calculations going on in my brain seemed to deafen me. I shook his hand, smiled, chit-chatted, but inside I was thinking: what could have made my Anna marry that sad bastard. This man is a serious drug-user, a liar and a sponger and this family is in deep, impending trouble. And so on. But it was the sudden humiliation I was feeling, and the retrospective anger. I was the one who had left Anna, I know, it was my stupid fault: but if I had ever for one second imagined she would have married someone like Frank Montrose on the rebound from me I would have sacrificed everything and anything to save her. And yet another side of my brain was saying: go very carefully. Call him 'Rory', whatever you do – don't let anything slip. Keep your counsel until you've figured out exactly what's going on.

LUCY DE VRIES. I sat beside Alex Tobias at dinner. He was between me and Lady M. He was perfectly agreeable. He'd been to Cape Town, we vaguely knew some people in common. At first I thought he may look good and he's obviously got money but like so many English guys I meet he's fundamentally boring. But he wasn't stupid and I always warm to intelligent people. Interestingly enough he paid as much attention to Rory as he did to Anna. Anna was across the table from him as far away as possible. There was a lot of careful reminiscing: people stepping delicately around their shared history.

Richard seemed out of it – he'd drunk a lot in the pub but it seemed to me he was stoned in some way. He didn't eat a thing.

ALEXANDER TOBIAS. Throughout dinner I kept half an eye on Frank/Rory. A good-looking man, one would have to say, but there was something swart and gypsyish about him that I found rebarbative. He gave no sign that he knew I knew who he was. He was perfectly friendly towards me. I noticed he went into the kitchen to supervise the serving of the pudding. Very much *chez lui*, very at home. Penny has turned into a real beauty: dark, gamine, her hair gelled into soft spikes, like black meringue. Smoky eye-shadow made her eyes lustrous.

ANNA MONTROSE. I thought Alex seemed a bit distant. Maybe meeting Rory affected him. Suddenly the concept of my marriage was no longer abstract but made flesh. After dinner Rory came up to me and whispered in my ear: 'I approve.'

ALEXANDER TOBIAS. Over coffee Lady Montrose was very forthcoming about the development of the estate. There is a company, Marchmont Enterprises Ltd, or something, which is run by Rory, as I must learn to call him, and someone called Peter Fuller-Baird, the estate manager. She implied that she had financed its setting-up: 'Some of the "family silver", had to go, you know how it is.' The company is paying for the conversion of the west wing into luxury guest suites, the establishing of a pick-your-own fruit farm and the stocking of the lake with trout. The fish will make their fortune, she says, people will pay hundreds of pounds a day to come and fish for trout at Marchmont, with everything catered for: food, accommodation, transport. The plans and schedule were very vague. 'I don't know what I would have done without Rory,' she said, 'he's a marvel.' The naivety is astounding. At one stage I noticed Richard make a signal to Rory and they both left the room. Rory returned alone ten minutes later.

ANNA MONTROSE. It felt strange lying in bed thinking of Alex in the Rose Room. But I was pleased Mamma had asked him: we could be friends now, I thought. Well, perhaps not friends – too much painful history – but we could see each other without anguish. Rory was very curious about how Alex had made his fortune. He analyses the movements of stock markets, I said, companies pay him for his advice and he writes reports about them that are published in funny financial journals with a circulation of about a hundred. How does that make you rich, he asked. You take your own advice, I said. So he's a journalist. No, he's an expert, I said. What's he worth, Rory asked. I said I'd only heard rumours: millions, I suggested. Rory came and sat on the bed and took my hand. What a terrible mistake you made, he said, grinning. I reminded him I hadn't had to make a choice: Alex had been long gone before I met you. Still, he said, imagine if you had all that money we wouldn't be bothered with bloody trout and raspberries.

ALEXANDER TOBIAS. I met Frank Montrose about ten years ago, briefly, at a weekend twenty-first birthday party of a friend of mine from school. It was a grand party at his parents' place in Perthshire. There was a shoot on the Friday and a ball on the Saturday. Frank Montrose was with, in every sense of the word, Hugo Stavordale. Both of them were wired for the whole weekend. There were a lot of drugs around generally and Hugo and Frank Montrose seemed to be supplying and consuming most of them. He wouldn't remember me but I certainly remembered him. Hugo Stavordale died two years later – suicide, apparently. Frank Montrose was left a lot of money, Hugo's flat in South Kensington and some paintings. The Stavordale family contested the will unsuccessfully. Frank Montrose went to live in Kenya in some style. That was the scandal and the gossip: and that was the last I'd heard of him until I met Rory.

LUCY DE VRIES. I woke up early and went for a walk. I saw Alex Tobias up on the scaffolding, poking about on the roof of the west wing, picking up bricks and lifting tiles. I didn't think anything unusual about it. Maybe he knew a lot about building refurbishment.

LADY MARCHMONT. Actually, it was Rory who suggested that we bring Alex into Marchmont Enterprises. Alex knew the family, he said, he loved the house – who could be better. I thought it was a super idea. We would give him a substantial share of the business in return for some capital investment. Rory said he reckoned it was best if Anna asked him – just to see how the land lay. I thought it was a marvellous idea.

RICHARD MARCHMONT. Alex asked me if I fancied a game of tennis. I won't play a 'game', I said, but I'll give you a knock up. I got tired after about ten minutes – he's clearly very fit, Alex – so we sat on the bench and smoked a cigarette. He started asking me about Rory, asking me if I'd ever heard of someone called Stavordale. I said no. There was something about his questioning that I didn't like so I told him straight: Rory is a great man, I said. He saved my life and he's keeping me pretty well clean and sober. I love him like a brother and I won't hear a word said against him. That shut him up. Of all the emotions I detest in this world I think jealousy takes first prize.

LUCY DE VRIES. I played tennis with Alex. He was good. But I'm good too and we worked up quite a sweat. After the game I knew he was looking at me differently – we can always tell, you know. We smoked a cigarette and walked back to the house. I need a shower, he said. I put my hand on his bum and said: care to join me? I don't know what made me quite so brazen. Anyway, it shook him up. I'm joking, I laughed, relax. Some other time, he said, but I could tell he didn't mean it. Penny must have seen us and she caught me on the stairs to my room. Hands off, she said, he's mine.

ALEXANDER TOBIAS. Things are becoming clearer. After lunch I had a chat with Lady Marchmont and dug out the information that the two Constable sketches had been sold and various bits of porcelain that her grandfather had brought back from China. They'd managed to raise about 150 grand. Probably 125,000 has gone into the pockets of Rory and his 'partner', Peter Fuller-Baird: certainly barely anything's been spent on the west wing. Then she started talking about the mortgage. What mortgage, I asked. It turns out they mortgaged the estate for half a million two years ago. She started rambling on about how once the income from the fishing and the guest suites started flowing they'd be fine. We've had a lot of bad luck, she said: the first lot of trout they put into the lake all died; the west wing was rotten and damp and she had a shockingly big, wholly unexpected demand from Lloyd's. The Marchmonts are plainly broke: it looks like everything is about to go down the pan.

PENELOPE MARCHMONT. I knew Lucy had the hots for Alex and I suppose that's what made me do it. And the fact that I'd drunk about three bottles of wine. After supper I said to him let's play a game of snooker. We went into the snooker room and he took the cover off the table. I didn't know you played snooker, he said. I know how to play strip-snooker, I said. I was standing beside him and I kissed him. He broke us apart very gently. We can't do this, Penny, he said. I started to cry – I was really drunk – why not, I said. Because of Anna. What's Anna got to do with anything, I said. Anna's a married woman. It doesn't matter, he said. Then he left me. What did he mean: it didn't matter?

ALEXANDER TOBIAS. After Penny tried to 'seduce' me I wasn't really thinking straight and went downstairs instead of upstairs. I turned a corner and at the end of the corridor saw two men. I stopped. It was Rory and Richard. They were in each other's arms. I couldn't tell if they were kissing. I backed off. They never saw me. I went out into the garden for a smoke, wondering what to do. When I returned to the drawing room only Anna was there. What happened to you, she asked. Everyone's gone to bed.

ANNA MONTROSE. It conceivably wasn't the ideal moment to bring up the question of money but I knew Rory wanted an answer as soon as possible and also it was probably the only chance I'd get to be alone with Alex. I poured him a brandy and we talked a bit about our missing four years. He seemed interested in how I'd met Rory. I told him about my holiday in Cape Town and the party. Oh, so it was South Africa, he said, not Kenya. How did you know he'd lived in Kenya, I asked. Something he mentioned – Alex was being very vague and evasive. I came and sat beside him on the sofa. Alex, there's something I want to ask you. Don't say yes, don't say no, just think about it. So, I asked him. He sat very still and his face was expressionless. How much do you need, he said. I told him what Rory said was the absolute bottom line. I put my hand on his and said: just think about it Alex. You know us and we all love you, you know that. I've never seen Mamma so happy this weekend. And if we could get the house up and running, all together, wouldn't it be amazing? Think of it as an investment, not a favour. You'd get your money back. Rory says we'll be making a profit in a couple of years. And then he kissed me.

ALEXANDER TOBIAS. The trouble was she was wearing that black velvet dress that I remembered, with the scoop neck and the long lace sleeves. When she came and sat beside me on the sofa I thought I'd stop breathing, my lungs seemed made of brass, immovable. The brandy went down my throat like fire. They needed £200,000, cash. An injection of capital – she said it so sweetly. I was barely listening: I was just aware of her sitting that close to me. And I thought: four years ago, with everybody in bed, we'd have slid into each other's arms and then gone up to the blue room and made love . . . That's what made me kiss her. And she didn't push me off. We kissed each other, her mouth opened and our tongues met and for a few seconds I felt my old life come back, as if nothing had changed – and then it disappeared when I broke away. Anna, I said – and I know my voice was trembling – you know that I love you. She sat there with her head bowed: I don't blame you, Alex, but please don't do that again. Please don't make me – I stopped her and apologized. I had to get away from her. I said I would think about her proposition, give them an answer the next day.

ANNA MONTROSE. Rory was awake when I went up. I told him quickly what Alex had said so he wouldn't sense my disequilibrium, my turmoil. Rory asked me if I thought Alex would do it and spontaneously I said yes. I don't know why: perhaps because it was obvious what Alex felt for me – what he still felt for me and what he would do for me, if I asked him. I thought that if he could help me in any way, he would. Rory was incredibly relieved and said that, for someone like Alex, 200 grand was like a taxi fare, that it wasn't as if we were asking him to mortgage his future to help us out. As I lay in bed I felt sad for Alex. After we'd kissed I couldn't bring myself to look at him. I couldn't see that blind devotion in his eyes, knowing all the time that I could never help him – that only he could help us.

ALEXANDER TOBIAS. I slept well. I woke early, had a bath and took a turn in the garden watching the sun rise. I felt good, confident, I knew exactly what to do. There was a heavy dew on the lawn and soon my feet were soaked. I looked round and Rory was standing on the terrace looking down at me. Shall we walk out with a couple of guns, he said. It's a fantastic morning for it. He lent me some gum boots and an old jacket and we wandered off to North End Wood with one of the dogs, a setter with a limp. I felt very calm being alone with him, not at all uneasy. I knew that Anna would have told him what I'd said. For the first time since coming to Marchmont I felt that the power suddenly all resided with me. We had a couple of shots at some wood pigeons. We could have had any number of rabbits but Rory said Anna didn't like us shooting rabbits, for some reason. Then he said: have you come to any kind of decision? And I said: not yet – Frank. He looked at me, oddly. Do you ever see anything of the Stavordales, I asked? And to my surprise he laughed, quite genuinely. You are a strange fellow, he said, keeping all this bottled up. I know all about you, I said, what you were, what you did, where you got your money. Does Anna know you were once called Frank? Of course, he said, she knows everything. It was my turn to laugh now. We headed back to the house. My name is Rory Francis Montrose, he said. When I went to Kenya I realized I wanted to change – didn't want to be a Frank any more so I took up Rory again. My mother calls me Rory. He looked at me, very squarely, not a flicker of insecurity in his eye. I was almost impressed. Anna knows everything, he repeated. There's nothing you can tell her she doesn't know.

LUCY DE VRIES. I saw them coming out of the woods with their guns. It was like something out of a sporting print: two English gentlemen with their guns and dog. It was a fantastic, beautiful morning.

ANNA MONTROSE. I was dressed and just about to go down to breakfast when he knocked on the bedroom door. He was wearing the clothes he'd arrived in, which I thought was a bit strange. He started talking about Rory in a low intense voice. There are things you should know about him, he said. Then he went on and on about drugs, Rory's gay past, that he had stolen money, the alleged suicide of Hugo Stavordale, that 'Frank' was his real name, and that even now he was having an affair with Richard. Then he grabbed me and began ranting about how he loved me, about how if I kicked Rory out he would do everything for this family. Renovate the house, pump money into the estate, everything. He kept saying that he had ruined his life and coming back to Marchmont had made him see what a disaster it had been to leave me. Tears filled his eyes. Think what I can do, he said, think what it would be like for us here at Marchmont. Divorce him, he said, I beg you: he's scum, a worthless liar, he's bleeding this family dry and he's fucking your brother behind your back. Get rid of him, marry me and everything will be all right. I didn't say anything: I let him spill it all out. Then I made him sit down. We're just asking you to help,

I said. We want you to share in everything. We'll pay you back. But he wasn't listening. Leave him, he kept saying, throw him out, be with me. I can't be with you, I said. You can, he said, he stood up and reached for me again. I love you, Anna, he said, we have to spend the rest of our life together. I'm pregnant, I said.

ALEXANDER TOBIAS. He was so clever, Rory/Frank. He had an answer for everything. It was as if he'd brainwashed Anna. Poor, sad Anna. Love is blind, they say. Rory had sunk all his money into Marchmont, she said: if the family went down he would lose everything. She knew all about his life as 'Frank'. He was young, he was wild, stupid – we all were. He was reconciled with the Stavordales. Richard was a damaged, sick person who leant on Rory for all emotional support. It was Rory who monitored his medication, and was weaning him off his anti-depressants, etc., etc. It made me sick. And I saw suddenly how I'd been used. The first major repayment of the loans fell due the following week. They were in hock up to their armpits. The bailiffs were at the gates, the banks poised to seize the estate. Do you happen to know any rich suckers? Rory must have said. Wasn't it curious how Lady Marchmont just happened to be in the food hall? I never go to Harrods, so somebody must have been following me. Do come down for the weekend, Alex, Anna would love to see you . . .

I remembered I stopped the car before I reached the south lodge and had a look back at the park and the lake. The day's promise had never materialized and the sky was filled with mousegrey clouds and the lake appeared cold and brackish, with a surface of tarnished steel. God, I thought to myself, what a farce. They can all rot in hell. I hope they lose every last penny. Rory and Anna and their brat. I drove back to London with the night coming on.

Visions Fugitives

'Keep straight on, and shortly **St Julien** (St Julien-sur-Meuse) comes into view. The village (completely ruined) is reached after crossing first the railway and then the small River Andon. Motor cars can climb as far as the church. Turn to the right after passing the church. Numerous German dug-outs and gun emplacements can be observed here. Down the lane about three hundred yards from the village there comes into view on the side of the hill **a very large American cemetery containing some 28,000 graves**. There is a fine view from here of the lower town and the valley of the Meuse (photo pp. 12 and 13).'

Paris. Yesterday. Watery November sunshine on glossy cobbles. A rime of sleet melted by breakfast. With sullen aplomb the waiter scooped our plates and coffee cups from the table. My daughter's hands were raw and scraped from shucking four hundred oysters the night before, her knuckles freckled with tiny, brilliant, forming scabs. I saw, as she handed me back the letter and the old guidebook, that her fingernails were bitten half way down to the cuticle. She looked beautiful, I thought, but deadly tired, her beauty draining from her.

'Who's the little girl with Grandma?' she asked. 'No, Great-grandma.'

I took the photograph from her. 'You look malnourished, Millie,' I said. 'It's your Great-aunt Sarah.'

'Malnourished . . . All chefs are malnourished,' she laughed. My daughter had been working in Paris since the summer. 'Do you know where you're going?'

'I'm heading for Metz.'

'Well, drive carefully. What's gotten into you, anyway? I thought you were on holiday. Is this wise?'

'I am on holiday. I'm seeing you. And I'm going to St Julien. I have to be there on the 4th.' I handed her a cutting from a French newspaper. 'This was what inspired me.'

She read the cutting: MAVROCORDATO S'EST SUICIDÉ.

'I still don't get it, Dad. Who's Mavrocordato?'

'He's a film director. Was a film director.'

INTERIOR. CAR. DAY.

The man lit his cigarette from the butt of the one he had just smoked. The girl reached across and lifted his sunglasses from his face and put them on. Lifted the sunglasses from his face and put them on. She stared sulkily through the windscreen, making a moue with her lips. 'I'm tired,' she said, 'I want to stop.' 'OK,' the man said, 'we'll stop at the next town.' He turned and looked at her. 'Baby.' 'Never call me Baby,' the girl said, 'never.' 'OK, Baby,' the man said. From the car a roadside indicator could be seen flashing by: it read 'St Julien 3 kms'. Through the windscreen there was a hazy view of a town ahead. A small town on a hill. An ancient church surrounded by cypresses. The man glanced over at the girl. (The naked woman is standing in what looks like an artist's studio, one knee, her right, resting on a *chaise longue*. Some sort of ornate wall hanging behind her. She is completely naked, her upper body turning slightly towards the left. In her left hand she holds a looking glass into which she stares. The fingertips of her right hand touch the underhang of her left breast, gently. She has bobbed, badly permed hair and the heavy makeup and dark lips of a soubrette. 1920s, definitely, perhaps earlier. Her shoulders are thin, girlish, and her head seems ever so slightly too large for her body. At the foot of the picture someone has written her name in a bold, cursive hand: Irène Golan.) 'OK, Baby,' the man said. He threw his cigarette out of the window. Exterior, day: the car turned off the *route nationale* and made briskly, at a careless lick, for St Julien, snare drum on the soundtrack going *tssssss-tup-a-tssssss, tsssss-tup-a-tsssss, tssssss, tssssss, tssssss.*

'Dear Mrs Culpepper –
Thank you for your letter. I do not know if I can be more precise but I will try. The village was in near complete ruins and was called St Julien, I think. I remember we crossed a railway line and then a small stream. There was a lower town and up on a hill beyond there was a church and other buildings, all fairly knocked about. I remember three fine ancient cypresses all broken down from artillery. The lower town was quiet, a few bodies here and there, but well cleared out. Captain Shaw sent our platoon forward up the road to the church. It was about three in the afternoon, quite mild, with a light rain falling. This was November 4th 1918 . . .'

In the photograph my grandmother is standing holding her daughter's hand in front of the sign. 'St Julien' stands out starkly, black on white, in what is a rather fogged, sun-faded print. All around them lie the ruins of the lower town. On the hill behind is the church with its shattered cypresses. My grandmother stands stiffly (I wonder who took the picture?), her daughter (my aunt Sarah) has turned her head slightly in her direction, as if to ask her a question. The date is 1920, some two years after my grandfather died.

I deduced that the noise must have been caused by a spontaneous rally of fifty dumpster trucks deciding to have a revving competition on Seventh Avenue, many floors below, true, but the sonic vibrations were palpable up here. Incredible. I was trying to listen to 'Variations on a Theme of Haydn' on my tape recorder and at the same time was going through my notes of the previous night's concert. The effort it was costing reminded me forcefully of the main reason why I left New York. I had just turned up the volume when my breakfast arrived. 'It's open,' I called, not looking round, hearing the metallic rattle of the room service trolley and the clink of glass and silverware as it made its shuddery, percussive way over to the window.

'Ah, Brahms,' said the waiter, organizing the table setting (now I did look round). His voice was light, the 'r' rolled slightly, in the French way.

He turned. That is, *she* turned. She was in full waiter's rig: starched bum-freezer jacket, black trousers, lace-up shoes, a black bow tie. Blonde hair held back in a taut chignon. Late thirties, I calculated, older than me.

'*Aimez-vous Brahms?*' she said with a smile, holding out the slim folder with the check for me to sign.

'I'm writing a book on him,' I said, noticing simultaneously the sudden hollowness in my chest and the fact that her name tag said 'Jay'. Odd name for a woman.

'I love Brahms,' she said.

'Me too,' I said. 'More than life.'

'. . . We were almost up to the church when the shells started exploding on the road. A whole bunch of us took cover in the graveyard but they had that targeted too. Lieutenant Povitch shouted at us to head back to the lower town. John and I with a dozen others had jumped over a low wall that bounded the cemetery. Ahead of us up the hill to the left we could see a ruined farm house and a big stone barn. It made more sense to take cover up there than risk the descent to the lower town. We set off, John was right behind me . . .'

My grandmother and her daughter Sarah stayed at the Hostelleric du Coq Hardi in Rochette, 'the original kitchen of which', according to their guidebook, 'has preserved its ample proportions and innumerable copper utensils'. My guidebook makes no mention of this establishment but I have decided to stay in the town anyway, if only to approximate to the spirit of this impromptu pilgrimage. The road from Paris is quiet and I am finding, to my vague surprise, that I am actually enjoying driving. I will stay somewhere in

Rochette and proceed to St Julien tomorrow, taking my time, making sure that as I walk up the hill from the lower town it will be around about three o'clock in the afternoon. If a light rain happens to be falling, so much the better.

That Haydn did not write the melody that inspired Brahms's celebrated 'Variations' is well known, but the designation is firmly established and so – So what? So we might as well stick with it. How to express that more elegantly? How to say that the notion that this fool has found a 'missing' variation is a crock, a brimfull, steaming, grade-A crock of –

Jay came into the bar and I put down my notes with barely a tremble, scarcely a rustle of paper. She was wearing a short black dress and her hair was still up, but more loosely, the result of some artful manipulation of pins and tortoiseshell combs.

We shook hands – it seemed unduly formal, but she was foreign, remember, she was not American – and she sat down beside me. She smiled at me as I *Sieg-heiled* through the gloom at the idle waiter.

'How's the demolishment going?' she said.

'The stiletto has been inserted between the seventh and eighth rib. We are half way to the hilt.'

'This new variation was meant to go where?'

'Another vodka martini and –' I said to the waiter and glanced round at Jay.

' – And another vodka martini, on rocks.'

'Between two and three. Variation 2 (a), I suppose. Absurd.'

'Obscene. May I?' She took one of my cigarettes from the pack on the table, broke off the filter tip and put the shortened filterless cigarette to her lips, a little off centre. I reached for my lighter but she was there first. But she frowned, not lighting her cigarette, thinking (thinking about Brahms?), the cigarette between her lips, slightly off centre, three uneven creases between her fine, dark blonde, frowning eyebrows. This is how I will always remember her, frowning, trying to imagine what possible kind of variation could have gone between number two and three. This is one of the ways I will remember her.

INTERIOR. ROOM. NIGHT.
The man leant against the window frame of the hotel room and placed his forehead against a cool pane. There was a flushing of water on the soundtrack (over) and the man did not look round. Irène Golan's round, impassive face, then the camera tracked down her body. Her small breasts, the swell of her stomach, her neat divot of pubic hair, her knees, her feet. Her name. Irène Golan. The man in profile: he closed his eyes. The girl was in the room, now, a stronger light coming through the left-ajar bathroom door. She wore a loose white t-shirt (the man's?) and black panties that did not quite conceal the cleft between her buttocks. The man moved away from the window. 'How many times did you sleep with Urbain?' he asked, in a reasonable voice. 'You can tell me, I don't particularly mind.' The girl was sitting down at the room's solitary table. Leaning forward slightly. From the configuration of the folds of her t-shirt, the convexities and concavities, it was possible to imagine that, beneath her t-shirt, her breasts were just resting on the table top – the underhang of her breasts just grazing the table top. She had an unlit cigarette in her mouth, just off centre, and had frozen in the act of removing a match from a book of matches. She frowned, possibly, you imagined, considering a response to this question. She looked directly at you, looked directly at you, and with two fingers took the unlit cigarette from her mouth, and said, 'France is really a beautiful country.' Cigarette from her mouth, turned and looked at directly at you, and said, 'France is really a beautiful –'

Jay carefully picked a shred of tobacco from the pink point of her tongue.
　'Do you want to –' I cleared my throat, 'Eat, stay here, try –'
　'– I'd like to go to a movie,' she said. 'I'd like to see, more than anything, *Visions Fugitives*. It's playing downtown.'

'Anything you say, Jay,' I said.

She looked curiously at me. 'Why do you call me Jay?' she asked. I explained.

She chuckled. 'Oh, that. I was only helping Jay out. I forgot to take his name off the jacket.'

I felt that slipping and sliding inside me once more.

'Well,' I said, 'you have me at a disadvantage. You know my name. I thought I knew yours.'

'It's Irène,' she said.

'. . . All the way up to the farm building John was right behind me. He was saying, "Come on, Bob, let's go, let's go, Bob." When we reached the farm we could see that it was in full view of the trench lines and gun emplacements in the upper town. Other men who had run up from the churchyard had taken shelter behind the barn whose walls were three feet thick, an ancient building. "Over there, Bob," John said to me. "That's for us, buddy." I can hear his voice in my ears as I write this. There was a four-yard gap between the end of the farmhouse and the gable end of the barn. John pushed me in the back and I hightailed it, ran round the corner of the barn and fell over. That's when I heard the explosion. Some tiles were blown off the roof and there was a lot of smoke. There were some hens inside the barn and they set up a mighty squawking . . .'

According to my grandmother's note in the margin of the guidebook she and Sarah ate 'some kind of stew' the night they stayed in Rochette, but neither of them had much appetite. I find a room in the Hôtel du Cygne (two stars) in the Place des Halles and, dutifully, eat a cartilaginous *daube de bœuf* in the Brasserie Centrale, five minutes from the hotel, an overlit establishment as doggedly functional as its name.

Walking home at night I reflect that there are few places quite so firmly closed and shuttered to the traveller as a French village after hours. Even the hotel front door is locked and it takes half a dozen rings to summon the amiable patron from his flickering TV.

I stand in my room and look down at the silent street, the shine of the street lamps picking out the dead cars in dewy, night-time monochrome. I have that sensation – you must know that form of self-consciousness that comes from being strangely alone – when every gesture, every scratch of the head, every throat-clearing acquires a curious, mannered significance. I feel I am performing, I feel I am being filmed. I feel I am playing out an abandoned scene from *Visions Fugitives*.

INTERIOR. ROOM. DAY.

The man sat in a wooden chair, smoking, and watched the girl sleeping. Birdsong, morning light squeezing through half-open shutters. The man was clothed but the girl – most of her beneath a sheet – was plainly naked. Irène Golan's face. The man picked through the girl's clothes searched her fringed suede handbag went through her coat pockets lit another cigarette sat down stood up walked round the bed. Smoking his cigarette walked round the bed and crouched down staring at her. The girl's face. The man's face. Irène Golan turned through ninety degrees. The man stood by the closed window. Stood by the open window. Two gendarmes in the street below. The man recoiled, turned and kicked the leg of the bed. 'Hey, get up. I'll bring the car round.' The girl woke and sat up in bed, slowly. Her right arm gathering the sheet to her breasts, modestly. She looked as if she had really been sleeping. The man left the room and the girl sighed – bored, irritated. With her free hand she pushed strands of hair back from her slumped and sleepy face. She yawned and a corner of the sheet slipped and nearly fell free. You wondered if they had made love the night before. There was the sound of the key locking the door. The girl did not even turn her head.

'. . . John was lying on the ground in the gap between the farmhouse and the barn. He was rolled on to his side. And he was very pale, white as chalk. But there was no mark on him, not a drop of blood. It must have happened instantly – I was told that concussive force of certain explosions can do this to you. There appears to be no evident cause of death, apart from this unnatural pallor, as if the blood as well as the breath has been driven from you. We pulled him into the lee of the barn wall and we waited until dark, at which point we made our way back to the lower town. I am sure it happened in a split second and it is inconceivable that he knew a thing. This is exactly as I remember it. I hope this is of some comfort. I should only add that he seemed very peaceful. The next morning our battalion was withdrawn from St Julien and we remained in billets at Verdun until the armistice.

Yours sincerely,

J. Robert "Bob" Quentin.'

Visions Fugitives (1961). **Un film de Jean-Didier Mavrocordato. Avec la participation d'Alain Hoffman et Julienne Jodelet . . .** I remember the poster. I remember the revival house in the Village running a season of *'nouvelle vague'* films from the '60s. I remember certain scenes in the movie with the recall of the the most pedantic cineaste. But the rest of it remains opaque. It was not that long ago, either. Twelve years, thirteen. I have never made any attempt to see the film again. The memory, with all its gaps, remains sharp, perfect but fragile, and I do not want it disturbed, do not want to shatter its perfect fragility.

'Mavrocordato is Swiss. I am Swiss. I think he used a village in Switzerland for this film which I know. St Julien, it's not far from my home.'

'Where's that?'

'Near Lausanne.'

The lights dimmed. The film began. On the screen the credits rolled and the abrasive, badly recorded jazz score filled the cinema. Tinny trumpet blare, hiss and tap of wire brush on snare drum. I don't think I had seen a black and white film in the cinema for over a decade. I watched, with the curiosity of an anthropologist, as Alain Hoffman and Julienne Jodelet strolled hand in hand along a promenade. Nice? Villefranche? Beaulieu? Juan les Pins? I find it hard to recall much more of the opening sequence of the film. In the shifting silver of the semi-dark I felt Irène gently take my hand.

Who was this Irène Golan? Why did Mavrocordato use that old photograph in his film? Cutting back to it repeatedly? As if it was a vision of absolute torment to taciturn Alain Hoffman, on the run with the exquisite Julienne Jodelet . . . I lie in my lumpy bed in the Hôtel du Cygne, my head resting on the solid bolster that passes for a pillow, and shuffle the images that slip into my mind. I will not sleep, I know, my mind going now in the perfect shuttered blackness of the room, in that dead calm of hotel noiselessness – which is not noiseless at all. A distant lorry changes gear on the *route nationale*, the chuckling of the central heating, the unexplained creaks and thuddings of an old building, the confessional whisper of a toilet flush somewhere below. Shhhhh.

You know those unhindering hours of the night when your thoughts will wander free, sometimes freighted with despair, but sometimes inspired and almost miraculous – this is one of those nights. And just before I begin to doze I think I have it, my Theory of Everything. It is to do, I decide, with mysterious parabolas – as if an event, a moment, is launched at your life like a projectile – a stone, a dart, an arrow – sent soaring in the direction of your life. One day it will descend, following its parabolic curve and hit you, or glance off you, or near-miss. It seems to me in the dazzle-dark of this shuttered hotel room that at times our individual lives are peppershot with these mysterious comings-to-earth. Much of the time they pass unacknowledged – or, if we do, we are only half aware of something happening to us. We stop and turn and take our bearings – we shiver, we ponder, we forget – but do not really understand that we have just intersected with a mysterious parabola. Even if we do, even if we grant that something has happened, something has changed, we do not understand because we cannot trace that parabola back to its starting place. We all know these moments of fleeting significance that touch our lives. The great problem, the abiding problem is to make some sense of them . . .

The bizarre death of John Culpepper in St Julien on 4 November 1918. Brahms's 'Variations on a Theme of Haydn'. Jay turning into Irène. (There's one: she recognized Brahms. What if she had not?) *Visions Fugitives*. Jean-Didier Mavrocordato's decision to film his *nouvelle vague* masterwork in the small town on the Meuse where my grandfather had died. Irène's misconception that it was filmed near Lausanne provoking our argument. Mavrocordato's suicide (that touched me, glanced off me, that one, but only because I am here in France). I would not be lying in my unyielding bed in the Hôtel du Cygne if John Culpepper had not pushed his friend Bob across the gap between farmhouse and barn first, instead of going himself.

'Brahms chose something deeply obscure and through the special alchemy of his genius transformed it into one of the best-known tunes in the orchestral repertoire. The melody he chose has nothing to do with Haydn, it forms the second movement of a *Partita*, probably by one Ignaz Pleyel, which may in turn come from some older, even more forgotten source . . .'

Irène stopped reading. She was sitting at the desk in my hotel room, my typescript in front of her. She was leaning forward slightly, resting on her elbows, and one could imagine, from the convexities and concavities of her dress bodice, that her breasts were just touching the desk top, that the underhang of her breasts was just grazing the desk top.

'Interesting,' she said. 'I didn't know that.'

'Keep going,' I said. 'It sounds better when you read it. Your accent makes it sound more intelligent.'

'I'm thinking of Brazil,' she said. 'I really think I should go to Brazil next.'

I poured some more whisky into her glass and added some ice cubes. My throat felt thick; I could think of nothing, absolutely nothing, to say. She put my typescript down and picked up the leather-framed photograph of my wife and children, my travelling photograph.

'What are your daughters called?'

'Millie. And Lucy. Lucy and Millie.'

'How old are they?'

'Six and four. Millie's the oldest.'

She stood up, her eyes distant, and strolled round from behind the desk, coming over towards me to collect her drink.

'It's wonderful that, no?' she said. 'To take something so obscure and make it so memorable.'

'What? Oh, you mean Brahms, the "Variations".'

'But we all do that, I suppose, don't we? In our own lives, in our own way. Or at least sometimes we try. We should try, when we have that chance, to do what Brahms did.'

'Yes. It's not so easy. I suppose we –'

' – Or maybe I should go to Mexique. What do you think, Brazil or Mexique?'

I took a few steps away from her, I had to, just at that moment. 'You know,' I said, 'there's no way that village was in Switzerland. That village was not in Switzerland, that St Julien. That was France, definitely.'

She laughed. 'Shall we have a row?' she said. 'How can you be so sure? Prove it.'

The man locked the girl in the room and she did not even look round at the sound of the key turning in the lock. When the man returned and opened the door again, the girl had gone. I can't remember if we saw her leave. I can't remember how the girl got out of the room.

It is almost three o'clock, overcast, with low, packed, mousegrey clouds, but no light rain falls as I walk up the steepish street from the lower town to the upper, although now all trace of a division has been erased by almost eighty years of building and development. I pass a dry-cleaner, a newsagent, a grocery store, a flower shop, an estate agent and an empty *patisserie* with a 'For Sale' sign slipped between the Venetian blind and the dusty window pane.

The church still stands some little way apart, islanded by a wide grass bank and a gravel path and the cemetery wall is high enough to obscure all but the tallest of tombs. I walk around the foot of the cemetery and pause a while in the lee of the wall looking up at the solid stone farmhouse on the hill's crest and to the left, beside it, a splendid old stone barn. Now there is a single-track, metalled road that winds up between back gardens on one side and a field cropped short by sleek, beige cows. I think of John Culpepper and his friend Bob Quentin sheltering here by the cemetery. In their place I would have made for the farm and those thick stone walls too.

EXTERIOR. STREET. DAY.

The sunlight was bright. The glare was over-bright, fuzzing outlines as if the exposure was wrong. It was difficult to make out the features of buildings in the street. The man stood there, in sunglasses, smoking. He stopped a passerby and asked him a question. It was impossible to hear what was being said because of the noise of the score and of the snare drum's insistency. The man's face looking up and down the street. The man walking towards his car. People passing turned and stared: it was clear that they knew this man was an actor (I remember thinking that, I remember noticing their expressions); they were bemused to see a film being made in their small town.

'You know, I've had a disturbing thought: he wasn't really your grandfather,' Irène said, moving to the door.

'No. But we always called him Grandfather Culpepper. I always thought of him as a kind of grandfather. My grandmother always talked about him, how he died in the war, a week before it ended.

That's how I know about this St Julien place, where he died. I've seen a photo. I recognized it.'

'Your grandmother married again – '

'In 1927. Had another child – my mother.'

She thought, pushing out her bottom lip. 'I tell you what, I'll bring you your breakfast.'

She leant forward and kissed me again, but quickly, on the lips. I reached for her. 'No,' she said. 'I'll see you in the morning. I have to go now.'

'Black coffee and croissants. For two. What was your disturbing thought?'

'Oh yes. Do you realize something?' She was standing in the doorway, leaning back in the doorway, her body canted backward, pleased with herself. I could taste her lipstick in my mouth. 'If your grandfather Culpepper hadn't gotten himself killed at St Julien – you wouldn't be here. Goodnight.'

She straightened, showed me the palms of her hands, shoulders shrugging, eyebrows raised, smiling – the girl who had won the prize with the last question of the quiz show.

'Black coffee and croissants,' she said. 'For two.'

How was I to know I would never see her again?

The duty manager looked at me patiently, and not at all intolerantly, as if his training had prepared him for all manner of bizarre requests, far more bizarre than mine.

'We do have a waiter named Jay,' he said, 'who works in our coffee shop. Jay Duveen. But he's been on vacation for four days. We have no member of staff with the name Irène. Not on our computer, anyway.'

He pronounced her name 'Eye-rain'.

He smiled, his smile was not unkind. 'If you could remember her last name, sir, it would be invaluable.'

Invaluable. It would be invaluable. Indeed.

'She's Swiss,' I said. 'Mid–late thirties, tallish, blonde. I imagine a friend of this Jay.'

'There are over five hundred employees in this hotel, sir. And I can't begin to tell you how many dozens of temporary staff we hire on a day by –'

'You've been most helpful.'

The gap between the gable end of the farmhouse and the corner of the barn is wider than Bob Quentin had remembered. I pace it out – sixteen yards. The farmer and his son stand respectfully some way off watching this strange, middle-aged American investigate a banal angle of their farmyard. 'Come on, Bob, let's go, let's go, Bob,' John Culpepper had said. I step out from the gable end of the farmhouse and pace out eight steps, stand equidistant between the farmhouse and the big stone barn. Beneath my feet is longish grass, muddied, trampled somewhat. Below me is the cemetery and beyond that the ugly semi-industrial outskirts of St Julien, the garages, the discount stores, the agricultural depots. The railway line is there and the slow-moving Meuse. I suppose, near as dammit, I am standing on the spot where John Culpepper died.

The afternoon light up here by the farmhouse is pewtery and cold, and a tarnished silver gleam comes off a loop in the river as the sky clears for an instant. I say goodbye to the farmer and his son (*'Mon grandpère, ah, était tué ici, en, ah, mille neuf cent dix-huit'*) and I walk down through the dew-heavy meadow towards the church. When I'm about two hundred yards from the church I pause and look back at the farmhouse and the barn and the gap of refulgent white sky between them. 'Over there, Bob, that's for us, buddy.'

Turning again, I see a small figure coming round the cemetery wall. A woman, wearing a dress – or a sweater and skirt – of the palest blue, striding out with a long, confident stride, setting off up the hill towards me. A blonde woman with loose shoulder-length hair. She waves and calls, and I think she calls my name, but I can't be sure. I can't be sure of anything any more because she looks familiar. Coming towards me through the dew-laden grass of the meadow on this cool grey afternoon is a vision, a vision of Irène.

'On leaving **St Julien** take G.C. 38. The road is interesting but in bad repair, and care must be taken for the next few kms. The view is impressive. Hill 238, across the valley, is literally ploughed up by the shell fire, while not a single tree is left (see photo, p. 18). After crossing the bridge over the Aisne and entering the town, the house on the left, no. 8, should be noticed. This is the old post house where Louis XVI was recognized during his flight in 1791. When the royal carriage stopped near this post house in broad daylight the postmaster thought he recognized the king. His fellow citizens mocked him, accusing him of seeing visions. The postmaster, convinced he was right, followed the carriage all the way to Varennes, where he caught it up, confirmed his suspicions and had the royal family arrested.

Several comfortable and reasonably priced hotels are to be found in the rue Chanzy.'

Fantasia on a Favourite Waltz

Clara Billroth handed the baby to Frau Schäfer and the child went gladly to the old woman, its cries diminishing to gurgles and whimpers. 'Say goodbye to your mama,' Frau Schäfer said uselessly, as she did each evening, taking the baby's wrist between finger and thumb and making the tiny fingers parody a farewell wave. 'Say "Goodbye Mama". Say it, Ullrich.' 'Please don't call him Ullrich,' Clara said, 'I don't like the name.' 'You've got to give him a name soon,' Frau Schäfer said, hurt, 'the child's nearly four months old. It's not correct. It's not Christian.' 'Oh, all right, I'll try and think of one,' Clara said and turned away, pulling her shawl around her as she went down the stairs, feeling the cold wind rush up from the tenement door to meet her. April, she thought: it still might as well be winter.

She walked briskly down Jägerstrasse towards St Pauli, a little late, her shoes pinching her feet, making her shorten her pace, making her favour the right foot over the left. The left was sore. Annaliese said that your feet were never exactly the same size, you should have a different shoe made for each foot. Annaliese and her nonsense. In what world would that be, Clara wondered? How rich would you have to be to have a different –

She saw the boy leaning against the gas lamp, holding on to it with both hands as if it were a mast and he were on the pitching deck of a ship in a stormy sea. As she drew nearer she watched him press his forehead to the cool moisture-beaded metal. The wind off the harbour was full of threatening rain and the gas lamps wore their mistdrop halos like shimmering crowns in the gathering dark. The boy, she saw, was about fourteen or fifteen with long hair – reddish blond – folded on his collar. His eyes were shut and he seemed to be speaking silently to himself. 'Hey,' Clara said, watchfully, 'are you all right?' He opened his eyes and turned to her. He was a stocky young fellow with good features, blue eyes, the thick honey-blond hair drawn off his forehead in a wave. 'Thank you,' the boy said, blinking his pale-lashed blue eyes at her. He had a distinct Hamburg accent. 'Migraine,' he said. 'You wouldn't believe the headache I have. But I'll be fine. I just have to wait until it's passed. You are kind to stop, but I'll be fine.' Clara peered at him: his eyes were shadowed with the effort of talking. Sometimes she had these headaches herself, especially after little Katherina had died and then when she was pregnant with the baby boy, whatever she would call him – with 'Ullrich'. 'All right, then,' she said. 'But don't let the police see you. They'll think you're drunk.' The stocky boy laughed politely and Clara went on her footsore way.

Clara arranged the front of her dress so that her bosom bulged freely over the bodice. The men liked that, it always worked. She tugged the front lower, arching her back, contemplating her reflection in the glass, turning left and right. She looked pretty tonight, she thought: the cold wind off the Elbe had brought colour to her face. She dipped her finger in the pot of rouge and added a little more to each cheek and a dab on her lips. She wanted to make a good impression on her first night; Herr Knipe would be pleased with her. She was early, too, none of the other girls were there and when she came through the bar the glasses were being polished and the dance floor swept. It appeared a prosperous place, this *Lokal*, not like the last one, there were even sheets on the bed. Herr Knipe seemed more generous too – keep half, my dear, he had said, and the more you work, the happier I am.

In the bar the pianist had arrived and was sitting on the little raised dais, playing notes again and again as if he were tuning the piano. She walked towards him to introduce herself – it was important to befriend the musicians, then they would play your favourite melodies. The pianist heard her footsteps crossing the dance floor and turned. 'Hey,' Clara said, surprised. 'Migraine-boy.

What're you doing here?' He smiled. 'I work here,' he said. 'How's the head?' Clara asked. He had the clearest blue eyes, all shadow gone from them now. 'Bearable.' He was trying not to look at her bosom, she saw. 'What's your name?' she said. He was too young to be working here, fourten or fifteen only, she thought.' 'Ah, Hannes,' he said. 'Hannes . . . Kreisler.' 'I'm Clara, Clara Billroth. Do you know any waltzes?' 'Oh yes,' said the boy Hannes, 'I know any number of waltzes.' 'Do you know this one?' Clara sang a few notes. 'It's my favourite.' Hannes frowned: 'You are not a very good singer, I'm afraid,' he said. 'Is it like this?' He turned to the piano and with his right hand picked out the tune. 'Yes,' Clara said, singing along, and then she saw him bring his left hand up to the piano and suddenly the dance hall was filled with the waltz, her waltz, her favourite waltz. She was amazed, as she always was, how they could take a simple tune, a few notes, and within seconds they were playing away – with both hands, no sheet music – as if they had known the waltz all their lives. Clara swayed to and fro to the rhythms. 'You're quite good, young Kreisler, my lad. Oh my God, look, there's Herr Knipe. I'd better go.'

Four men – forty marks, twenty for her, a fair start. A fat sailor, then his little friend. Then some dances. Then a salesman from Altona who proudly showed her a daguerrotype of his wife – she hated it when they did that. Then a dark, muscly fellow – Norwegian or Swedish – who smelt of fish. Clara sniffed at her shoulder, worried that it had rubbed off on her. He had heaved and heaved, the Norseman, took his time. None of her tricks seemed to work. Took his own sweet time.

She finished her beer, pulled the sheets back up and tucked them in. She was unhooking her shawl when there was a knock at her door. It was Hannes. 'Hey, little Kreisler. Thank you for playing my waltz.' 'It's quite pretty, your waltz,' Hannes said. 'I like the tune.' 'Want some beer?' Clara said. 'No, I must go,' Hannes said. 'I came to say goodbye.' 'I'll see you tomorrow,' Clara said; she noticed he was looking at her breasts again. 'No, no, I'm going away,' he said. 'To convalesce. I'm not very well.' He smiled at her wearily, 'I can't take any more of these migraines. I think my head will explode.' Clara shrugged, 'Well, I hope they get someone as good as you on the piano.' They walked down the stairs to the rear entrance together. 'That was real class tonight, Hannes, my boy. You're a talent, you know.' Hannes chuckled politely, the sort of polite chuckle, Clara thought, that told her he knew full well just how talented he was. They paused at the door, Clara tying her shawl in a knot, pulling it over her head. 'So, hello and goodbye, Hannes Kreisler.' Then she kissed him, as a sort of goodbye present, really, and because he had been nice to her, one of her full kisses, with her tongue deep in his mouth, to give him something to remember her by, and she let him fumble and squeeze for a while at her breasts before she pushed him away with a laugh, clapped him on the shoulder and said, 'That's enough for you, my young fellow, I'm off to my bed.'

It was funny how everything could change in a year, Clara thought, as she wandered through Alster Arcade looking at the fine stores. She liked to do this before she went down to St Pauli for her evening's work. '47 had been, well, not too bad, but '48? . . . My God, not so good. If only Herr Knipe hadn't died. If only Frau Schäfer hadn't gone to live with her son in Hildesheim, if only the baby had been healthier, not so many doctors needed. Money. All she thought about was money. And everywhere there was revolution, they said, and all she could think about was money. She looked at her reflection in the plate glass window of Vogts & Co. She should put a bit more weight back on: the gentlemen didn't like skinny girls these days. She sighed and went to stand in a patch of sunlight 'to warm my tired old bones,' she told herself, with a chuckle, 'for a moment or two'.

There was a big piano store across the street, the pianos in the window lustrous and glossy, their lids up, the grained wood agleam with wax polish. The early summer warmth meant that the double doors of the shop were thrown open and she could hear over the noise of the cabs and the horse trams the demonstrator inside playing away at a waltz. Dum dee dee, dum dee dee . . . Good God in Heaven, she thought, that's my waltz.

It was little Hannes Kreisler all right, Clara saw, though not so little any more, the back was broader, the jaw squarer, the hair longer, if anything, playing away on the small stage in the centre of the great emporium, but he wasn't calling himself Hannes Kreisler, these days. The fancy copperplate on the placard that advertised the demonstrator's name (and his address for piano lessons) read 'Karl Wurth'.

Clara strolled into the shop, grateful that it was busy, thinking that with a bit of luck no one would tell her to leave for a while. A small crowd stood in a semicircle around 'Karl Wurth', listening to him play. It was her waltz, that was true, but it was different also, the tune was freer: it kept changing, changing pace and rhythm and then coming back to the original notes. She edged closer, watching Hannes play, seeing that he was reading music, there were sheets propped in front of him, concentrating, staring at the notes. The music grew faster and then finished in a kind of a gallop and a series of shuddering chords, not like a waltz at all. He slowly took his hands away from the keyboard. There was applause and Hannes looked round with his fleeting smile and gave a small dipping bow before he stood up and stepped away from the piano, taking his sheet music and removing the placard with his new name.

'Well, hey, if it isn't the famous pianist Herr Karl Wurth,' Clara said, tugging at his coat tail. He turned and recognized her at once, she saw, and that pleased her. 'Clara,' he said, 'what a surprise.' 'How's the nut,' Clara said reaching up and tapping his forehead. 'How's the brain-ache?' 'Much better,' Hannes said. 'I spent last summer at Winsen. Perfect. Full recovery. Do you know it?' 'Winsen? Oh I'm never away from the place,' Clara said. 'That was my waltz you were playing. You've even written it down.' He had rolled his sheet music up into a tight baton. 'Here,' he said, handing it to her. 'It's a present.' 'How will you play it, if you give it to me?' she said. 'Oh, it needs improving. I'll do some more work. It's all up here,' he touched his head, lightly. 'So, Clara, still at Knipe's *Lokal*?' he asked. 'He's dead,' Clara said, 'Tuberculosis. It all changed. I've moved – to a place on Kastanienallee. They could do with a decent pianist, I can tell you. So if you're looking for a position, I'll put in a good word.'

Hannes was about to speak but another boy appeared beside him, carrying a music case. 'And who might this charming young lady be?' the boy said. He had lively, mobile features, dark hair and a pointed chin. 'This is Clara,' Hannes said. 'An old friend. And this is my brother Fritz. Who's late.' 'My apologies,' Fritz said, and bowed to Clara. 'He – that one –' pointing at Hannes, 'is a slave driver,' he said and stepped up on to the stage and opened his case, taking out sheets of music. 'I have to leave,' Hannes said. 'I've a lesson to give.' 'We all have to earn a living,' Clara said. 'On you go. I'll look at the pianos.' They shook hands. 'What's the name of your *Lokal*?' Hannes said, lowering his voice, 'Maybe I'll pass by.' She wanted to tell him but she decided not to. 'Oh no, it's not the place for you, Hannes Kreisler Karl Wurth.' 'I'll find it,' he said. 'Kastanienallee isn't so big. I probably worked in it. I worked in a lot of these places.' So she told him the name: Flügel's. What was wrong with that, she argued, he was almost a man, he was earning some money, why should she turn away the chance of earning some money herself? 'Please take this,' he said, handing her his scroll of sheet music again. 'A souvenir.' She took it from him. 'See you soon, Clara,' he said, but they both knew that was very unlikely, still, you never could tell about a man and his appetites. 'For sure,' she said, 'Come by any time after six. We'll have a dance.'

She managed to look at the pianos for a few minutes before one of the floor managers asked her to leave. As she walked past the demonstrator's stage Fritz Wurth smiled at her and nodded goodbye. Except his name wasn't Fritz Wurth at all, she now saw as she glanced at his placard, it was Fritz Brahms. Brahms. What were they like, these boys? First Kreisler, then Wurth, now Brahms – it was all a game to them.

She rode in the omnibus down to St Pauli, trying not to think of the floor manager's expression as he had asked her to leave. To distract herself she unrolled the sheet music Hannes had given her. Hannes had been kind, decent, he had remembered her. All written by hand, too, the little squiggly black scratching of the notes. How can they play from that? His brother had been polite also. She read the title slowly, her lips moving as she formed the words: 'Fantasia on a Favourite Waltz'. A souvenir. A nice gesture. She said it out loud, softly: *'Phantasie über einem beliebten Walzer'* . . . There were some decent people about in the world, not many, but a few of them. Hannes. It was a good name, that, short for Johannes . . . Yes, maybe that was what she should call the baby. Hannes Billroth.

She was still musing on the baby's new name when she arrived at Herr Flügel's *Lokal*. Hannes Billroth – it had a ring to it. It was only when she took her position by the bar, and the pianist started thundering away noisily at a boring old polka, that she realized she had left the music behind her in the horse tram. It made her angry at her carelessness, for a moment or two, before she asked herself what she could possibly do with such a manuscript anyway, and certainly that ape pounding away on the piano wouldn't have been able to make head nor tail of it, not something so delicate and beautiful. *Phantasie über einem beliebten Walzer*. I ask you. Head nor tail.

The Ghost of a Bird

Thursday

Patient 39 was admitted this morning. I put him in the ground-floor room of the Belvedere wing, the one that gives on to the herb garden. I didn't see him myself, but the nurses said he was comfortable and that he ate a little treacle sponge and custard. We had been told that he had begun to speak since emerging from the coma, but he didn't utter a word.

The facts as we know them. Patient 39: male, early twenties. Discovered naked and unconscious after the heavy fighting at Villers-Bocage, near Caen, on June 12 1944. No identification was found on him, but he is most likely British, judging from his dental work, though it's conceivable he could be German. He showed general scorching and contusions over his body. His feet were badly burned and his left side over the ribs, second degree, and there were copious shrapnel wounds on his back and buttocks. According to the preliminary records seventy-four men were reported killed in action that day in the battle at Villers-Bocage, sixteen are missing believed killed, thirty-four bodies remain to be identified (owing to the ferocity of heat in the burned-out tanks). Enemy casualties are not known. We must also consider the possibility of baled-out aircrew, USAF and RAF. But the short odds are that he is a British soldier.

The wound. A piece of shrapnel entered the right parieto-occipital area of the cranium and lodged there. Resulting inflammation caused adhesions of the brain to the meninges and engendered further trauma to adjacent tissues including the left hemisphere of the brain. The shrapnel was removed in the field hospital but the inflammation has provoked irreversible damage to posterior regions of the left and right hemispheres. The scar tissue has stimulated a partial atrophy of the medulla. Prognosis? Very difficult.

Friday

I saw Patient 39 today for the first time. He was sitting in the herb garden in his dressing gown staring intently at a clump of tall blue salvia that was shifting sinuously to and fro in the gentle breeze. I picked a flower and handed it to him. He tilted his head noticeably in order to focus on it (there must be problems with vision). I said the word 'flower' to him several times. When I tried to take it away from him he would not let me.

He looks very young, does Patient 39, no more than a boy. The scarring on the back of his head is intensive, very buckled. I told the nurses that we could let his hair grow back, now.

Tuesday

Patient 39 recognizes me, it seems. He canted his head and smiled when I came into the room today. He is eating normally (but only with a spoon) and his bowel movements are regular. His burns have healed; the wounds in his back also. From the neck down he is a healthy young man.

I placed a paper and pencil in front of him to see if he would make any mark or sign. He picked up the pencil and rolled it in his fingers as if he were enjoying the friction of its hexagonal shape on the palps of his fingertips. He looked at me and said one word: 'flower'. This was the first word he had spoken since he arrived here.

I showed him how to use the pencil but I could see that the effort of making a mark on the paper was immense. He managed some tiny cursive squiggles, very faint as if he was afraid to press down too hard.

Tuesday Night

The salvia's stem is ridged, square in section. This must be the pencil–flower link. After he had made his tiny marks on the page I noticed him smelling his fingers. Touch, smell . . . If the vision is very partial perhaps the route to take is a stimulation of the other senses.

Thursday

He started speaking again today. Disconnected words. I wrote them down.

'I feel . . . I feel . . .'

'Wednesday night . . . Make it Wednesday night.'

'*Je t'aime pour toujours.*'

'My head is very . . . Hurting me.'

Then he pursed his lips and whistled, tunelessly. Then he started to repeat a name, mumbling it at first.

'Sylvie.'

Then back to Wednesday, Wednesday and then, 'I feel my head is very hurting me.' It was a sentence of sorts.

'Who is Sylvie?' I asked him. He couldn't answer and I saw sudden tears form in his eyes so I pushed him no further.

It was like seeing an ancient rusted engine trying to splutter into life: a spark, a piston turns, a fart of exhaust smoke. And then nothing.

Sylvie/salvia – of course. The French phrase was odd: but he's clearly English with an educated accent. A young officer? A tank commander? I've sent the information I've gleaned and the few precise facts – height, weight, colour of eyes, colour of hair – to the War Office.

Friday

I played Patient 39 some music today. The adagio from Rachmaninov's Second Symphony. He listened with huge concentration. When I took the needle from the disc he seemed as if he wanted to say something.

'It's very . . .' He stalled, as if searching his mental lexicon for the right word. He shrugged.

'Beautiful?' I said.

'Beautiful?' The word meant nothing to him. Then he smiled. 'It's very *dry*,' he said, with a look of triumph on his face.

The words are coming, but at random and with associations of meaning that I can't identify.

This afternoon when I looked in on him on my usual round of the hospital he seemed unusually alert.

'I need a bicycle,' he said.

'A bicycle? Why?'

He thought for a while. 'I don't know,' he said. Then he sat down at the table and drew something on the sheet of paper. He showed it to me: two wobbly circles joined by a bar – a rudimentary, schematic bicycle, certainly. Then he remembered something and added two looped, L-shaped extensions.

'A bicycle,' he insisted.

I told the nurses to book in an optician for the next day.

Wednesday

Patient 39 has his spectacles yet he still tilts his head to see. The optician said he had done his best but the prescription was something of an estimation. The spectacles make him look younger, if that were possible, but Patient 39 seems glad to have them – as if he had reclaimed some vestige of his old self from the time before the trauma suffered in the battle. He handles them carefully; he looks at his face in the mirror as if he sees someone he vaguely recognizes.

We had something approaching a conversation.

ME: How are you?
39: I'm, yes, I feel . . . I feel I am . . .
ME: Better?
39: I'm sorry. I don't know.
ME: Would you like to go for a walk?
39: I don't know.
ME: Who's Sylvie?
39: Sylvie . . . Sylvie . . . She's . . . She's Sylvie.
ME: Is she your wife?
39: I don't know.

He sat for a while thinking, then he stood and led me outside. It was one of those late summer mornings, full of sunshine yet with a coolness in the air, a presaging current of the cold days to come. He pointed up at the sky.

'What is that?'

'Sky?'

'No, what is that?' he made a spreading motion with both his hands.

'That is blue. The colour blue.'

'Blue.' He thought about this for a second or two and said, 'Sylvie is blue.'

Tuesday

The papers came from the War Office. It seemed conclusive evidence so I went to find Patient 39. He was on the south lawn walking along a gravelled path, occasionally stooping to stare at something – an insect, a quartz pebble – that caught his attention.

When I was about ten yards away, I called out.

'Gerald?'

There was no reaction.

'Lieutenant Gault? Lieutenant Gault?'

He still didn't turn, so I circled round and came back down the path so he could see me. I asked him how he was.

'I feel . . .' he thought. 'Feel fine. Yes, fine.'

I told him papers had arrived from the ministry.

'We think we know who you are,' I pointed at him. 'We know your name.'

'My name?'

'Yes. Your name is Gerald Gault. You are twenty-three years old. Your family live near Thame, in Oxfordshire.'

He smiled at me. His eyes were candid, his expression mildly interested. It was apparent I might have well been talking Gaelic.

'Are you sure?'

Thursday

I know a great deal about Lt Gerald Gault of the 4th County of London Yeomanry. I now have photographs of him at various stages of his life. I have his school reports. I have the details of his army medical. I have several letters he wrote to his mother and father (he is an only child). I have a copy of *Penguin New Writing* containing his short story 'The Ghost of a Bird'. I can track his life from nursery to prep school (where his father was headmaster) to his minor public school. He did not go to university but joined the army in 1941 at the age of nineteen. After Sandhurst he saw active service in North Africa then was shipped home to England in 1943 with bad pneumonia. It was during his convalescence that he began writing.

'The Ghost of a Bird' was published in early 1944 when Gerald Gault had begun training with his regiment for the invasion of Europe. It is a strange, almost surreal tale (therefore not entirely to my taste) about a young English soldier in the North African campaign who, lost and separated from his unit, comes across the body of a dead German in the desert. He takes the personal papers from the body and amongst them finds the photograph of a girl. On this photo is written: '*Je t'aime pour toujours, Sylvie.*' In a series of overlapping hallucinations the soldier has a short but intense love affair with this Sylvie. It's not entirely clear, but the likelihood is that the soldier then dies of thirst. The narrative point of view changes. Back in England, the young soldier's parents receive a small bundle of their son's personal effects: amongst them is the photograph of Sylvie. The boy's parents are consoled by the thought that at least during their son's short life he had been in love and had been loved in return.

The pages detailing the fancied affair with Sylvie are rapt and overcharged. Gerald Gault is clearly a virgin.

Monday

Mr and Mrs Gault sat anxiously in my consulting room as I explained the many handicaps their son was suffering from as a result of his brain injury: extreme memory loss, traumatic aphasia, partial vision. Mr Gault was a rosy-faced, bald man, trimly moustachioed. Mrs Gault, a handsome woman with a sharp patrician accent, wore pearl earrings and a pearl necklace. I imagined she had had great plans for Gerald.

'He can't see?' Mr Gault asked.

I explained: as far as we could tell only half of Gerald Gault's field of vision was functioning. 'If he looked at a page of a book he would only see the left half. He can read but it takes considerable effort: you'll notice how he moves his head to bring the seeing half of his field of vision into play. He has to piece together the visual world he occupies, just as he has to struggle to make his verbal world comprehensible.'

'How long before he gets better?' Mrs Gault interrupted.

'We have no idea.' I paused. It's always best to be a little blunt on these occasions. 'I should warn you: it's almost a hundred per cent certain he won't know who you are.'

Mrs Gault laughed at my preposterous assertion.

Tuesday

I took Gerald to the Star and Garter at noon today. He was wearing his own clothes (brought by his parents). The pub was quiet, and the wide unmatted flagstones of the dark snug-bar made the room cool. I brought him a pint of bitter and offered him a cigarette. He used to smoke, apparently, but he refused and when he saw me light up and exhale it made him smile. 'I can see the air you breathe,' he explained.

Mrs Gault had accepted a cigarette in my consulting room after her collapse. As she smoked I could sense her discomfort growing: her shame at her behaviour crept up on her, obliterating her misery like an advancing tide. She became curt and hostile towards me. Not that I blamed her: even I still find the memory of Mrs Gault's shocked response to Gerald's absence of reaction as she greeted her son disturbing. How she wilted before his candid, oblivious stare as she uttered his name and touched his face – and how she screamed and wailed as we struggled to lead her away – but Gerald clearly had no idea what was going on.

He sipped his beer.

'Good,' he said. 'I like it.'

'You know the war will soon be over,' I said.

'I was hurt in this war.'

'Yes . . . Can you remember how you were hurt?'

He frowned. 'I remember the sky. How it was . . . blue. And how it was not cold.'

'Hot.'

'Yes . . . Hot. And Sylvie was there.'

Heat. The desert? Or memories of his burning tank? An account of the action at Villers-Bocage places Gerald Gault and his Cromwell in the middle of a line of tanks ambushed in a Normandy lane by the 501st SS Heavy Tank Battalion. The German Tigers were impervious to British return fire and the column of British tanks was severely mauled. Many tanks, unable to move in the narrow lanes, blazed fiercely before exploding. Gerald was seen climbing from his tank, his uniform on fire. And then the tank erupted in a billowing fireball. Whether his clothes were ripped from him by the explosion or whether he removed them himself is not clear. The wound in his head was caused later, it seems likely, when another tank near by exploded, hurling him through a hedge (many wood splinters were removed from his body) into a field beyond, where he was discovered later in the day when the Germans temporarily withdrew. Twenty-five British tanks were destroyed that afternoon and twenty-eight other tracked vehicles.

I bought him another pint and asked him some more questions about his parents. I could see him struggling to fit the vague memories of these strangers' visit into the concepts of 'mother' and 'father' – concepts that did at least seem somehow familiar to him.

'She was my mother . . .'

'Is your mother. They came yesterday,' I prompted. 'She became very upset. Do you remember?'

Then he stood up.

'Please, I have to go . . .' He touched his groin.

The lavatory of the Star and Garter was in a whitewashed lathe and plaster shed on the edge of the small carpark at the rear. I lead Gerald through the saloon bar and down a shadowy passageway to the back door and steered him into the odorous gents.

'I'll see you in the bar,' I said. 'I'll order some sandwiches.'

The meagre sandwiches arrived but there was no sign of Gerald. I looked into the gents but he had gone. Then I saw him across the road some thirty yards off and called his name.

'There you are,' he said, relieved, coming over. 'I couldn't find.'

'Did you come back to the pub?'

'The pub?'

'Where we had our drinks.'

'I'm sorry, I don't know.'

I took him back inside and showed him our coats, our drinks and the stiffening rounds of sandwiches. It distressed him to see how quickly he had forgotten everything, how quickly the residue of fresh impressions was wiped away, allowing no memory of a way back to form, even one so recent as a few minutes ago.

We walked back to the hospital each in a deep and preoccupied silence. I was thinking that this severe short-term memory crisis made a solitary life virtually impossible to lead: Gerald Gault could lose himself and his known world within seconds.

Preliminary Diagnosis

Patient 39 (Lt Gerald Gault) is severely handicapped, though at first glance this does not seem apparent to the casual observer. The damage to the posterior sections of his brain has incapacitated his ability to process, analyse and retain information. Despite the patchiness of his field of vision, Patient 39, with effort, can see. It is in his understanding of what he sees that the problem lies. He can see a middle-aged man and a woman but cannot recognize them as his parents.

The injury has also affected his use of language. He can retain bits of information. He knows when he needs to go to the lavatory but having gone there cannot piece together the route back. His life has become an endless series of labyrinths.

Wednesday

Gerald sat in a deckchair in the herb garden. He was leaning back looking up at the patches of blue sky between the swift clouds.

'What day is it?' he asked.

'Wednesday.'

'I think it was on a Wednesday that I was hurt.'

'Can you finish this sequence? Monday, Tuesday, Wednesday –'

'– Thursday, Friday, Saturday, Sunday, Monday.'

'Excellent. Now what day comes before Friday?'

'I don't know.'

'Never mind.'

We sat quietly for a while.

'When I see blue I think of Sylvie.'

'Why?'

'Because of the desert, when I was lost.'

Saturday

Mr and Mrs Gault came again today and spent an hour or so with their son. Gerald had understood enough of their relationship (I had explained again who they were, why they wanted to see him) to address them as mother and father, but it was clear this was an act of *politesse* rather than affirmation that anything had changed.

The great difficulty – perhaps tragedy would be a better word – with Gerald is that the frontal lobes and anterior sectors of his brain remain undamaged: thus he still has the capacity to recognize his defects. He knows how badly he is damaged and how his world was fractured and he struggles, as much as his strength permits, to overcome his problem. I can see how intensely he suffers as he tries to reconstitute his world and his life. Yet in a deep sense he remains a man, a human being.

Monday

I took Gerald to the cinema today, to a matinee. We watched an anodyne film about a young couple falling in and out of love before love triumphed at the end. I told Gerald to squeeze my arm when he didn't understand what was happening. Not a very scientific experiment, but from the almost continuous pressure on my arm it was apparent to me that only the very simplest acts of everyday life – walking down the street, opening a door, getting out of bed – made any sense to him. The rest was incomprehensible. When at the end the couple duly made up and kissed he was still baffled.

Later, walking back to the hospital we tried to analyse what the difficulty was.

'Everything was so fast,' he said.

'What about the girl?'

'Yes, I liked her.'

'Did Sylvie look like her?'

He nodded his head vigorously as he thought.

'Yes . . . I think the same . . .' He touched my hair.

'Hair. Sylvie had blonde hair?'

'Blonde hair. Yes.'

Wednesday

Gerald has been trying to write. He handed me these lines today, product of several days' effort.

'My name is Gerald Gault, I am twenty-three years old. Sometimes I get sad at how pathetic my life is. But I want to prove I am not a lost cause, that my life is not hopeless. I need to learn to remember. I need to have the kind of mind I had before I was hurt. I need to find Sylvie so we can be together again. When I am together with Sylvie I will be a man like other men. We will get married and we will live in a house by the sea. We will have two children – a boy and a girl. We will be very happy.'

Sunday Night

I was called out to see Gerald. He had asked for me most insistently, the nurse said. When I went into his room he was in his pyjamas and dressing gown.

'My head is hurting me,' he said. 'Things are changing in my head.'

'I don't think so, Gerald,' I reassured him. 'Every day you grow a little better. You're beginning to write. Slowly, slowly you're beginning to understand more.'

He delicately touched the back of his head where the scars were. 'No, I think . . .'

'Show me where your nose is, Gerald.'

He looked at me. 'Nose?'

'Point to your eye.'

He screwed up his face. He was like a man in a dark room looking for something precious he'd lost. If only he could switch on a light.

'My eye . . . I don't know.'

I ordered a sedative and the nurse put him back to bed. Just as I was leaving he said, 'When is Sylvie coming to see me?'

'One day soon.'

'I want to see the blue sky and Sylvie, like in the desert.'

I went back over to him.

'Do you remember the desert?'

'When I was with Sylvie, yes. The sky was very blue.'

'Do you remember the dead soldier? The German soldier?'

'No. Sylvie was there. She said: *"Je t'aime pour toujours."*'

I looked down at him. He took his spectacles off, folded them and laid them on the bedside table. He smiled, happy with his memories of Sylvie.

'Goodnight, Doctor Moran,' he said.

Monday

Gerald Gault died in the night of a massive brain haemorrhage. I went to look at his body and as far as I could tell it appeared as if his death had been both instantaneous and dramatic. His mouth was slightly open and there was a perceptible arch to his brows as if he had been caught in the middle of uttering a phrase such as 'Oh, really?' or 'How interesting!' I telephoned his parents and was glad to speak to his father, though half way through our short conversation I could hear Mrs Gault's choking, throat-raking sobs in the background as she guessed from her husband's expression and his posture – the hunched shoulders, the back half turned – what the news must have been.

I went out into the hospital gardens and strolled the gravelled pathways for ten minutes or so. Building blue-grey clouds in the east screened the morning sun, though occasionally sharp and vivid passages of blue meant that the lawns and arbours were bathed in sudden sunlight. A fresh sturdy breeze moved the tops of the elms and the ash trees where they lined the small stream and the noise of their growing whisper masked the domestic drone of an aircraft coming into land at the RAF base. Impromptu currents of air shook the rhododendron bushes and the laurels, making them shudder and thrash as if some beast were trapped or lurked behind their dense leaves. Pentecostal, I thought, or valedictory? And for a moment I allowed myself to picture this agitation of late-summer wind as Gerald Gault's soul taking final leave of the hospital and its precincts.

Gerald Gault's soul. Patient 39's soul . . . What did it add up to? In the few weeks that I had known him it was plain to me that Gerald's case – his peculiar and particular agonies – was among the most complex and perplexing that I had ever seen. That part of his undamaged brain that most sustained him had been a memory of something his imagination had once produced. His imagination had not been damaged by the shrapnel that had penetrated the back of his head and what became real to Gerald Gault was a consoling phantasm, a dream, an urgent wish. It was more solid and tangible to him than the fragmented physical world that he found so hard to shape and comprehend.

A love of the colour blue and false memories of a non-existent girl called Sylvie were all that remained of Gerald Gault after his terrible injury: such fragile, ephemeral foundations – too insubstantial a thing to build a new life on? Perhaps that is all any of us require. As I walked back to my office I saw a thrush stabbing at worms on the cloud-shadowed lawn. Patients were being urged indoors by the nurses. A door banged somewhere. The wind tugged at my tie and jacket and spots of rain began to patter on my uplifted face.

The Mind/Body Problem

He looks at his father. His father is on the phone confirming the bus to the airport. One hand holds the phone, the other a 20 lb barbell. His father, a huge man, is wearing tiny swimming trunks that only just contain his buckled genitalia. He turns his hairless, tapered caramel body to reveal that one buttock has freed itself from its sling of magenta spandex.

He looks at his mother. His mother puts the finishing touches to her meal replacement drink: she adds two sliced bananas and sets the blender to pulse.

His name is Neil Tobin (it's the same name as his father, annoyingly). He is nineteen years old, six feet tall, weighs nine stone four, and suffers from asthma, psoriasis and, he's now almost 100 per cent sure, some form of near-persistent arrhythmia in his heart. He takes out his inhaler and gives himself a couple of squirts. His mother, Tanya Tobin (she's American), comes in to the conservatory where he's sunbathing and asks him yet again if he's sure about the gym, honey. Yes, I'm sure, he says.

Open University course A211 – Philosophy and the Human Situation. Summer holiday essays are a choice between 'Can minds exist independently of matter?' and 'Are minds really nothing but matter?' He knows what this is. This is the mind/body problem.

The coach is full of bodybuilders, male and female, members of Neil and Tanya Tobin's gym/health club 'Body's East'. The proprietors stand outside the bus in their trainers and track suits bidding farewell to their son. The bodybuilders are off to Florida for two weeks and will then fly to Las Vegas for the finals of Mr and Ms Olympia. Neil reassures his mother that he'll be fine. The club'll be quiet, Tanya observes, as most of its regular members are travelling to Florida for the finals. Neil agrees, bids them farewell, kissing his mother, shaking his father's big hand. Enjoy, enjoy.

Neil begins his reading: 'In philosophy the mind/body problem asks the question whether there is a mental sphere of existence separate from the physical sphere, and if so, how do the two interact? If I cut my finger how does my mind know it hurts?'

'So,' says Lion Davy, looking knowingly at Xanna North, 'We got a new boss.'
　'Yeah. You'd better watch your step, Lionel,' Neil says.
　'Lion.'
　'Lionel.'
　'If you call me Lionel you have to call her Sandra.'

Neil adds some Angostura bitters to the glucose mixture until it turns a pale pink. He tastes it: suitably unpleasant and astringent. He reaches for his Portuguese dictionary and, on his label machine, types out: 'NAO PARA VENDA COMERCIAL' and sticks it on the plastic bottle. He suspects that the injunction is ungrammatical but he doesn't care, the foreign languages always work. He'll say it comes from Brazil. He puts the bottle with the others in the cupboard under the reception desk and locks it with his key.

As his mother predicted the gym is indeed quiet. The ranked machines – the ab-benches, leg-presses, stair-climbers, the squat racks, the cycles, the steppers, the treadmills – stand idle. Someone comes in for a Jacuzzi. Xanna's aerobics class at ten o'clock has three clients (school holidays). Lion spends his day polishing, dusting, waxing the floor. He used to be a cleaner until he started to work on his body.

'One more extreme position argues that human bodies are simply a form of complex machine (today we might rather say physico-chemical system) working purely according to physical principles. In such a depiction of the human being there is no room for consciousness, as we would routinely describe it.'

Later, Neil passes an hour on the net looking vainly for a prescription skin cream with a mild water-based cortisone. He's grown some-what suspicious of the heavy cortisone creams his dermatologist happily prescribes. Neil is sensing a thinning of the skin, not to say aggravation, of those hard-to-treat plaques of psoriasis that badge his body (the elbows, the backs of the knees, the baffling, spreading patch an inch to the left of his navel).

For want of other clients he sells Xanna his Brazilian steroid drink for £18 (staff discount).

'It's brilliant, apparently,' Neil says.

'Where you get this stuff?' Xanna asks. 'Nao para venda . . . What's that mean?'

'I track it down on the web. Then I source it through my contacts.'

Xanna turns away, already twisting off the cap. 'New member's in,' she says.

Neil heads up the stairs for the gym with the new member's membership swipe card. The name on the card says D. Babcock. In the gym he sees Lion and three of the usual regulars – Chuck, Dave, Nigel – on the weights. He mouths 'new member' to Lion and is pointed towards the far corner by the big floor-to-ceiling window that looks obliquely out on the promenade and the English Channel beyond, grey like streets. D. Babcock turns out to be a young woman. She's doing a barbell squat and Neil can see that not only is she shredded, she's big, damn big.

'We can think of ourselves biologically and we can think of ourselves historically. The idea that we can conceive of ourselves in any transcendental way is nonsense. Everything we know about our nature is the product of our limited experience and all too fallible biology.'

Body's East draws the serious male and female bodybuilder from a large catchment area – as far as Brighton in the west and Dover in the east (as well as the bread-and-butter aerobics/health-club crowd). Tanya has modelled the club on Floridan enterprises where she used to live and work and both she and Neil Snr put its renown and success (the Tobins make a good living) down to the slick US feel (its can-do efficiency, the piped music, the incredibly friendly staff) that they have aped here on the south coast of England. But Neil Jnr knows that many people patronize the club for all the exotic grey-market supplements he secretly supplies from 'abroad'.

The new member (showered, changed) comes into the shop where Neil is refilling shelves with supplements, protein boosters, RTGs and MRPs. She buys a can of XXX-POWR-FUEL.

'Is this any good?' she asks

'Well,' Neil says, 'it has protein stacked with Ectdysteron – which is useful – and there's no high cyclamic index maltodextrins. After your workout you need a good osmotic, glycogen load carb source. It's not bad. We have our own house brand – better.'

'Right. Yeah . . .'

He can spout this kind of detail for hours. Neil hands over her change and introduces himself. She tells him her name – the D stands for Doreen, Doreen Babcock. He talks to her about the gym, the services they offer, and hints at the possibilities of acquiring bodybuilding supplements not available without prescription. I get them from abroad, Neil says, meaningful: Mexico, the former Soviet Union, the Eastern Bloc . . . She looks intrigued. She's very small, barely five feet, and in her loose sportswear her muscle mass is mainly concealed. Many of the serious women bodybuilders, Neil has noticed, are extremely petite – his mother being a case in point. Doreen's corded throat and the dilated bas-relief trees of her vascular system (on her neck, her forearms) show the effort she puts in. Her jaw muscles bulge and broaden what would have been a pretty face with a snub nose – if she weren't looking so drawn from her exercise. She has a small shading of acne just below her ears – a real give-away. Neil knows what she's doing to herself and what she's taking. She's going for a competition cut: massive fat-burn, maximum definition. He wonders if she's a pro. Her dyed blonde hair is naturally curly and her accent is local. She's been recently transferred from Brighton: she works in Barclays Bank on Teasdale Street.

A couple of days later Neil goes into the Barclays Bank and moves his account there from the HSBC. Doreen Babcock is a personal account executive and she looks smart in her official navy blazer and skirt. The material of her jacket strains across her broad, tapered back but her legs, Neil observes, are surprisingly slim and normal. In her uniform she looks top heavy, unsteady on her very high heels. Neil has almost £10,000 in his account. They make a date for a drink later that evening.

Back in the club Neil tries to make a start on 'Can minds exist independently of matter?' but finds it hard going. As far as he can determine, at this early stage, the mind/body problem provides you with a choice of three fundamental positions (three positions with many sub-positions of increasing complexity). You can believe that there is nothing but mind; you can believe there is nothing but body (or matter, or physical substance); or you can believe that both exist. He reads on, but with decreasing concentration: he keeps thinking of Doreen Babcock. Later, he sells £200 worth of GH.DYASIC.250 tablets to a man (a friend of Dave) who says he's come down from London specially. The man asks, lowering his voice, if he can get this new Hungarian-manufactured human growth hormone that he's read about in one of the underground magazines. Neil says he wouldn't touch that Hungarian stuff but he can get him SOMABLOK. What's that? The man says. It blocks somastatin: it's the best, Neil avers, simply. I'm the only place you can find it in the UK, but it's pricey. The man orders £500 worth.

That evening in the pub, The Golden Anchor, Doreen asks for a fizzy mineral water. Neil orders his usual vodka and tonic. Doreen studies the rubric on the bottle, checking the electrolytes and trace minerals. 'I need more zinc,' she says. Then she takes about nine pills, as far as Neil can count, glugging them down with swigs from the bottle.

'Are you using gear?' he asks, knowing the answer.

'Yes,' she says. 'Do I look that freaky?'

'What's your stack?'

'AQLASTERON.'

Neil winces. 'That's a monster. You take these unadulterated AAS products. You're asking for trouble.'

'AAS? AS, surely.'

'Anabolic-Androgenic Steroids. That's what they are. You know what anabolic means?'

'Of course: muscle-building.'

'You're building muscle with synthetic testosterone. That's where the androgenic comes in: "man-making". You have to be careful. Men and women – all sorts of things start to happen.'

'Well, it works.'

'I can get you something better than AQLASTERON, something called TESTOMAX. No side effects.'

For the first time Doreen Babcock looks at him with genuine interest.

'*Cogito ergo sum*. Wittgenstein: If a man says to me, looking at the sky, "I think it will rain, therefore I exist," I do not understand him.'

Neil walks Doreen to her bus stop through the orange glare of the promenade lights. The glow makes Doreen's skin look a jaundiced yellow, her acne spots like dark freckles. Neil pauses to use his inhaler.

'Are those dermal patches?' Neil points at the round sticking plaster on her calves. 'I couldn't help noticing.'

'I'm injecting there,' she says. Since their TESTOMAX conversation Doreen has opened up about her steroid cycle.

'Site-specific fat burner?'

'An oil.'

'Jesus. You must be desperate.'

'Yeah. It's not working, either. I need to bulk my calves, fast – the oil seemed the only way.'

'Lagging muscle group?'

Doreen nods. She seems close to tears, suddenly, as they walk on in silence. Neil makes a vow: I am going to save this girl from herself.

'Cut out the oils,' he says. 'I've got this amazing fat burner: a gel.'

Neil boils up a thousand branded analgesics in a saucepan, just enough for the logo to disappear. Then he spreads them on a tea towel and rakes his fingers through them to speed the drying. The partial boiling takes off the pill's industrial sheen and makes them look cruder, more home-made. Neil's great revelation was the discovery that many bodybuilders are attracted by bad packaging. The true supplement searcher wants something that looks smuggled, contraband, under-the-counter: the more makeshift the packaging therefore the more authentically illicit and potent, so the formula goes. Neil prints out on his home-printing set: 'TESTO-MAX: BEISPIEL NUR ZU VERKAUFEN', and sticks the label on a small, oblong, utterly plain, recycled-paper pillbox . . . He'll get Doreen on to this stack tomorrow.

That night he lies in bed listening to his heartbeat through his stethoscope. Ba-dum, ba-dum, ba-dum-dum-dum-dum, ba-dum, ba-dum. Both his parents, he knows, when they were semi-pro bodybuilders in competition in the 1970s and '80s, were regular anabolic steroid users. He has heard them extol the values of smuggled Mexican steroids and their astonishing cheapness – a vial of DECA for $2.75 (they used to inject their AAS quota in those days). He was born in 1984. A year before his mother won the NPC Junior USA championship. He sees the photographs every day when he enters the gym, sees his mother's white smile as she holds the columned trophy aloft, sees also the perfect cross-striation on her biceps and thigh muscles. Tanya was ripped, peeled to perfection. He is the steroid progeny of two carefree steroid users and he knows this is the source of his asthma, his psoriasis, his allergies – and now the changing rhythm of his heart. He feels a rage build within him. He knows what this is, too, an anger peculiar to those who use supplements: 'roid-rage', they call it. He lets the roid-rage rinse through him for a while, then calms himself with the knowledge of all the good work he is doing down here in the south-east of England.

'Gilbert Ryle argued coherently against the idea that the mind was a non-physical entity related in some way to the body. This position was stigmatized by him when he invented the concept of "the ghost in the machine".'

Doreen is now on Neil's regime – his stack. Four TESTOMAX, three times a day, two GH.DYASIX.250 three times a day, his MRPs, his site-specific fat-burner. He has squeezed two tubes of hair gel mixed with some horse liniment into a small jamjar and labelled it 'DERMABLAST'.

In the gym he watches her rub the gel into her calves.

'It's hot,' she says. 'It burns. Brilliant.'

'Careful you don't get it in your eyes,' he warns, 'it can hurt like hell.'

She is truly grateful, she says, as she writes out the cheque for £346. She's clean, he realizes: nothing toxic is going into her body any more – now all he has to do is to cajole her into eating properly.

Mind over matter: Doreen Babcock is going to be his exemplary model.

The day is sunny and warmish but with a gusty breeze off the Channel that makes the small clouds hurry inland, the wide crescent of beach edging the bay mottled with moving shadows. Neil and Doreen find a hollow in the dunes that shelters them from the breeze and spread their travelling rug. Neil does not remove his jeans and t-shirt but Doreen strips off to reveal a small ultramarine bikini. Her body is the colour of varnished oak and probably just as hard, Neil thinks. He has seen so many powerful bodies in the gym that he's no longer surprised by the grotesque distortion of her musculature; but he has also seen enough to realize that she is in formidable shape – the pecs, the delts, the abs, the bis and tris, the glutes, the traps, the hams, the rhombs, the lats and quads. Her balled shoulder muscles are the size of rugby balls. Her breasts have virtually disappeared, Neil notices, from all the testosterone she's taken plus the muscle gain and non-stop fat burn. Her bikini top is more a symbolic gesture to a lost sexual characteristic than a device designed for holding, cupping and concealing.

Neil does not undress because the patch of eczema by his navel is the size of a beermat and is not responding to any of his powerful creams. He notices how relaxed Doreen is with her near nudity; how she settles down on the rug to apply her suntan lotion and, as she does so, she checks with her fingertips – prodding, squeezing – certain muscle groups – her thighs, her abdomen, her hamstrings – almost like a farmer assessing a prize steer. She and her body are at peace, he concludes with some bitterness, while he and his body are involved in a nasty little civil war.

Sometimes he feels he lives in a world of overwhelming materiality. He senses his chest tightening with pressure – Stress? Pollen? Doreen? – and takes a couple of squirts from his inhaler.

Trying to think of something else, trying to return to the world of the mind, he asks Doreen a question.

'Doreen. If I said to you, "I think it is going to rain, therefore I exist," would you understand what I was saying?'

'Of course – specially if you were lying there beside me.'

But Doreen is in an excited mood and doesn't want to explore arcane aspects of Neil's mind/body-problem problem. The TES-TOMAX is working, she claims, really working. She has more energy; her bench presses have increased by 10 lbs in a week, she's less tired after her workouts. She's upped the time she spends on her calf muscles – more weights, more reps – and can boast a half-inch gain already. She stands and shows him. Clenching her lower right leg to reveal the two tensed plates of muscle, like separate frozen chicken breasts, one large, one smaller, under the beige, oiled carapace of her skin.

Lunch. Neil drinks a can of beer, eats a cheese and tomato sandwich. Doreen has a protein shake and three apples. She offers Neil one, but he tells her he is allergic to apples.

They go for a walk along the beach, Doreen walking on tiptoes the whole way, working on those lagging muscle groups in her calves. While they walk she tells him she is going to the States in ten days. She's giving up her job in the bank: she's entering a competition in Orlando, the ANBC Empire Classic.

'Bit drastic, isn't it?' Neil says. 'Won't Barclays take you back?'

'I'm not coming back – not right away – I'm thinking of turning pro,' she says.

'Oh. Right. I thought you might be thinking of that. Yeah . . . Congratulations.'

'There's only one problem,' she confesses. 'I need a new name. I can't be a professional bodybuilder called Doreen Babcock.'

Neil knows what she's asking. 'Leave it to me,' Neil says.

Neil spends that evening analysing and categorizing names of female bodybuilders. Certain key types emerge. The most popular, as far as he could determine, are what he would classify as: German,

Swedish, Girl plus Girl, Trash plus Traditional, Solitaries, Armenian, Slavic, Alphabet Soup, Hooker, Alliterative, Italian, Home-on-the-Range and onomatopoeic. Or any combination of the above. On these principles he draws up some random selections for Doreen: Shona Dalburian, Sunrise Kruger, Maiayani, Vanessa-Anne April, Alamaba, Shirleen Simpson, Trixxxi Olafsen, Nyralene Kowalski, Skyye, Maggie Steelmaster, Omega Dubrovnik, Trish Malateste, Helga Gudrunsdottir, Ludmilla Francis, Yellow, Carrie-Mae Tuesday, Oklahoma Banks, Zonella Zay, Pearleen Gunther, and so on. He compiles a list of what he regards as a hundred acceptable names.

'Opponents of Dualism never succeeded in giving a satisfactory account of the feeling we all have of personal identity. They could not account for the special relationship that exists between the elements that make up a person's mind and that particular physical object which is that person's body.'

'And another thing,' Doreen says, as they walk along the prom towards the restaurant, 'my vascularity is better and I don't get headaches.'

'That's a because TESTOMAX is a natural product,' Neil improvises, 'extracted from a plant, *tibullus terrestris*, that grows along the banks of the Black Sea.'

'You could make a fortune,' she says, 'if you marketed this properly.'

Neil mentally lists the side effects of excessive steroid use in women bodybuilders: coarsening of the skin, acne, stretchmarks, roid-rage, deepening voice, hirsutism, clitoral enlargement, cholesterol increase, headaches, high blood pressure, kidney malfunction, water retention, stomach aches.

'You risk kidney malfunction,' he eventually says.

'But,' she says, 'how do you gain serious muscle-mass, otherwise?'

'Fair point.'

They are scrutinizing the menu in Zebulon, a new restaurant that has opened in the refurbished Grand Hotel. As far as Neil can tell, Zebulon generously offers food from at least seven different cuisines – Pacific Rim, straight Asian, Tex-Mex, English, US, Indian and Italian – and the odd idiosyncratic mix of several, best symbolized by the house sandwich: a bacon, egg and brie ciabatta. Tom Yum prawns with a lime and lemon grass salad sounds good, but he is worried about his creeping shellfish allergy. His eczema patch is the size of a side plate now. Goan chicken curry or the 'Ultimate Nachos' also tempt. Doreen is ready to order.

'Does the chicken caesar salad have anchovies?'

'Yes,' says the waiter, who sounds Russian, 'and you can have extra.'

'Right. I'll have a chicken caesar with extra anchovies but with no chicken, no croutons and no dressing.'

'Ah, anchovies,' Neil says. 'More omega-3 fatty acids. Excellent.'

Neil orders steak and kidney pudding with a flamin' salsa sauce on the side. He takes his list of names out of his pocket and slides it across the table towards her.

Neil walks Doreen across the carpark of Body's East towards her car. She opens the door, turns and kisses him, full on the mouth. His arms go round her and his palms rest on her lats. It's like hugging a wide-screen television. Even in her heels she's seven inches shorter than he is. Their pose is awkward: she flattens her face on his chest, he rests his chin on the top of her head.

'Can you hear it?' he says. 'My heartbeat's irregular.'

She's not listening. She raises her face to him. 'Thank you, Neil,' she says.

'What for?'

'Maggie Steelmaster.'

'What do we see when we look at our fellow human beings? The bulk of their behaviour is as unpredictable as the weather. We intuit that they have mental lives – minds – of one sort or another but beyond that we arrive at perplexity.'

Before she leaves for the States Doreen – as a form of thank-you present – takes Neil to Glyndebourne to see *Cosi fan Tutte*. It is his first opera. Doreen, to his vague surprise, tells him she loves opera and *Cosi* is her favourite. Moreover, she seems familiar with the place – this theatre in a country estate – and knows what to do, what the form is. Neil learns that she usually comes to Glyndebourne with her father – in fact he has given up his ticket for Neil.

In the interval they sit on the lawn with their picnic, Doreen removing the bread from her smoked salmon sandwiches, allowing herself a rare sip or two of Neil's champagne. She has been recently on the sunbed and her even, dense pro-tan is immaculate. Neil tries to imagine her on stage in her micro-kini, ripped and pumped, depilated, dehydrated, oiled and slippery with collagen posing oil, and feels a rare sexual quickening. He reaches for her hand.

'I'm going to miss you,' he says.

She's not listening, her mind's on something else. 'Neil,' she says, 'What's your opinion about beef plasma?'

'For some thinkers, the mind is more confidently and immediately known than anything that is material. If this view is followed it is natural to begin to become sceptical about the very existence of the material world.'

'It seems incredible,' Doreen writes two weeks later, 'but the fact that I came third in Orlando means I now have a sponsor – Busta-Tech. I even have a car! I told the people at Busta-Tech about TESTOMAX – so expect a call! I couldn't have done this without you, Neil (and TESTOMAX!). By the way can you send me some more? If I get a top ten in Ms Olympia I'll be staying on here for a year or so. I'm frying my calves in the gym and it's working, it's really working. Lotsa luv, Maggie.'

*

Neil's tutor, Francis Parkman, hands him back his essay and compliments him on it. Then asks him if he'd like a drink. They stroll across the near-empty campus of Sussex University towards the students' union. As part of his Open University degree Neil is spending a few days at a regional centre meeting tutors and attending seminars. Parkman suggests that he applies to do a degree at the university itself. Neil is flattered but seems unsure. Think about it, Parkman suggests, he's confident something could be sorted out.

In the union bar Parkman brings their drinks over.

'So,' Parkman says, raising his pint in a toast, 'minds can exist independently of matter.'

'Yes,' Neil says. 'And matter can exist independently of minds. I see it every day, believe me.'

'So you're a Dualist.'

'If you say so.'

'Well, you arrived at a conclusion and it was a well-argued essay,' Parkman says. 'What made you come up with the concept of the placebo?'

Neil tries not to think of Maggie Steelmaster. Of Doreen Babcock turned Maggie Steelmaster. 'My parents run a gym,' he says. 'It was just something that occurred to me.'

The job, as the men promised, only takes a day. Neil pays for it himself so his parents have no complaint – but they still can't see what the fuss is about. Neil looks up at the new sign: the same colours – but finally correct. That sign has bugged him for years: he has minded about that sign. Now the gas-flame-blue neon of 'Bodies East' is shimmeringly reflected in the rain-pocked, glossy black puddles of the carpark. One problem solved, at last.

The Pigeon

'You ask me: what is life? That is like asking: what is a carrot?
A carrot is a carrot and that's all there is to it.'
Anton Chekhov

He wakes up at 6.17 a.m. because of the pressure on his bladder
and reaches under the bed for the pot. He sits on the edge of the
bed and raises the hem of his nightshirt and pisses without standing
up – like an old, sick man, he thinks. This summer they would
install a proper lavatory, one that flushed, and they would build
the guest house for the men to sleep in: the women could stay in
the main house. How civilized.

He dresses, pulling on the clothes he discarded on the floor the
previous night. Sometimes an old shirt is more comfortable than a
fresh, new one, he thinks. We're like animals, we prefer our own
familiar smells. He stands in front of the looking glass and runs a
comb through his hair and his beard. His hair seems to be thinning
and he wonders for a moment if that could be a new symptom of
his illness. The thought of becoming bald fills him with horror. He
is only thirty-four, in God's name, yet at times he looks and feels
twice that age. How handsome he was at twenty! How did that
young, burly peasant lad turn into a querulous, pernickety invalid?
His own father has ten times more energy.

Just before he leaves the room he sees Lika's letter on the bedside
table and now he remembers why he went to bed so angry and
why he slept so badly. He picks it up and folds it away in his jacket
pocket. She was trying to tell him something, in her cryptic way,
but he needs some coffee before he can attempt to decode her
flirtatious chatter.

In the breakfast room no plates have been laid out and the lamps are not lit. In the kitchen he can hear Mariushka shouting at someone. Roman? No, Efim – he's not fed the chickens . . .

Olga, the kitchen maid, comes in and gives a little cry of shocked surprise seeing him sitting there at the table.

What's wrong, Olga? he says, keeping the irritation out of his voice. She moves around the room lighting the oil lamps.

Oh, I just didn't expect to see you, sir.

Did you know I was in the house?

Of course, sir, you came a week ago.

And when I'm here do I not come in for breakfast every morning?

Yes, sir, you do.

So, in the morning it's not unreasonable to say that you might expect to see me sitting here waiting for my breakfast.

I don't understand, sir.

Be a good girl and fetch me some coffee.

He takes out Lika's letter and spreads it on the table in front of him.

'Dear naughty uncle, dear gentle daddy, I beg you on my knees to come to Paris where your adoring and adorable Lika needs to see you –'

A scratching on the floor, like a few seeds in an empty gourd, and he looks up to see Quinine, his dachshund, waddle into the room from the kitchen.

Hello, fatso, he says and clicks his fingers. Quinine wanders over and sniffs at his fingers and looks at him resentfully because there is no food on offer.

Have we ham, Mariushka? he calls into the kitchen.

No ham.

Have we veal?

Veal, yes, sir.

Bring me some bread and cold veal with my coffee.

Quinine stands there, his front feet bowed and his paws splayed, and then yawns.

You shall have food, he tells his dog, just be patient.

'Dear naughty uncle, dear gentle daddy . . .' He has asked her many, many times not to call him uncle. But now 'daddy' – even though she's only twenty-four, this is intolerable. He begins to compose his reply in his head: 'My dearest toddler, my darling little munchkin . . .' but he could already hear Lika's low and hearty laugh. How she would find this amusing – strapping Lika, with her broad shoulders and small, soft breasts, her flaxen hair, her lazy, hooded eyes that looked as if she were perpetually about to fall asleep. 'Flaxen', that's the word for her hair: its blonde exuberance, its preposterous, curling mass . . .

He hears his father kick off his boots at the kitchen door and pad across the floor.

Oh, it's you, his father says as he enters, have you calmed down yet?

What *is* the man talking about? he thinks as he watches his father cross the room searching his pockets for something.

Olga comes in with the coffee.

There you are, sir, hot as lava.

Thank you, Olga: now what about some milk, some bread, some cold veal? She's running back to the kitchen. And a damn cup!

He stares at the pot of coffee. There's a small bunch of cherries painted on the side. Or are they tomatoes? What is it Potapenko calls me? King of the Medes.

Still in a bad mood, eh? says his father, filling his pipe. If you go to sleep angry it can ruin your digestion for a week. Don't say I didn't warn you.

In the yard Roman is stacking new pairs of cart shafts. He looks round.

Morning, sir, wonderful morning. They talk about the weather, how last week's rain ruined the clover.

He asks Roman: who ordered these cart shafts?

I did, sir.

Are the old ones finished? Broken?

Oh, no, they're fine, sir.

So why do we need new ones?

We always order new cart shafts before the summer haymaking.

He looks round and notices Quinine, fortified with veal, snarling at the yard dog.

Have you seen my sister? he asks Roman.

In the vegetable garden, sir.

He walks through the yard and around the side of the house past the veranda towards the vegetable garden. He can see Masha earthing up the young potato shoots, but urgently, furiously, as if a flood were coming or a tempest and this was her last chance to complete the task. Everybody in a sour mood today, he realizes.

Morning, he says. I'd offer to help but I'd drop down dead.

Which might be best for all of us, Masha says.

I refuse to respond to this, he thinks.

We have to get rid of that yard dog, he replies instead. He'll eat Quinine for lunch one of these days.

Masha says nothing.

What have I done, Masha? Tell me and I'll make amends.

It's what you're *not* doing that outrages me, she says, finally turning to face him.

He sighs. But I like Potapenko, he's my friend.

Your 'friend' is having an affair with your mistress. I'm sorry to be the one to tell you but you should know.

Of course I know, I'm not that stupid. Anyway, Lika's told me. She wrote to me about it.

Masha balances her fork on its tines, lets go and watches it fall to the ground.

That is possibly the most disgusting thing I've heard.

Look, we're all grown-ups. We're not children –

It's a grotesque betrayal of you, she says, of your friendship with him, and of our hospitality to him. How can you see him, how can you go travelling with him?

He's excellent company. He looks after my affairs brilliantly.

Masha stamps past him out of the garden. Call yourself a man, she shouts over her shoulder.

I just want Lika to be happy, he yells after her. Life's too short.

He goes to his study. As he clears a space on his desk he notices that someone has placed a sheet of paper on top of the manuscript of his latest story on which is written the title 'The Man with the Big Arse'. He crumples it up with a smile. Potapenko. But then thinks: what was he doing in my study?

He tries to draft out a reply to Lika but finds it difficult going so he reads her letter again and senses his anger returning. 'All the women in this hotel look at me askance as if they know some secret about me. Come and rescue me, daddy dear, and we will travel together – Switzerland, Sweden, Morocco. You would be well in Morocco with its palm trees and endless sunshine. Perhaps I'd let you have a dancing girl or two . . .'

He looks at the date at the top of the letter and makes some elementary calculations. Of course, Potapenko was in Paris too, now. So how could she write like this to him? Was she waiting for Potapenko to arrive or had he just left her?

In new acid-biting anger he picks up his pen. 'Accept a farewell kiss from an old man, Lika, my darling. She who travels alone, travels furthest. Let me sit here on my estate with my memories and my problems. Kirghiz, the bay gelding, needs the horse doctor. We have only seventy ducklings this year. Last week's rain has ruined the clover. Tell your smart Parisian friends of the things which preoccupy me –' He crumples up the piece of paper. No: revolting self-pity. He must find a way of being careless and care-free, brilliant and witty. That's what will wound her: his vast insouciance.

Lunch is eaten in almost silence. Masha refuses to respond to his few attempts at mollifying her. He compliments her on the white salmon, on the cucumbers, but she pays no attention. His father – who enjoys seeing his children quarrel – eats noisily with a smile on his face. His mother, who hates confrontation of any kind, seems to shrink into herself, often closing her eyes as if she's at prayer. At the end of the meal his father belches and is careful to make a small sign of the cross in front of his gaping mouth.

He goes for a walk, longing to be alone. Quinine follows him for a minute or so then grows bored and waddles back home. He skirts the orchard and strolls down the lane towards the river. A sudden, stiffish breeze combs the leaves of the willows – their silver undersides glinting in the sunshine like a flashing shoal of fish darting amongst weeds. Too complicated a simile, he thinks, admiring the graceful, supple willows nonetheless, as they bend and recoil to the invisible urgings of the wind. Across the watermeadows he can see the mill on the outskirts of the village. In the east heavy clouds build. More rain, just when the clover looked like it might recover. Yes, of course, he must talk about Potapenko. How perfect: a long letter to Lika about Potapenko and their plans for the Volga trip – from Iaroslavl to Nizhni and then down the Volga to Tsaritsyn and from there to Taganrog. Nothing could be more telling, nothing could better convey the scale of his utter indifference to her betrayal.

He takes out her letter and a pencil to make some notes and his eye is caught by a few phrases: "This is a cold unfriendly city of secrets and whispered rumours. Your poor Lika eats pastries to console herself and is turning into a giantess. Will you still love me if I'm fat, beloved intolerant uncle? They say it helps you sing better which is why all opera singers are fat. When I'm back with you I'll sing you a lullaby – '

Then the thought comes to him: it's not all about Lika . . . After all, there's the prospect of the three-week holiday in the company of Potapenko, a holiday in the full knowledge of what has gone on between him and Lika. Perhaps the Volga trip's not such a good idea after all . . . But he has to meet Potapenko in Moscow, anyway: they have to sort out that business with Suvorin. He walks on, absentmindedly hitting out with his stick at the nettles and burdocks growing alongside the river path. He should see Aleksandra in Moscow: lithe, dark Aleksandra who wants him so fervently. That last letter had been extraordinary – with its talk of heat and ardour and French kisses . . . Which reminds him: he has to talk to Blago-veshchensky about establishing a proper post-office at Lopasnia. That would mean letters every day, and parcels too, without having to go all the way to Serpukhov –

He hears his name being called and looks round to see Efim running towards him, a piece of paper fluttering in his hand.

He is glad of the summons, he tells himself. Whatever nonsense it may portend at least it's some kind of a distraction – take his mind off Lika and Potapenko.

Beside him, Roman taps Cossack Girl, the new mare, on her haunches with the end of his whip and whistles at her through his teeth.

Come on, Cossack Girl, show the master how fast you can go. Come on, my lovely girl.

She tosses her head and mane, the flies bothering her, and plods along steadily.

Why has she got no bridle? he asks Roman.

She can't take the bit, sir.

So you just harness her with rope? It doesn't look very smart.

If I put a bit in her, sir, we'd be off the road in a second.

Did you know this when you bought her?

Oh, yes. Yes, yes.

They have reached the outskirts of Talezh. Roman gently wheels Cossack Girl into a right turn and the railway station comes into view.

Where are you going?

To the school, sir.

We're going to the new school, not the old school.

Ah, right. And where would that be, sir?

Behind the courthouse.

Roman heaves on the reins, dismounts and leads Cossack Girl round in a 180-degree turn before climbing back on board. They set off again.

*

He sits patiently outside the headmaster's office, waiting. The headmaster's secretary is heating up the samovar so they can have some tea. She brings him a plate of small sugary cakes. He declines. She apologizes for the third or fourth time and says the headmaster will be with him in a matter of minutes.

While she busies herself with the samovar he takes out Lika's letter and smoothes it on his knee. 'You mustn't be cross with me, ogre-ish daddy-monster. I hardly see Potapenko because his wife is here with him and we must keep our secret. To everyone in this horrible hotel I'm a married lady. So write to me as Madame and not Mademoiselle and don't be angry with your lovelorn, getting-fatter-every-day, sweet-toothed, not-so-little Lika . . .'

'Secret'. How many times had she used the word 'secret'? A sudden, aching image of her comes into his mind as he reads this. That time when they spent three days at the Hotel Loskutnaia. He had come back unexpectedly and, wanting to surprise her, had tiptoed through the hall and peered round the door of the sitting room. She was standing in her nightdress looking out through a gap in the muslin curtains at the street, a wand of sunlight setting her hair ablaze. But her eyes were unseeing: she was thinking, frowning, as if she were trying to remember some elusive fact, her lips pushed forward in a pout, one hand idly caressing her plump left breast. He watched her for twenty seconds before he coughed politely and she turned to greet him, the frown and the pout erased by a widening smile on her broad, beautiful face.

He follows the headmaster down the wooden stairway (creaking like a caveful of bats) towards the courtyard.

Are these new stairs?

Everything is new, sir.

Then this joinery is lamentable.

We cannot find the craftsmen, sir. They've all gone to the cities, looking for money. We do our best with the dross that remains.

The headmaster steps into the courtyard and turns to face him. He is a lean man of average height and horribly bald – little tufts of hair around his ears and above his neck. He has let the whiskers on his cheeks grow long in compensation and consequently looks like a monkey. An oriental monkey – what were they called? Macaques? Gibbons?

There you have it, sir, the headmaster says ruefully. What should we do?

He looks around the courtyard. Three storeys: the ground floor stone, the top two wood. The bust of Count Nicolai Khobotov on its granite plinth squarely in the middle. The headmaster raises a pointing hand, dramatically.

At the level of the eaves a net has been strung covering the entire area of the courtyard below. In the middle of the net a pigeon is trapped fast, its wings askew, its feet splayed, almost as if it were trying to turn on to its back but had been frozen halfway through the manoeuvre.

He steps out into the courtyard and looks up at the hapless bird. A pink claw paddles the air.

It's alive, he observes.

Very much so, the headmaster says. That is our problem.

Why did you have the courtyard netted like this?

Against the pigeons. They would perch on the statue, you see. They defecated on the statue. After a weekend the statue would be grey with pigeon filth . . . The headmaster lowers his voice, takes the soft right wing of his whiskers in the fingers of his right hand and draws it to a point. Count Khobotov is our honoured patron, the honorary chairman of our school board, the headmaster explains. He most honourably allowed us to name the school after him. He honours us with impromptu visits –

– Does he live near here?

One of his estates is close by. He comes each summer.

I never knew that.

Imagine if he came and saw his statue despoiled . . . The headmaster swallows, and places his hand on his throat. The net was the only solution. Have you any idea how much a net of this size costs? Or of the price demanded to fix it to the eaves, to hold it stretched securely in place, summer and winter, spring and autumn?

I've no idea.

Close to a thousand roubles.

He looks at the headmaster and feels sorry for this troubled, nervous man. But something is nagging at the back of his mind.

Why have you asked me to come here?

Because of your gift, sir.

My gift?

He remembers: last year he had given the new school at Talezh money to buy text books.

How much did I give you?

A thousand roubles, sir.

He paces around the courtyard waiting for Roman to return. Pacing around the courtyard under his very own net, he realizes. A thousand-rouble net that he has paid for to prevent the bust of Count Khobotov being shat on by pigeons . . .

He has suggested to the headmaster that they take down the net and free the trapped bird, but he has been assured that the cost of finding workmen to do this job and then to replace the net securely would be prohibitive. It was clear to him, in his further discussions with the headmaster, that he was there to take responsibility. The headmaster's logic ran in this manner: his gift had purchased the net, therefore he should take responsibility for the resolution of the current net/pigeon problem.

The headmaster appears and asks him if he would like more tea and cakes. He declines.

Has this ever happened before? he asks the headmaster.

Once. Last autumn, the headmaster says.

And what did you do?

Nothing. A pigeon was trapped and we couldn't reach it. The bird died and we left its corpse there. Unfortunately it took many months before it decomposed and ultimately disappeared. Some of the younger pupils were distressed . . . The dead pigeon was very visible from the upper classrooms, you see. Week after week, month after month.

And what with Count Khobotov taking up his summer residence . . .

Precisely. That's why we sent for you, sir. As it was only thanks to your generosity that we were able to fit a net in the first place.

Yes.

We felt you should be consulted.

Roman comes into the courtyard with the shotgun.

Shall I do it, sir? He asks.

No, no, I insist. This is my net after all. Whose gun is this?

A friend of my brother, sir. He's a blacksmith. Lives right by the church.

He breaks the gun and checks that there is a cartridge in each barrel. Then he steps into the centre of the courtyard and aims upward. The bird suddenly begins to try and flap its pinioned wings as if somehow it knows it has only seconds to live.

He aims and he fires – both barrels simultaneously. The pigeon disappears in a cloud of feathers and shredded flesh and bone. There is a hole in the net the size of a man's head.

As the noise of the shotgun blast reverberates around the courtyard he is aware of a ringing in his ears, as if a small shrill bell is being vigorously shaken somewhere close at hand, and he suddenly realizes – with absolute, cold clarity; with absolute, cold certainty – what Lika was trying to tell him in her letter.

Supper proves to be another silent meal but he doesn't mind as he has no inclination to talk. Masha remains furious with him. His father still enjoys his children's wordless animosity and picks his teeth with particular enthusiasm for over a quarter of an hour. His mother has gone to her bed with a migraine.

After the meal is cleared away he takes a tumbler of vodka into his study and settles down to try and complete his short story. He writes a page or two and begins to relax: it's going well. He calls for another tumbler of vodka. He knows he shouldn't drink too much but an agreeable mood of creative endeavour is on him and he wants to encourage it. That evening he hardly thinks at all about Lika, Potapenko and their impending child. Hardly at all.

WILLIAM BOYD

ON THE YANKEE STATION

William Boyd's first collection of short stories offers more style, suspense and sheer entertainment.

Adolescent sex in a Scottish boys' public school, oddballs on the seedy side of America, murder in a quiet Devon cottage ... Comical, ironical or lacerating – wit is the keynote of these stories, which include two early adventures from the career of Morgan Leafy, glorious anti-hero of the prize-winning *A Good Man in Africa*.

'Funny and sad, spare and yet robust ... stories that I advise everyone to buy their dearest friend' *Listener*

'His writing, with nods in the direction of Borges and Nabokov, combines violence, comedy and experiment' *Time Out*

'He takes on depressing netherworlds like glitterless Los Angeles. He tells of failures, obsessions, hopeless loves ... and he's funny, witty and wise' *Company*

'Crisp, wry, energetic ... the author slips with ease from one narrative manner to another, reproducing the exact tones of a girl in a sideshow or an articulate psychopath ... nothing in this accomplished collection is less than diverting' *The Times Literary Supplement*

WILLIAM BOYD

STARS AND BARS

'One of the comic masterpieces' *Daily Telegraph*

All Henderson Dores dreams of is fitting in. But America, land of the loony millionaire and the subway poet, the down-home Bible-basher and the sharp-suited hood, of paralysing personal frankness and surreally fantasized facilities, is hard enough for an Englishman to fit into. Henderson could never shed enough inhibitions to become just another weirdo. Or could he?

'William Boyd has a way with the Englishman abroad ... His humour, timed to a tee, always raps out the truth' *Mail on Sunday*

'Extremely funny ... Boyd does not pass up a single comic turn' *Sunday Telegraph*

'Splittingly shrewd and engaging ... with an extra and uneasy little something fretting away at the ribald content' *Guardian*

'The wry laughter never stops ... a master of witty manipulation' *Observer*

WILLIAM BOYD

THE DESTINY OF NATALIE 'X'

'*The Destiny of Nathalie 'X'* should not be missed … Each story has its own very specific, new and singular voice' *Daily Telegraph*

'The intense visual quality draws the reader into a world where betrayal and fear are the dominant themes. This pithy and evocative style is reminiscent of the young Hemingway. William Boyd displays in this collection his great talent as a master of fantasy, farce and irony' *Sunday Express*

'Boyd can establish a character in a single sentence and a situation in a single paragraph. Every aspiring writer – and many an established one – could benefit from a lesson in the arts of concision and precision from him' *Evening Standard*

'In the title story of his bracing and sometimes stunning collection *The Destiny of Natalie 'X'* he writes, exquisitely, the most quixotic exposé of Tinseltown I have read since Scott Fitzgerald's *The Last Tycoon*. It is a fairytale infused with the brimstone of truth' *Scotland on Sunday*

'Fine, precise writing and effective formal invention … as good as anything in Boyd's novels' *The Times*

WILLIAM BOYD

If you enjoyed this book, there are several ways you can read more by the same author and make sure you get the inside track on all Penguin books.

Order any of the following titles direct:

Visit www.penguin.com and find out first about forthcoming titles, read exclusive material and author interviews, and enter exciting competitions. You can also browse through thousands of Penguin books and buy online.

IT'S NEVER BEEN EASIER TO READ MORE WITH PENGUIN

Frustrated by the quality of books available at Exeter station for his journey back to London one day in 1935, Allen Lane decided to do something about it. The Penguin paperback was born that day, and with it first-class writing became available to a mass audience for the very first time. This book is a direct descendant of those original Penguins and Lane's momentous vision. What will you read next?